Table of Contents

....1
The Rakes of St. Regent's Park Series.......................................3
Author's Note..4
Summary..6
Prologue..8
Chapter 1..14
Chapter 2..20
Chapter 3..29
Chapter 4..36
Chapter 5..47
Chapter 6..55
Chapter 7..65
Chapter 8..76
Chapter 9..82
Chapter 10...91
Chapter 11...102
Chapter 12...116
Chapter 13...125
Chapter 14...135
Chapter 15...142
Chapter 16...153
Chapter 17...160
Chapter 19...181
Chapter 20...188
Chapter 21...195
Chapter 22...204
Chapter 23...212
Chapter 24...221
Chapter 25...227
Chapter 26...238
Chapter 27...246

I0614884

Chapter 28 254
Chapter 29 262
Epilogue 277
Author Note #2 280
Author Biography 283
More Books by Karyn Gerrard 284
Sneak Peek of The Detective and the Baroness 286

The Viscount of Shadows

The Rakes of St. Regent's Park #6
By
Karyn Gerrard

The Viscount of Shadows (The Rakes of St. Regent's Park #6)

Copyright © 2023 by Karyn Gerrard

KG Publishing

Vers 1.0

PRINT ISBN: 978-1-7386845-7-1

Cover art by © EDH Professionals

Rakes of Regent's Park Series

IN A PRIVATE MEETING place, in an old bank office behind Colosseum Terrace on Albany Street, a group of gentlemen attended a gathering. It had nothing to do whatsoever with financing, investments, or stocks—unless you counted moral bankruptcy. The central rules of this club: no serious attachments to anyone and the pursuit of one's pleasures, especially of the carnal variety, were of the utmost importance.

But weariness and boredom were setting in. Along with something more worrying: loneliness. A disquiet of the soul. These bad-boy peers of Victorian London were damaged, hiding their inner torture beneath a thin veneer of devil-may-care dissoluteness.

It takes an exceptional group of women to capture such men's hearts and see past the outer shell. The ladies are determined to live and love in their own way, with no relinquishment of their independence and no compromises. How satisfying to find that these progressive men are in total agreement.

Author's Note #1

Book #6 is all new material!

The Rakes of St. Regent's Park consists of the following books (so far). Will there be more after book 6? I never say never.

Since this is a continuing series, and various characters from past or future books appear, I may slip into the point of view of one of those characters for a short scene. I only do it to enhance the current story or at a future plot.

The hero of this book, Oliver Wollstonecraft, is the grandson of Aidan, whose story you find in *Love with a Notorious Rake* (Men of Wollstonecraft Hall #3). That series takes place fifty years before this one.

☺ NEWS: I just signed a 3-book contract with Dragonblade Publishing (historical romance), and the series will be a spin-off of The Rakes of St. Regent's Park! It is called The Duke's Bastards, and Mitchell Simpson, the secondary character in this story, will be the hero of the first book, *The Detective and the Baroness*. It is coming soon!

THE RAKES OF ST. REGENT'S PARK SERIES
Book 1: Protecting the Duke
Book 2: The Baron and the Mistress (Revised Edition)
Book 3: Knight of Christmas
Book 4: The Duke of Pain
Book 5: The Not So Perfect Duke
Book 6: The Viscount of Shadows

Each historical romance author does their own world-building, much like authors in fantasy, paranormal, or other genres. Each author has their own set of characters and peers. That is why my characters from different historical books pop up in my writing. They are all part of my particular historical romance world.

See the detailed author's note #2 at the end of this story for specific historical details.

Summary

Oliver Wollstonecraft, Viscount Tensbridge and recent member of The Rakes of St. Regent's Park, has a secret: he leads a double life. He sits on a progressive parliamentary committee by day, crafting laws to benefit the less fortunate. But by night, Oliver tests those values, acting as The Sentinel, a masked protector of the underprivileged. Nothing shakes his stoic resolve until he comes to the aid of a bold and fiery woman who turns out to be a lady detective. She awakens emotions Oliver believed were well hidden.

Claudia Ellingford has secrets of her own. The illegitimate daughter of a villainous duke, she spent the past ten years surviving on the streets. Recently hired by The Galway Investigative Agency, Claudia relishes her exciting new occupation. But nothing prepared her for seeing a masked man lurking in the shadows and patrolling the alleys of a notorious section of London. What is more shocking is that the stuffy viscount who hired her is the vigilante that stirred her dormant desire.

Claudia and Oliver become swept up into a perilous situation, with a vicious criminal determined to discover The Sentinel's true identity. But what is also in danger is their hearts, facing their doubts, and finding a path to lasting happiness.

Prologue

AUGUST 1898
London, England

MARY O'TOOLE HAS BEEN alone and living on the streets since age sixteen. Society, judgmental as they are, saw her as a tramp, a dosser, and a vagrant. And since she was a woman, she'd been referred to as a strumpet, a tart—and a prostitute, to name a few insulting terms. No doubt, the two women sitting across from her in the Ten Bells pub in the East End of London assumed such. Mary couldn't make out their expressions, for they kept them maddingly impartial.

One of the ladies was quite tall, the other about average stature for a female, and Mary guessed her height lay between the two. Both women stared at her with clear-eyed astuteness.

"I am Althea Galway," the petite one declared. She reached into her leather case and placed a card on the table. With the tip of one finger, she slid it across to Mary.

Mary picked up the offered card. "The Galway Investigative Agency. Looking for a lost soul? There are plenty around here, love," she observed sarcastically.

"We were searching for *you,* to be exact. Since you take lunch here, Olivia Durham suggested we seek you out at the Ten Bells. You came to her rescue this past spring. Do you recall the incident?" the taller one asked.

Mary remembered everything. Olivia Durham had been cornered in a dark alley by two repulsive men who had abducted her from a duke's town house. Mary, along with her compatriots, came upon the scene. Pulling a knife from her garter, Mary stood them down, threatening to cut them from their throat to their bollocks. Perhaps she hadn't quite verbalized that aloud, but she thought it. And tempted to do it if they hadn't fled like the cowards they were and no doubt still are.

Mary tucked the card in her ample cleavage. "I remember Olivia. Pan tells me she married her duke. The best to her and all. She doesn't owe me anything. I sought out the job at The Velvet Vine as she suggested. Thank her for me, yeah?"

Miss Althea Galway inclined her head to the tall woman next to her. "My older sister, Eleanora Galway-Bamford, and co-owner of our agency."

Mary nodded in acknowledgment. How impressive. You did not hear about two sisters running an investigative agency every day. Good for them.

"Olivia, now the Duchess of Watford, recommended you for our agency. We wish to hire you," Eleanora Galway stated.

What?

"You cannot be serious," Mary balked.

"We most certainly are," Althea Galway replied firmly. "You know the streets, are smart, can handle yourself with a knife. You would be perfect for undercover work and other assignments. We cannot pay the wages you earn at your present labor, but we offer steady employment and adventure."

Adventure? Mary had quite enough of that in her life. As far as money was concerned?

"I am not earning as much as you think," Mary said, her mouth quirking into a half-smile. "And I am not ashamed of how I made money to survive these past years."

Mary had taken the position at The Velvet Vine and Tackle brothel to see that her friends had a comfortable and safe place to stay. It had taken intense negotiating with the owner and manager, Pan, to take them all on, with Mary agreeing to assist him in running the club while smoothing the rough edges off her friends. As part of the deal, Mary declined to serve customers in *any* capacity. To her utter astonishment, Pan had agreed.

"We offer room and board, all meals included. You would have your own room," Eleanora Galway interjected. "And as to your current work? It is not a factor to us."

Well, that was good to know about her present living. Anyone working at a brothel in whatever duty was looked down upon by humanity. As far as a room, she had her own now; in fact, it was Olivia Durham's old one.

"I don't know nothing of being an investigator," Mary stated, embellishing her faux Irish accent.

But the notion had taken root. Mary was weary of street life, not knowing where the next crust of bread was coming from or if she would have a roof over her head for more than one night—these past months had been a blessed reprieve from existing on the streets. And to use her survival skills in a compelling career? To begin a new chapter, a diverse journey? It was enticing—very much so.

"We will train you. You read; do you write as well?" Eleanora Galway asked.

"Aye."

"Most of our clients are women seeking a divorce, but we have had a few significant cases beyond that," Althea Galway stated. "You would be living at our place on Cleveland Street. Our cousin, Sybil

Norton, lives at the residence with another investigator, Edwina Callen. The rate of pay would be two pounds a week. To start."

It was less than she made now, but not by much. It was an excellent wage, more than a senior clerk at a bank makes. It would be hard to leave her comrades after all they had been through. Mary needed to confer with them. But she knew that they would encourage her to pursue a new life.

Wait. Galway-Bamford?

Mary hardly read the papers, for who had time, let alone the coin, to buy one on a steady basis? She often retrieved newspapers from the rubbish bins and read them to her ladies. But her sharp recall flipped through her well-ordered memory to an article of a lady investigator marrying a duke. Again, this is not something you hear about every day.

She swung her gaze toward Eleanora. "Are you the Duchess of Allenby?"

"I am. And my sister is about to marry the Duke of Chellenham. But we are still running our agency." The duchess pointed to the cane leaning against the table. "At the moment, Althea does not move around as well as she used to, and we have more clients than we can possibly take on. It is why we approached you. We need the assistance."

Well, you could knock Mary over with a feather. Dukes? How fascinating. "Don't you want to know anything more of my past?"

Althea shrugged. "Not particularly. That is your business. If you take this job, we would prefer that you leave the life behind—it is a condition of employment. We require all your energy and focus to be on the investigative work. Your street smarts will be invaluable in this regard."

The wheels in Mary's mind turned the information over, examining it thoroughly. Leave the life behind? Not a problem. She tapped her fingers against the table. "You don't know me. Yet you both are willing to take me on. Why?"

"Because Olivia recommended you, and I trust my friend implicitly. And sitting here conversing, I can see you are frank, confident, intelligent, and perfect for our needs. If you prefer a trial period to see if you would like the work, we can arrange it," Althea replied.

Mary took a sip from her pint mug of bitter. "Can I get back to you? I need to think this through. I want to speak to the owner and my compatriots before deciding."

"That is satisfactory," Eleanora responded.

"Let me tell you a little about myself, for 'tis best you know this now. My name is not Mary O'Toole. I'm twenty-six, the illegitimate daughter of a duke, and I've been alone and on the streets since age sixteen. And though you may hear a slight Irish accent, I'm not from Ireland. Although I lived on Eaton Place the first years of my life, as soon as my so-called duke father tired of his mistress—my mother—we were turned out." Mary dropped the accent and spoke in perfect upper-crust English. "The succeeding addresses made their eventual slide into abject poverty."

The sisters exchanged astonished looks.

"Do not tell me your father was the Duke of Chellenham, my fiancé's late father. He was a disreputable rake of dubious morals," Althea whispered. "He left children in all corners of London and beyond."

"No, my birth certificate states Claudia Ellingford. My mother put my father's last name on the certificate because she thought it sounded posh, even though my father is not legally designated on the official documentation."

"Whinstone," Althea Galway whispered. "My God."

"The very one," Mary replied. "I see Whinstone's reputation precedes him."

"Olivia's case," Eleanora Galway interjected, "Whinstone was the villain, her husband's stepfather. He planned Olivia's abduction. What are the odds?"

"It is a small world in the scheme of things. And I am not surprised by his villain status." Hell's bells, her so-called father was worse than she had initially supposed. So, he was behind Olivia's terrible ordeal? Miserable bastard.

"Whinstone is currently in prison, and plans are in motion in the House of Lords to have his dukedom stripped from him," Althea Galway added.

"A good place for him. May he rot." Mary frowned, thinking back, going to her father on bended knee, begging for a couple of pounds so she could find clean lodgings to care for her sick mother. The cruel man had her turned away without even granting her an audience. Good riddance to him.

Mary stood and extended her hand to the women, and they shook it. "I will send word to the address on your card. Give me at least ten days to mull this over."

"Very well. And if you agree, we will have a more comprehensive interview and discuss the agency and the cases you may be involved in," Althea Galway replied.

Mary pulled her shawl across her shoulders and strode from the pub with her head held high. The ladies could pay for her lunch.

Mary did not examine fate closely or believe in the "everything happens for a reason" declaration. But she could not ignore this strange and unexpected twist in her life journey.

It may be time to become Claudia Ellingford again.

Chapter 1

LATE SEPTEMBER 1898
London, England

Mary O'Toole took those ten days to consider the offer. With the encouragement of her friends, she began her new life using her real name, Claudia Ellingford. Claudia carefully folded and gently placed Mary in a drawer. While Claudia was grateful for the protection the Mary O'Toole persona afforded her, that part of her life was over.

Tonight, she lurked in a dark alley, following a baronet, Sir Tristan Nottingham. Her first assignment with The Galway Investigative Agency was a divorce case. Her partner for the night, Edwina Callen, awaited her in a hansom cab on the next street.

Claudia received a few weeks of training, but the practical application to learn investigative skills was imperative. Lady Catherine suspected her husband, Sir Tristan, of stepping out, and the lady in question had had enough of the man's infidelities and wanted solid proof to present in court.

Sir Tristan was unquestionably seeking out the lower forms of vice in the East End if he was heading where Claudia imagined. Not that there were many dilapidated buildings left in this section of Bethnal Green, as a clearance was ongoing by the London County Council. But the underprivileged and criminals would find another locale to take over. The city of London had done evictions for decades—neighborhoods razed to make way for the above and below ground railway and supposed urban enhancement.

The East End was not alone in these types of slums, as pockets existed throughout the city, as Claudia came to discover when she and her mother found themselves in Notting Dale —or the *West End Avernus* as it had been referred to recently in the papers—or hell on earth as the locals called it. Many also recognized the area as The Potteries and Piggeries, where fifteen people shared a toilet and forty out of a hundred children did not live to see their second birthday.

Claudia shook away the horrid memories and concentrated on the task at hand.

Sir Tristan moved with a swift and decided purpose, his long cloak snapping in the wind. Sir Tristan traveled deeper into the rookery through twisting, dank alleys and secluded courtyards. Sounds of off-key piano music filled her hearing. The man was heading toward Kelly's Paradise, which was anything but. The back alley venue offered an abundance of cheap gin, gambling, bawdy shows, and sex.

To blend in with the locals, Claudia wore a tattered dress with a patched shawl wrapped around her head and shoulders and fingerless lace gloves. And she had two knives on her, one in the holder attached to her garter and a smaller one in her boot.

The doors were propped open since it was a warm night. It allowed a semblance of fresh air to circulate. Not that the air was clean and crisp, far from it. Claudia stood in the doorway and peeked in. Customers packed the place, and a tobacco smoke haze hovered over the crowd. On stage, four scantily dressed women performed a lewd dance, eliciting hoots and applause from the general male audience. In one darkened corner, a man had a woman against the wall, rutting her, with a small group of men watching as if it were part of the show. Perhaps it was.

Claudia scanned the crowd and located Nottingham. By all accounts, he was good-looking if your preference ran toward smug, middle-aged elites. The baronet already had a pint of bitter in one hand and a plump woman in the other. He buried his face in the woman's generous bosom, his mouth latching on to the barely-revealed nipple peeking out of her low-cut blouse. The woman laughed naughtily, whispering in his ear.

Someone grabbed Claudia's shoulder and spun her about, pulling the shawl from around her head. The garment fluttered to the ground. Three men stood before her; their gazes were lascivious and threatening. She had expected this, as a woman alone was unsafe in this area.

"Here, sod off and all!" she yelled, using her Irish accent. "I belong to Grindhouse Pete, eh? So, you'd best shove off and leave me be, you bleedin' muckshites!" Claudia had no idea if Grindhouse Pete was still in control of this part of the rookery, but the men's hesitation meant the name still carried some weight.

"Pete won't mind if we have a taste," one man rumbled. "I've never had me a redhead afore. Wonder if she's red—down there?" The other men chuckled salaciously.

"A taste?" She slowly raised the hem of her frayed plaid dress, giving the men a flash of leg. Claudia stealthily reached for her knife. "A taste of what, ducks?"

With the men now distracted, she grabbed the knife from her rawhide holder and swung around in an arc, making contact.

One of the men screamed, his hand covered his cheek. Blood oozed between his fingers. "The bitch cut me!"

Before Claudia could react or reply, someone dropped down from above. In a flash of dark leather, the tall man—she assumed it was a man considering the width of the shoulders and the muscular build—battered one of her attackers with what appeared to be a truncheon.

He then spun to face the other men, pulling a large dagger from his coat. "This is my territory," the muffled voice dangerously hissed as he held the blade to one of the men's throats. "Leave now if you want to live."

The men needed no further inducement. They grabbed the beaten man, brought him to his feet, and hurried out of the alley. The tall man turned to face her as he tucked the knife away.

His territory?

Be damned if she would wait for this leather-clad rookery boss to lay his hands on her. Claudia lifted her leg and kicked him right in the bollocks. Or at least she hoped so, as ascertaining the target remained challenging in the dark. She must have made at least partial contact as the man descended on one knee, his breath expelling in wheezing gasps.

"I was trying to help you," he bit out.

"I don't need any assistance," she replied, speaking in her own voice. "I had the matter under control. Who *are* you?"

The man grunted as he stood. "The Sentinel, at your service."

What?

"You're a vigilante? Really? Why?" Vigilantes were not unheard of in the seedier sections of London, and many people considered them a necessity, considering there were segments of the city that coppers refused to police. Someone had to protect the poor. But Claudia thought those urban tales came from a London of long ago. How interesting.

"And who are *you*?" he asked, disregarding her questions.

She took a step closer to get a better look. The man was encased in leather from head to toe, from the long coat, waistcoat, shirt, trousers, boots, and scarf around his head. Claudia could not tell if the mask hiding his facial features was leather. Perhaps not. He slipped his truncheon into his belt, the dagger under his coat, then pulled his floppy hat lower over his brow to conceal his eyes.

Claudia reached into her cleavage and handed a card to him. "I am with The Galway Investigative Agency. Sorry about the kick. I thought you were a rookery boss."

"I'll live," he mumbled. Claudia surmised that he took the card and slipped it in his coat pocket, for it was too dark to read the thing anyway. "Then go about your investigating and be gone. It is not safe hereabouts. And you shouldn't carry anything that can identify you."

"I am aware it is not safe," she bellowed. Although Leather Man had a point about the card, she would never admit it aloud. Althea and Eleanora had mentioned it might be best not to carry identification. Claudia should have surmised they meant the business cards as well. Live and learn.

He stepped toward her, but Claudia held her ground. He clasped her arm and brought her in close enough that she caught a brief and faint whiff of bergamot and lime. She always had an excellent sense of smell. The odor was an expensive men's cologne, meaning this man was not working class. Though the mask muffled his voice, he did not have the cadence of the lower stations of society.

She raised her chin defiantly, catching his gaze—and a brief glimpse of light-colored eyes, though she could not quite make out the shade. Blue, gray, or green? It was hard to tell. The Sentinel pulled her into the shadows, causing her to gasp and grab his arm. Solid muscle flexed under her grasp.

"A further word of advice," the deep, muted voice intoned. "Before kicking men in the bollocks, ascertain if they are friend or foe." He nuzzled her neck, causing a frisson of awareness to pass through her. And a jolt of excitement.

He released her arm and stepped farther back into the darkness.

"I will do as I like!" she called out.

But she was talking to damp, foggy air. The Sentinel had disappeared.

HE COULD BARELY SEE straight from the pain radiating throughout his body. Luckily, he only received part of the impact from that summary boot to the bollocks. If she had caught him full-on, he would still be groaning and drooling in an embryonic position in that filthy alleyway.

But as he loped away, he could not help but admire the woman. She stood up to those men, even cut one.

And she worked for The Galway Agency; what were the odds?

He could also not help but notice her obvious attractiveness, at least, what he could make out in the darkness: all that red hair with streaks of fireplace flame. Because of her disguise, he thought he was coming to the rescue of an unfortunate prostitute.

But when he brought her in close, enough to have those luscious curves tease and arouse him? It stirred emotions he had not experienced for a long time. Perhaps his pain was a specific stiffness that had nothing to do with being injured.

But enough of this, the night was still young, and he had other territories to cover tonight.

But as he traveled through the dank streets of the East End, the bold lady detective remained at the forefront of his thoughts.

Chapter 2

EARLY OCTOBER 1898
London, England

Oliver Wollstonecraft came from a large, boisterous family—close-knit to a fault. But the past five weeks had brought sorrow to the clan as there had been two funerals in rapid succession. Oliver had no sooner returned to London after the first funeral when, over two weeks later, he had to return to Wollstonecraft Hall in Kent, their medieval-age country seat, for the second one.

The first memorial was for his 87-year-old great-grand-uncle, Garrett Wollstonecraft. A mountain of a man, the half-Scotsman had lived a happy and adventurous life. His uncle was already missed, especially by his wife, children, and grandchildren.

But Oliver's 81-year-old grandfather, Aidan Wollstonecraft, the Earl of Carnstone, untimely death a mere ten days after they had buried Uncle Garrett—cut deeper. Oliver had been close to his grandfather, perhaps more than his father. They had joined Tremain Hornsby, Viscount Hawkestone's progressive caucus from within Parliament, with Oliver sitting at his grandfather's elbow, soaking up all he could learn. Oliver was the heir apparent, after all.

With his grandfather's passing, Oliver took on the courtesy title of Viscount Tensbridge since his father, Julian, was now the earl. This new title would take getting used to, as Tensbridge was the only courtesy title attached to the earldom. Everyone was "my lord-ing" him now.

But for Aidan Wollstonecraft, still vibrant, to die in his sleep? It was not blasted fair. Oliver thought the man would live to be one hundred years of age. It showed that one never knows when death will strike, although both his great-great-uncle and grandfather had long, productive, and loving lives. Living well into one's eighties was a rare feat in this day and age, and Oliver knew what a blessing it was to have them in his life for so long. Everyone would sorely miss them.

How does one process grief? Oliver deduced it was a process since numerous emotional reactions were involved, such as overwhelming sadness, the shock turning to anger, and the disbelief that the person in question was gone. Time heals all wounds and all that. But not really. He supposed one learned to cope with the loss, but managing did not mean forgetting, and Oliver knew his family would never forget Uncle Garrett or his grandfather Aidan. Not. Ever.

Exhaling, he headed into the parlor, where his grandmother reclined in her favorite chair, staring out the window. A cup of tea sat before her, not touched.

"Grams," Oliver gently murmured as he kissed her cheek.

His grandmother gave him a shaky smile as he took the seat opposite. "My dear."

"How are you holding up?" Oliver asked, then he wished he had not. It was an asinine question, and one people uttered when addressing grief. His grandparents had been married for fifty-three years; Grams had lost the love of her life, her partner. Her dearest friend. A significant loss, indeed.

The story of their introduction was a crucial part of the family lore. The first meeting was at a sanitorium where Aidan Wollstonecraft recovered from opium addiction. The subsequent encounter at a cotton mill where Aidan had been undercover as a mill supervisor gathering information on the horrific working conditions. The stuff of legends.

But what was also legendary was their love story.

He could only hope to aspire to his grandparents' marriage. To find your soul mate, to love, desire, and respect until death. At least in Oliver's eyes, it may be an impossibly high standard for anyone to achieve.

What was the primary legend attached to the Wollstonecraft name? The talk of a curse, that women of the family—either born or married into it—had a short lifespan, and how the Men of Wollstonecraft Hall in 1845 broke that tragic, centuries-old vexation by all of them finding love within the year. Succeeding generations may scoff in private at such a turn of events. Oliver figured if his family believed in such a curse, he could not dismiss it so cavalierly. Those who gave the curse credence included his grandfather Aidan, great-uncle Riordan, great-great-uncle Garrett, great-grandfather Julian, and his namesake, his great-great-grandfather Oliver.

"Under the circumstances, I am well," The dowager countess replied, pulling Oliver from his thoughts. "I am still shocked, for I believed I would go first, and I keep telling myself not to go to pieces. We had a wonderful life, and I could not ask for more—except to see my children and grandchildren content and at peace. Which brings me to Bryan."

Bryan was his 22-year-old younger brother and a complete rogue. And a massive pain in the arse.

"I know this will be inconvenient, but when you return to London, please keep an eye on Bryan?" His grandmother continued, her expression beseeching. "I know your father will not ask it of you, for he believes Bryan must make his own mistakes to become a better man. While I agree to a point, there is much in your younger brother that reminds me of your grandfather's early years, and not in a good way."

His grandmother picked up her cup and sipped her tea. "You may not know that your Uncle Garrett found your grandfather in an opium den, almost near death. The family decided to place him in my father's sanitorium. I cannot explain the depths Aidan had sunk to chase the dragon, which I believe is the term. I do not want Bryan to suffer the same fate. It would break me."

"Do you know of something I am not aware of?" Oliver asked. Is Bryan skulking around opium dens? Although, he would not put it past his reprobate and selfish brother.

"No, but I want to avoid such a downfall. I will not worry as much if I know you are watching out for your brother. I know you are busy, but please do what you can. I gently suggested he stay with you at the viscount residence, but he said he had rooms elsewhere, an iron-clad rental agreement he could not break."

An iron-clad rental agreement? It sounded like a fabrication, or perhaps not. Blast it all, playing nursemaid to his spoiled younger brother, was not on his list of urgent items to accomplish this autumn. He had yet to learn where his brother holed up while in London.

"Bryan and I would not make compatible housemates anyway, Grams. But I give you my word to keep a watchful eye."

His grandmother audibly exhaled, closing her eyes briefly as if highly relieved. "Thank you; I knew I could rely on you. When are you returning to London, my dear?"

"In two days. Rett is coming with me and will stay at the Tensbridge residence. I will see to it Bryan travels with us." Garrett was his late great-grand uncle's grandson and namesake, though he went by Rett to avoid confusion. Oliver and Rett had grown up together, the same age of twenty-seven and more brothers than cousins. Rett was also his best friend.

"Rett told me he is staying with you, for I asked him to also watch out for Bryan. You will keep me informed?"

"I certainly shall. Are you staying here?" Oliver asked.

"No. Your father offered, but he is the earl, and this is his home now. I need time away. And your Aunt Abigail has invited me to stay with her indefinitely. We are good friends. If anyone understands what I am going through, it is Abbie. I will be traveling there next week, and it is not far. I will have a set of rooms, and I will have my possessions moved there." His grandmother smiled. "Your father's place, Tensbridge Estate, is now yours. I do hope you will come and stay there soon."

Though the Tensbridge country home had a lofty-sounding name, it was not that large or much of an estate, although his great-grandfather, Julian, had built a significant extension on it. Well-situated near a pristine lake and woods, it was Oliver's childhood home, and returning there as the sole occupant would feel strange indeed. The family lived within a few miles of each other, so there were always Wollstonecrafts around. Not that Oliver minded. His childhood was nearly idyllic compared to the other members of the club he recently joined, The Rakes of St. Regent's Park.

Oliver stood, then leaned down to kiss his grandmother on the cheek once again. "I shall do so soon."

She stroked his cheek affectionately. "Make the home your own; decorate it any way you wish. There are numerous furnishings in storage; some are recent purchases."

"Isn't there an entire warehouse filled with decades worth of cast-offs?" There. A hint of a smile from his grandmother.

"Your great-great grandfather's study furnishings are there. You might like your namesake's desk as it is quite ornate."

Oliver patted her hand. "A fine suggestion. Early next year, I will seek it out. I promise to make use of the furniture. See you at dinner."

Oliver departed, exhaling as he entered the main hallway.

Rett stood, leaning against the wall with his arms crossed. "So, when are we leaving?"

"I told Grams in two days. Bryan will be traveling with us."

"But not staying with us. Grandmama tried to get me to agree to take him in. I said it was up to you." Rett took Oliver's arm and pulled him into the library, closing the door with his boot. Rett could easily steer him since he was broad of shoulder and close to three inches over Oliver's six feet, one-inch height. Rett bore a resemblance to his late grandfather, except Rett's hair was brown with threads of auburn rather than full-on red.

"No. I explained to Grams that our all staying together would not work out. Bryan shouldn't be underfoot."

Rett arched an eyebrow. "And discover your nocturnal activities as The Sentinel, you mean?"

"Keep your voice down," Oliver hissed through clenched teeth. "I shouldn't have told you."

"I am glad you informed me about it since I am joining The Rakes of St. Regent's Park. Are any of those men involved with your do-gooder watchman persona?" his cousin teased.

"No. And I do not wish for the members to know. It is my business." Although, Oliver wondered if Damon Cranston, the Duke of Chellenham, and Althea Galway at least suspected since The Sentinel came to their rescue about seven weeks ago.

Rett sat in one of the chairs, waving Oliver to sit opposite. "This group, is it all charity work? While admirable, I am also interested in the original purpose of the assembly. Vice. More specifically, sex and where to get it. Discreetly and safely, of course."

"Aspiring to be a rake in the truest sense?"

Rett smiled. "Well, here and there. Now and then."

"There are unmarried members of the group who still like to indulge in various vices; you can commiserate with them."

Rett arched an eyebrow. "And you?"

"I have gone to a few gambling dens with various associates, mostly with Asher Colborne, Baron Wenlock, but brothels? No. I do not like paying for sex as there are too many variable outcomes—like a sexual disease. And the women involved have a hard enough life without me increasing their toils."

"Are you still a—you know," Rett mumbled. "Never mind, none of my business."

No, it was *not* anyone's business. But technically, Oliver still was a virgin. It seems odd in this day and age, where sex is available everywhere you turn. At age twenty, Oliver allowed an older widow of a baronet to escort him to her home. They had indulged with plenty of sex play of the oral variety, but he balked when it came time to do the actual act. The reaction had surprised him and angered the widow. He had a few encounters since, with plenty of kissing and touching and nothing else.

Oliver could not say why he stayed away from sex. It wasn't because of religious or spiritual reasons. Perhaps he was a man who wished *not* to share an intimate act with total strangers. He wanted to know and care for the person. Maybe even be in love, or the beginnings of it. It's an eccentric notion for someone in the peerage, but there it is.

Also, it was as he said to Rett. Acting as The Sentinel meant he had seen enough of misery in the slums without adding to it. He had joined The Rakes more as a cover than any genuine interest in debauchery. It was often difficult to keep from rolling his eyes when some of the men bragged of their conquests. But Oliver ultimately decided not to stand in judgment of anyone—of any societal class. He was glad the group also took on charity endeavors these past months.

"I do not go out every night as The Sentinel. I refuse to become obsessed with rescuing all of humanity. There is no possible way for me to save everyone in dire straits. But what little I do gives me a sense of purpose," Oliver said. At least, he tried not to become obsessed. Sometimes, what little he accomplished was not near enough.

"I can see that," Rett murmured. "Our family's foundation is good works to further benefit humanity. In our own way."

"Exactly so. Perhaps you might like to give it a go. We can fashion an outfit to fit that huge frame of yours."

"You are mocking me," Rett replied dismissively.

"I am deadly serious. Think on it. Although, we will have to get you in better shape. I instructed the Tensbridge staff to turn the smaller library into a gymnasium. You can join me in vigorous exercise."

"I am sorry now I agreed to stay with you," Rett grumbled.

Oliver laughed heartily. "Come now, think of the adventure. Who doesn't want to be a hero? You may even find some of it fun. And you will be doing a good turn, besides."

"Fine, I will think about it. What of your servants? Are they aware of your hero status?"

"The butler, Dalton, is aware. Father never had a valet in town, and I aim to continue that tradition. I came home one night with a stab wound in my shoulder. Dalton attended me, very handy with needle and thread." Oliver had stayed at the Tensbridge town residence during the summer and early autumn while his parents remained in Kent.

Rett's eyes widened. "Stab wound? How is that considered a fun adventure?"

"Well, it's not. The blackguard caught me by surprise, and the wound was not all that deep. Anyway, regarding Bryan. I am considering hiring an investigator to follow him and report his comings and goings. Not around the clock, but sufficient enough that we know what he is up to."

"Which frees you up for other activities," Rett snorted.

"And you. Let us face facts; who wants to spend valuable time following Bryan?"

The luscious lady from The Galway Agency entered his mind, though he could not ask for her specifically. That fiery red hair, her bold expression. Confidence oozed from her every pore. Oliver wished she had given her name—but he would discover it soon enough.

"I agree," Rett replied. "Hire someone."

Oliver smiled. "And I have just the investigative agency in mind."

Chapter 3

"I DON'T UNDERSTAND why we are taking one of the family carriages when we could be in London in less than an hour by train," Bryan groused, slumping lazily in his seat.

"Because we want to talk to you privately," Oliver replied, losing patience already, and they were barely out of Kent. "And we want to use the carriage while in the city. The family does not have one in London at the moment, not until Father returns next month."

"You should try and convince Father to buy one of those automobile contraptions. Easier than keeping a stable of horses within the city."

Bryan made a valid point for once. "I will discuss it with Father next I see him."

"Or why have a carriage at all? There are hansom cabs aplenty to hire," Bryan continued.

"True. But what if we wish to travel farther afield? And those automobile contraptions, as you call them, are small. There is not enough room for more than one or two people. At least the current models."

"How do you know anything about it?" Bryan asked.

"I recently entered into an investment scheme within my club. I own shares in The Daimler Motor Company," Oliver replied.

"Automobiles. They might be useful in the short term, but over the long run? You will lose money in your investment," Bryan stated with a wave of his arm.

"I don't agree," Oliver retorted. "I have made a study of—"

"Oh, who bloody well cares?" Bryan groaned, his bored expression back in place. "What I want to know is how long do we have to wear this?" he whined, pointing to the black armband on his left arm.

Rett rolled his eyes. "Up to six months is the general society rule. But in our family, it is three months. And stop your bloody whinging. We are in mourning. Show the proper respect." Rett met Oliver's gaze. "I want to smack him one."

Oliver understood and agreed with the sentiment. "Grandfather and Uncle deserve your esteem. I agree with Rett. Stop acting the mealy-mouthed brat."

His brother sniffed. "Grandfather always preferred you, being the heir and all that nonsense."

"Bryan, where *are* you staying? Surely the location is not classified?" Oliver asked, deciding to change the subject before his growing annoyance spilled over.

Bryan shrugged. "I suppose not. I am staying with Shinwell and Linton at Shinwell's town house in Notting Hill."

Viscount Shinwell and Lord Romeo Linton? Troy Beckingham, the viscount, and Rome Linton, the second son of the Duke of Coldbridge, were part of The Rakes of St. Regent's Park, although they had not attended that many meetings since joining some months ago about the same time as Oliver.

He never cared for Shinwell at the first meeting. Oliver found there was something—off—about the man. His arrogance and indifference? Shinwell made it more than plain that he had joined the group for debaucheries, not charity. And Rome? The man recently became Christian Bamford, the Duke of Allenby's stepbrother, when Rome's duke widower father married Allenby's widowed duchess mother. But Rome had made no effort to get to know Christian better, even though Christian had made overtures. To Oliver's mind, that showed a decided lack of character.

"Who are you, the mascot?" Rett snorted.

"How droll, Cousin," Bryan retorted. "Yes, I am younger, but they have befriended me and shown me an interesting side of London."

"Notting Hill is a little out of the way for a peer to have his town residence," Oliver murmured. "I thought the area was more upper-middle class and a draw for artists and the like."

"You really are a snob, aren't you, Brother?" Bryan sneered. "It suits us, and there are nearby entertainments."

Oliver frowned. Nearby was Notting Dale, a slum enclave within Notting Hill. About forty-odd years ago, the author, Charles Dickens, said of the area, "a plague spot scarcely equaled for its insalubrity by any other in London." In plain English, it had been an open sewer, attracting the worst of London, even to this day. A feeling of unease bloomed within Oliver. Perhaps his grandmother was correct in her assessment of Bryan. Young, impressionable, reckless, and yes, stupid. Oliver added the adjective for it fit.

Oliver settled back in his seat. "You will be keeping contact with us, little brother. You are to check in at the Tensbridge residence every Friday. In person. At ten o'clock sharp—in the morning."

Bryan sputtered. "Be damned If I will!"

"I am afraid Grams insisted on it. Do you wish your allowance to be cut off? One word from me to Father and Grams, and you will be forcibly returned to Wollstonecraft Hall secured to the carriage's roof, trussed like a Christmas turkey. Tread carefully and stay out of mischief."

Bryan crossed his arms, sulking. "You are a miserable bastard."

Oliver turned to gaze out the window. As the oldest and now heir apparent, he had to be.

ELEANORA GALWAY CALLED a gathering in The Galway Agency meeting room (the former study at Cleveland Street). Around the table was Eleanora, The Galway sisters' cousin, Sybil Norton, Edwina Callen, and Claudia.

"First, let me relay the good news that Althea came through her operation with flying colors. After her release from the hospital, she will be convalescing at the Allenby town house; no doubt tended to by the Duke of Chellenham."

After being hired, Claudia was informed that Eleanora's sister, Althea Galway, had experienced a recent health crisis. Although the details had not been revealed to the agency employees, it concerned Althea's leg, and she would no doubt need to use a cane for some time while recovering.

"But as soon as she feels more herself," Eleanora continued, "she will return to work. I imagine it will be a few weeks, not months."

"Oh, that is good to hear," Edwina enthused. "And when is the wedding to take place?"

"Before Christmas, I believe," Sybil interjected. "A small affair."

In other words, no employees are invited. Not that Claudia minded one way or the other. She liked the ladies in this agency well enough but decided it was best to keep things courteous and professional. This new direction in her life had thrown her for a loop more than she thought it would.

"And on to business." Eleanora organized her notes. "Viscount Tensbridge contacted me. He wishes to hire our agency to do surveillance work on a family member that he and the family are concerned about."

"Viscount Tensbridge, coming here?" Sybil exclaimed. "Brilliant! More aristocratic customers are just what we need. Think of the fee we can charge!"

"Who is Viscount Tensbridge?" Claudia asked, looking around the table.

"Oliver Wollstonecraft, heir to the Earl of Carnstone," Eleanora replied.

Edwina bit on her lower lip. "Oh, dear."

"What is it, Edwina?" Eleanora asked.

"I cannot be involved with the case, as I have a prior dealing with the viscount," Edwina relayed quietly. "Well, before he became viscount. Several weeks ago, Mr. Wollstonecraft asked me out to tea. It did not go as well as I had hoped, for he dropped me here, and I haven't heard from him since. Rather rude, I must say."

"Allenby told me that Tensbridge has been attending two family funerals in Kent these past weeks. It is why he is now Viscount Tensbridge," Eleanora replied.

Edwina flushed. "Of course, I should have realized. Regardless, it is best another take the case."

"Perhaps you are correct," Eleanora said. "Claudia, this will be your first solo investigation. How goes the Sir Tristan situation?"

"The past several nights, we have followed him to three brothels and two gaming hells. I have secured testimony from some of the workers at these places. Edwina need only take a few nights to wrap it up," Claudia responded.

"Excellent work, the both of you," Sybil smiled.

"It was mostly all Claudia," Edwina said. "She was very convincing in her disguise."

No one knew of her past except the Galway sisters, and they did not even comprehend all of it. But it would be polite to acknowledge the compliment.

"Thank you, especially to Edwina. She is an astute supervisor." Claudia gave Edwina as warm a smile as she could muster. This was another thing the investigative sisters were unaware of, nor were her former street worker associates. Claudia was all but dead inside. Emotion hardly entered any facet of her daily life.

It was a protective gesture, a means by which to avoid being hurt. Claudia was self-aware enough to understand that aspect. But feelings had been chipped away in her past—and because *of* her past. How could they not be? That is why encouraging any close friendships would not be prudent. The other ladies undoubtedly found her aloof at times, but Claudia had no choice. The behavior had become ingrained in her daily dealings with individuals.

"Viscount Tensbridge will be here in three days at two o'clock. Claudia, I wish you to sit in on the meeting."

Claudia gave a short nod. The conference continued for another twenty minutes, discussing upcoming cases. The sisters could pick and choose as they had more inquiries for their services than they had time to pursue them all.

When it was adjourned, Edwina took her aside. "He is quite handsome," she whispered.

"Who?"

"Oliver Wollstonecraft, the new viscount. He will be pleasing to look at, at any rate. Tall, with dark wavy hair, and well-formed. *Very* well formed, from what I could tell. Those shoulders."

"Will you step out with him again, if he should ask?"

Edwina bit her lip once again. "No. Although an initial spark, there was nothing under the surface. I felt uncomfortable the entire time we were together. I had no idea he was an heir to an earl when I first agreed to an afternoon stroll. Had I known, I would have refused."

Claudia scoffed. "And yet the Galway sisters have snagged dukes; why should that stop you? Never say anyone is above you. It puts you at a disadvantage in life. Just a bit of advice. From a colleague."

"But not from a friend?" Edwina asked shyly.

And here it is.

Claudia should throw up that frosty, defensive wall she had used many times over the past several years. "I think it best we stay co-workers."

"Oh, what utter nonsense," Edwina exclaimed, ignoring Claudia's detached tone. "We live here together; we will work on some cases as a team. Why not? When was the last time you had a close friend?"

Claudia pursed her lips. "My mother. And she died ten years ago."

Edwina slipped her arm through Claudia's, causing her to stiffen. "Then it is high time you had one. I will tell you now, I am persistent, but I will not badger you. You will warm to me; wait and see. We can start by sharing a cup of tea and a plate of biscuits tonight. Mrs. Bartle makes the most delicious, frosted shortbreads. Eight o'clock. Let me know if you are available."

For the life of her, Claudia could not bring herself to shake off Edwina's arm and say something horrible to her to drive her away. "Fine," she mumbled. "I will let you know."

Edwina chortled cheerfully. "That's the spirit."

Edwina then winked and headed toward Sybil to discuss the Sir Tristan case.

Perhaps taking this job was not such a sagacious decision after all.

Chapter 4

VISCOUNT TENSBRIDGE was ushered into the Galway Agency's conference room at two o'clock. Edwina Callen had not exaggerated; the man was handsome to a fault. Tall, with that lean musculature that Claudia imagined all women find appealing. His clean-shaven looks showed off his cheekbones to his advantage, and his thick, dark, wavy hair and flawless skin merely added to the prevailing picture of an indolent but beautiful aristocrat who had the world by the tail.

Mrs. Bartle, the housekeeper, accepted his coat, hat, and gloves and hastened from the room.

"Viscount Tensbridge, I am Eleanora Galway, and this is Claudia Ellingford, who will be taking your case."

The viscount took Eleanora's hand and bent over it, then slightly twisted toward Claudia, giving her a short nod of acknowledgment. How intriguing that the man's gaze had not met hers. Or maybe it wasn't interesting at all.

Once seated, he turned toward Eleanora. "I will come straight to the point. I require surveillance on my younger brother, Bryan Wollstonecraft." The viscount reached inside his suit coat and pulled out a photograph. Placing it on the table, he slid it across to Eleanora. "This is recent, as I received an Eastman Kodak folding camera as a gift."

Eleanora smiled. "We also have one. Miss Ellingford recently learned to use it if you wish the surveillance to include photographic evidence, my lord. That will be an extra charge."

"Of course. Include any photographs when necessary, but I believe most of this investigation will be undertaken at night. I do not expect a twenty-four-hour, seven-days-a-week report. Just a general accounting of his comings and goings. The family believes he has fallen in with a disreputable crowd and wishes to avoid any—complications."

The viscount brought forth an envelope, sliding it across the table to join the photograph. "This is the address and the names of the men he shares a residence with."

"He is not staying with you, my lord?" Claudia questioned. "Seems to me that if you wish to keep tabs on your brother, you'd keep him under your roof—and thumb." Typical of a peer handing off his family responsibility to another.

Eleanora glowered at her with eyes widened as if to say, "What are you doing?"

Tensbridge gazed at her for the first time since entering the room. Claudia almost gasped audibly. His eyes were a shade of gray-green she had never seen before, and they were quite mesmerizing. And so was that plump lower lip of his.

"What do you suggest, Miss Ellingford, that I lock him in a room?" his lordship questioned sarcastically. "He is twenty-two years of age, an adult, at least by the legal terminology. The family suggested he stay with my cousin and me, but Bryan refused. There we are."

Claudia didn't care for his sardonic tone and bit back a retort. Instead, she seized the envelope and tore it open. Her heart sank when she saw the address. His lordship's wayward brother lived in Notting Hill on Clarendon Road. Right next to Notting Dale, the aforementioned West End Avernus, a location she swore she would never return to. She could not refuse to take the case. It would mean elucidating why. And to reject her first solo case? Not wise.

"Is there a problem, Miss Ellingford?" Tensbridge asked gruffly.

"No, not at all, my lord," Claudia replied. "What can you tell me about Viscount Shinwell and Lord Linton?"

"I do not know them all that well. They joined The Rakes of St. Regent Park the same time as I—"

An undignified snort escaped Claudia's lips before she could restrain it. What an outlandish name for a men's club. Rather foolish, really.

"You *are* aware that your superior's husband, the Duke of Allenby, is a senior member of that group?" Tensbridge stated, with one thick eyebrow cocked.

Claudia arranged her features to show neutral indifference. Hell's bells, no, she was *not* aware Eleanora's duke husband was in the group or of the group's existence at all.

You are off to a great start, Claudia.

Her eyes narrowed as she glared at the viscount. "Thank you for informing me, my lord." There was no keeping the slight sneer from her voice. Claudia cleared her throat—best to change the subject. "I will begin the surveillance tomorrow. What are your brother's habits? Is he an early riser? Are there any clubs or pubs he likes to frequent?"

"That is why I hired *you*," Tensbridge sniffed haughtily. "As far as an early riser, I suppose Bryan is similar to the rest of the indolent upper classes and rarely ventures out before noon."

"It must be why you asked for a two o'clock appointment, my lord," she smiled sweetly.

The corner of his mouth quirked. An actual reaction: was he amused, annoyed, or perhaps both? It was difficult to tell as the man was so self-contained.

"We will start tomorrow. How can we reach you, my lord?" Eleanora asked.

"At the Tensbridge house, 5 Hill Street, Mayfair. Next to the Coach and Horses," he replied. "But I am not at home most evenings or some afternoons. Better to send word first to my butler, Dalton, to arrange an appointment."

Next to a public house, how convenient. And only home some evenings. Not a surprise there, either. Claudia exhaled. She must stop being so hypercritical of a man she knew nothing of. But peers and wealthy gentlemen generally had good cause to rile her contempt. Starting with her miserable father and to every man of the elite and gentry class she had come across while living on the streets.

By the restrained expression of annoyance on Eleanora's face, Claudia was about to be reminded of treating all clients with respect, regardless of their station in life.

It's best to nip this in the bud.

"Excuse my tone," she offered contritely, looking to Eleanora and Tensbridge. "I meant no disrespect. It appears I tumbled out of the wrong side of the bed this morning. I will throw myself into this investigation immediately, my lord, including discovering more about your brother's housemates."

Tensbridge nodded. "Thank you, Miss Ellingford. I must be off. Meetings at Parliament." He stood, and Eleanora called for Mrs. Bartle.

Claudia stood as well and came to stand before him. *Those eyes.* Not a shade she will soon forget. "I would like to arrange a sit-down interview with you, my lord, perhaps at the end of the week? I can give you my preliminary report and ask more in-depth questions regarding your brother." She added a brief smile to show the appropriate amount of eagerness.

"Is it just me you disdain, or my entire class?" His voice was low, his gaze intense. Standing this close, she could see a ring of gold around the irises of those extraordinary eyes. There was a tiny mole above his upper lip. How distracting. The man really was a handsome specimen. A flutter moved through her insides.

Attraction? It's best to dismiss that immediately.

"Oh, it is the entire class. Nothing personal at all, my lord. I will restrain my derision in the future, I promise."

There, the hint of a smile. It makes the viscount all the more appealing; drat it.

Mrs. Bartle handed Tensbridge his coat, hat, and gloves. "Good. Then I will see you Friday afternoon at two o'clock to hear your first report." He nodded and left the room.

"Claudia," Eleanora began.

"I know. I do apologize; that was not well done of me."

"Mrs. Bartle, please bring us a tea tray. When is my next appointment?" Eleanora asked the housekeeper.

"Not until half past four. I'll fetch the tea." She hurried off, leaving them alone.

Eleanora pointed toward a chair, and Claudia sat. "It was *not* well done, and it cannot occur again. The agency treats all clients respectfully, regardless of class, gender, race, or other classification. Let me tell you about The Rakes of St. Regent's Park. You might wish to take notes." Eleanora was not overtly angry; she spoke matter-of-factly. Regardless, Claudia heard a slight admonishment in Eleanora's tone. Claudia felt her cheeks grow hot. *New life, indeed.* Claudia nodded in response and pulled out her notebook and pencil—the ones Althea said she should always have on her.

"Indolent peers formed the club twenty years ago to seek excitement and adventures in moral iniquity. Over the years, the membership has ebbed and flowed. It now consists of a small group of friends and acquaintances, of whom most are married now. In the past months, the group's purpose has turned to more of a charity bent, but the few unmarried members still pursue certain vices."

Claudia wrote furiously.

"The current membership includes my husband, Christian Bamford, the Duke of Allenby. Gideon Broyles, the Duke of Watford. Damon Cranston, the Duke of Chellenham, and Althea's intended. Asher Colborne, Baron Wenlock. Merritt Redfern, Viscount Tolwood. Troy Buckingham, Viscount Shinwell. Oliver Wollstonecraft, Viscount Tensbridge. Mr. Gregory McFadden and Lord Rome Linton. And my husband tells me Mr. Rett Wollstonecraft, a cousin of Tensbridge's, will join the group." Eleanora spoke slowly, pausing after each name, giving Claudia time to write everything in her notebook.

Mrs. Bartle brought in the tea. On the tray were a plate of sandwiches and another of assorted biscuits, homemade ginger and store-bought Peek Frean and Company Garabaldis, a flat raisin biscuit, and chocolate-covered digestive biscuits. Claudia was famished.

Eleanora poured the tea. "The unmarried ones are from Tolwood onward. As far as Viscount Shinwell and Lord Linton, who is the second son of the Duke of Coldbridge, I do not know much about them. The Duke of Coldbridge recently married Christian's mother, making Rome my husband's stepbrother. But they are not close, though Christian has tried to include him in the family."

Eleanora passed her an empty plate and then held out the platter of sandwiches. Claudia took five wedges. She would say this of The Galway Agency: the food was plentiful and well prepared. Even better than at The Velvet Vine. It certainly improved over one meal a day at the Ten Bells.

"Shinwell has a reputation," Eleanora continued as she held out the platter of biscuits. "I suppose you could refer to him as the main rake now that Chellenham is engaged to my sister. If Bryan Wollstonecraft is staying with Shinwell, then the young man will be pulled into Shinwell's pursuit of depravity, I have no doubt. Linton, as well. I will ask Christian to ask around about the two men discreetly."

It astounded Claudia that a duke would be assisting his wife with investigations, but credit where it was undoubtedly due. Perhaps not all aristocrats were soulless bastards.

The bell sounded, and Mrs. Bartle rushed down the stairs. A few moments later, she entered the room and announced. "The Duchess of Watford."

Claudia stood and watched a beaming and beautiful Olivia Durham, now Olivia Broyles, a duchess, cross the threshold. Olivia held out her hands, and Eleanora took them.

"So good to see you, Eleanora." She turned toward Claudia and smiled. "Mary. Or rather Claudia." Olivia embraced Claudia, startling her into inaction. "You can hug me in return," Olivia whispered. Feeling awkward, Claudia patted Olivia's back.

They parted. "I stopped in to see Althea," Olivia continued. "What a scene! Damon fluffed her pillows and poured her tea. Who would have thought?"

Eleanora laughed. "Certainly not me. I thought Chellenham was an unrepentant rake, but I was mistaken, as he genuinely loves Althea and is completely devoted to her. Mrs. Bartle, please bring another cup."

"At once, Miss Eleanora." The housekeeper departed as the women sat at the table.

"Your housekeeper doesn't call you, "Your Grace'?" Olivia asked.

"While here at Cleveland Street, I am Eleanora Galway. Besides, Mrs. Bartle is like family. I would never insist on addressing me as such."

"I am not interrupting anything?" Olivia asked as she removed her gloves.

"Oliver Wollstonecraft was just here," Eleanora replied. "He has hired the agency, and I was filling in Claudia about The Rakes."

Olivia grinned. "A handsome cluster of naughty men, to be certain."

"Olivia, sorry to interrupt," Claudia interjected. "I meant to call on you before this, but I have been busy with training. I know you were told about my real first name, but I wanted to tell you in person about my actual last name, at least the one my mother put on my birth certificate. My father is Whinstone. I am Claudia Ellingford."

Olivia's friendly smile disappeared. "Whinstone?"

"Yes. The duke kept my mother in a few rented rooms at Eaton Place. He didn't come around much and hardly paid me any mind. Then we were dispatched to other places, each address heading toward absolute poverty until he cut us off altogether. Things went from bad to worse. My mother fell seriously ill, and I asked Whinstone for money to care for her in a decent room. But he refused to see me."

"Oh, that horrible beast," Olivia seethed.

"My mother died soon after, and I was alone. I had no one to turn to."

Olivia placed her hand over Claudia's and squeezed it in support. "I know, for it happened to me when my adopted father abandoned me in London. There is nothing worse than being alone on the streets."

Claudia nodded, unable to speak. A haze of hot tears glistened in her eyes as unfamiliar emotions swelled, but she blinked the tears back. Try as she might, there was no keeping the reaction in check, not when speaking about this. This bleak part of her life caused irreparable harm, scarring her soul and damaging her ability to deal with people and properly regulate her emotions.

"Whenever you are ready to talk about it, I'm here," Olivia whispered. "For I understand more than anyone." More loudly, she said, "Gideon and I are staying in London for the rest of the autumn and part of the winter as renovations continue at Foxmont. I want us to see each other, Claudia, and Gideon wishes to know you. He understands you are not related to him by blood, but there is a tie through marriage. Soon, I will tell you about Whinstone. You know he is in prison?"

Watford? What *would* her tie be to Olivia's husband? Illegitimate stepsister?

Hell's bells.

"Yes, Althea had mentioned Whinstone's imprisonment. We will talk of it later to be sure."

Olivia released her hand from Claudia's. "You will find no finer friends than the Galway sisters. Allow yourself to be open to new relationships, Claudia. I know it won't be easy to trust—anyone. But do make an effort. I still find it problematic."

Claudia nodded. A lump had formed in her throat. Trust. It will take work. She could try.

Olivia understood her well despite not knowing each other long. Claudia found Olivia's frank revelations and observations refreshing. Yes, if anyone comprehended living on the streets, Olivia would. Perhaps discussing it with someone when she is ready will lessen the nightmares and permit her to deal better with people and feelings.

Olivia patted her hand in reassurance and turned toward the doorway. "Ah, Mrs. Bartle. Thank you." The housekeeper placed a plate, and a cup and saucer before her. "I am hungry."

Eleanora poured the tea. Then, the platters were passed around.

"I am holding an afternoon tea in two weeks to raise money for Chellenhome," Olivia declared as she placed numerous sandwich slices on her plate. "Althea said she would attend. I wish for you both to attend, as well."

Claudia choked on her tea and coughed. "You can't be serious. Me? Among rich ladies? No, thank you."

"Like me, you are a daughter of a duke," Olivia replied firmly. "Illegitimate or not, you can hold your head up in any company, despite Whinstone's reputation and recent doings. Besides, it is for a good cause. Chellenham is my half-brother, and he owns Chellenhome for Foundlings."

The Duke of Chellenham was her half-brother? Which meant the late duke was her father. "Hell's bells," Claudia muttered.

Eleanora laughed. "There is quite a lot to fill Claudia in on."

"There is. Eleanora, your cousin, Sybil, and the other investigator, Miss Callen, are also invited," Olivia said as she sipped her tea. "It will be my first social event as the Duchess of Watford. I am nervous, and I need my friends there for support."

"We will gladly attend, won't we, Claudia?" Eleanora stated as she reached for the biscuits.

What choice did she have? She had other options, but why decline when Olivia acted so kind and compassionate? Despite her initial instinct to refuse, Claudia decided to accept. She might as well make an effort, at least for this tea party situation. "Yes. Very well. But I don't own a proper dress for a fancy afternoon tea."

"We will go shopping. I will pick you up tomorrow morning at ten. You can spare me two hours?" Olivia asked. "We might even have time for tea at Lyon's Tearoom."

A tearoom? Another first for Claudia. Since Bryan Wollstonecraft would no doubt be still abed, Claudia sighed. "Yes. But I agree to this under protest. I do not mix well with the elites."

Eleanora snorted. "And you think we do? Join the club, Claudia."

Olivia raised her cup and chuckled lightly in agreement.

Claudia was swept up into these ladies' lives whether she wanted it or not. Trying to remain disconnected will prove to be a challenge. On all fronts. Including finding Tensbridge attractive. That had been the most astonishing revelation of the day.

It would be best to set that aside for several reasons. Handsome or not, Viscount Tensbridge embodied what Claudia could not abide: the arrogant, indolent peer who disdains everyone below them. She had encountered worse examples than Tensbridge, but he disturbed her in ways beyond his stuffy manner. What had that Sentinel bloke stirred up inside of her that a stranger also piqued her interest? A client, no less.

Claudia shook her head. It is best to dismiss it, as nothing could ever come of it.

Chapter 5

IN A CROUCHED POSITION, Oliver waited on a rooftop overlooking the corner of Pottery Lane and Portland Road in Notting Dale. It is not that he lacked faith in Claudia Ellingford's investigative skills. Still, he spent the past few days pouring over maps of the area, familiarizing himself with the streets and back alleys of Notting Dale. Oliver wanted to see for himself what his brother was up to.

The slum had seen its worst days mid-century, when sewage and pig slurry ran in rivulets along the streets and fed into old clay pits, turning into a lagoon called The Ocean. The noxious hole was filled in some years ago, but the filth and stench of the area remained. The pig owners, along with most of the criminal element, were also driven out in the past two decades, but poverty and crime persisted in a tightly packed neighborhood of five streets.

When at Parliament yesterday, he asked the other members of the Hawkestone Progressive Caucus (as they were now calling themselves) about Notting Dale. Oliver was informed clearances were already underway and that by 1910, a mix of public and private housing would be in place. It was an ambitious plan, and after inspecting the site, he was skeptical it could be achieved.

Although some of the makeshift shacks had already been pulled down in some sections, all that remained were empty lots with piles of rubble or wood. Irish travelers had moved in on those vacant blocks of land with their colorful caravans. They were next on the list to be cleared, or so Oliver had been told.

Oliver watched Claudia—yes, he was thinking of her by her first name—stroll along Pottery Lane. She wore a brassy gold wig and the same outfit she had worn when he encountered her in the East End. Every one of his nerve endings pinged with awareness at the sight of her. Even in disguise, her very presence had his insides in a whirl.

A man, staggering down the street, stopped and leered, no doubt suggesting all sorts. He roughly grabbed Claudia's arm, and Oliver stood and ran along the edge of the crumbling roof toward them. But Claudia raised her skirt, pulled out her knife, and held it to the man's throat. The startled drunk stumbled away as fast as his short legs could take him. Oliver halted and smiled. She didn't need his help at all. At least not tonight. But he knew that anyway. He had complete confidence in Claudia's abilities. She was bold and fierce. Perhaps that caught his attention more than her beauty. Although she tried to hide her emotions, they slipped out, mainly when she made no bones about her low opinion of the upper class.

He turned and headed from whence he came. The buildings were so close that he could travel from roof to roof in most circumstances. Most buildings were two or three stories, hopefully not too dangerous if he had to jump to the ground. Glancing at the sky, Oliver scowled. It looked like rain, so he would make this an early night. Not too far away, in an abandoned building, he had hidden a sack containing his street clothes.

A scream and a torrent of curses reached Oliver's hearing. He halted and observed a rickety set of stairs hugging the side of the building heading right to the street. Grabbing the roof's edge, he swung downward, silently resting in a crouch position on the landing, his hand splayed in front of him.

"Gimmie the money, you hag!" the man growled, jostling the woman so hard her head bobbed back and forth.

"I earned it, 'tis mine, you daft gobshite!" the woman screamed.

The man hauled off and slapped her hard, then punched her midsection, causing her to drop to the ground. That was more than enough. Oliver took the stairs two at a time, then jumped in front of them. With a swift motion, he grabbed the truncheon from his belt and shoved it into the man's soft belly, bringing him to his knees.

He groaned. "Ya feckin' shite!"

With a lightning-swift motion, Oliver gave him a bash on the temple with the cudgel, hard enough to knock him out. The man lay unconscious on the broken, dirty cobbles.

Oliver held out his hand to the woman to assist her with standing. "I'd leave him there. He will awake soon enough."

Once on her feet, the woman spat in the insentient man's direction. "Aye, he deserved it and all. He tried to take me laundry earnings. I don't work bloody fourteen-hour shifts as an ironer to have this layabout snatch me money. Aye, he's me husband. Doesn't do a stitch of work and lets the kiddies run wild; he does. Anyways, thanks and all."

Oliver touched the brim of his floppy hat. "The Sentinel, at your service."

"Well, ta. Too bad you won't be around the next time I get paid. I'd best hurry off, settle the rent, and buy food afore he steals it all to purchase gin. Obliged to you."

"Are you well?" Even in the dark alley, he could see the red welt on her cheek from the slap.

"Kind of you to inquire, but 'tis typical of the men 'round here. I manage, as do others." The woman smiled at him, showing broken teeth. Then she turned and hurried down the street.

If only those snobs in The House of Lords could see how others live, perhaps they would be moved enough to do more—wishful thinking, as most of the upper crust could not give a hang for anyone less fortunate.

"Well, if it isn't Tall Leather Man, once again. You're called The Sentinel, right? What are you doing in this slum section of the city? Following me, perhaps?"

Oliver swung about in the direction of the feminine voice.

Claudia Ellingford.

Well, damn.

CLAUDIA HAD HEARD THE commotion and arrived in the alley in time enough to see The Sentinel put the boots to a drunk and hear his conversation with the washerwoman.

The changes in The Piggeries since she had lived here almost ten years ago astounded Claudia. While still a slum, it was not nearly as horrifying as her reminisces. There was more industry, like numerous steam laundries, which the woman The Sentinel had rescued no doubt worked.

"No, I am not following you."

Claudia raised an eyebrow in disbelief. "So, it's a coincidence?"

"It is. I do not spend my time just in the East End."

Claudia stepped closer and leaned in.

"Are you sniffing me?" his deep voice rumbled.

"Just seeing if you are wearing that expensive scent again."

"I don't wear a scent."

Well, she could argue that point, for she certainly smelled one the last time they had met. And it was an enticing aroma.

The man sprawled on the cobbles started to moan.

The Sentinel touched the brim of his oversized hat. Blast, she still couldn't see his eyes. "Good evening, Lady Investigator. Stay safe."

Before she could blink, he disappeared around the corner. He *had* followed her, for Claudia did not believe in coincidences. This time, she wouldn't let him slip away into the shadows. Claudia rushed along in the same direction he headed but couldn't see him. Then, she glanced skyward. By the light of the moon, partly covered by gray clouds, she saw a man's silhouette running along the edge of the roofs. Claudia picked up the pace, keeping the mysterious figure in her sight.

She turned the corner, and—no Sentinel. What did he do, drop into one of the buildings? Some of these places looked as if they were about to be demolished. Good. The whole area should have been razed decades ago. Claudia scanned up, then down the street. With hands on her hips, she huffed in exasperation. She stood there for several minutes, wondering where to go and what to do next.

An arm looped about her waist from behind, causing her to gasp. She was brought up against hardened muscle. "Don't reach for your dagger. I mean you no harm."

The Sentinel.

Claudia hadn't heard him come up behind her at all.

Oh, he is good.

"Hell's bells. You shouldn't do that."

His hot breath trickled across her neck, sending shivers through her—and not from fear. His mask must be made of material that allowed him to breathe easily but thick enough to muffle his voice. He nuzzled behind her ear. "You're not wearing any scent, either."

"Too much of a giveaway," Claudia murmured.

"Yes, I will remember that." He trailed his gloved hand over the curve of her hip, leaving heat in its wake.

About to turn around and face him, numerous raised voices headed in their direction.

"This way, yeah? He ain't got too far. Beat me, will he?"

"We're with you, Charlie!" another yelled.

The Sentinel clasped her hand. "Come with me."

"We can fight them," Claudia stated emphatically.

"Not tonight."

They started running along Portland Road, with the sounds of numerous pairs of boots hitting the cobblestones not far behind. Keeping up with the man's long strides wasn't exactly easy, but Claudia managed it. They turned into an alley, and The Sentinel propelled her between a half-demolished shack and another building. She glanced over her shoulder to see him pulling loose boards across the narrow entrance behind her.

"Quiet," he whispered.

The vigilante knew his way around The Piggeries, for how else could he know about this hiding place? The Sentinel looped his arm around her waist again, pulling her against him. Only this time, there was something hard and prodding at her back. Was the man aroused? While that should disgust her, it did not. Instead, Claudia rolled her hips against that noticeable hardness, causing a hissing, low moan to escape his lips. Feeling bold, she reached behind for his hand and brought it to her breast. Already, her nipples were hard. When had she ever had such an immediate and sensual reaction toward a man?

Never. Not like this.

Until tonight.

She found Tensbridge attractive, but the reaction paled next to the one she experienced with this masked vigilante.

The Sentinel froze for a moment, then cupped her breast. She wasn't wearing a corset, only a thin chemise, so when his fingers brushed by her nipple, she was the one moaning. He rubbed against her, massaging her breast, and Claudia let her head fall back against his muscled chest. How tempting to lift her skirt—

"Check that alley, Andy!" a voice yelled.

They stopped moving, although he kept his hand on her aching breast. Claudia held her breath as the man stomped along the broken cobbles. Thankfully, there was no light from this angle, not even from the moon. The Sentinel reached into her low-cut gown and clasped her breast. He had removed his glove at some point, so they were skin against skin. How had he managed that? Claudia bit her lip to stem the passionate moan from escaping. He rolled her nipple between his fingers, causing her to grow wetter.

Emboldened, Claudia reached behind and laid her hand against that prodding hardness. She didn't dare grip it (not that she could do it effectively as she wasn't a contortionist), or the leather would creak. As best as Claudia could, she ran the tip of her finger along his length. Impressive. The feel of him only heightened her passion. How surprising to find she even possessed any.

When the man called Andy moved the boards, all he would see was darkness. The Sentinel wearing all black would melt into the shadows. They stayed perfectly still.

The man pulled the boards aside. "'Tis nothin' here!" Andy yelled.

The sound of the boards banging against the wall and retreating footsteps allowed Claudia to expel the breath she had been holding.

The Sentinel pulled his hand from the front of her gown and stepped out of her reach. "Wait here. I'll check to see if it is safe."

Then he did the strangest thing. He moved aside Claudia's hair, leaned in, and kissed her neck. Soft lips made contact on that sensitive spot at the curve of her shoulder. He must have pulled his mask up far enough to kiss her. The man was incredibly deft at silently moving about and removing a glove or lifting his mask without making a sound. Claudia spun about, not manageable in such a narrow space.

But he was gone.

"Hell's bells," she whispered.

Striding out of the hiding place, she made her way to the head of the alley, glancing up and down the street. Deciding it was safe, Claudia pulled her shawl over her head and strolled toward Pottery Lane.

Every nerve ending was alive and thrumming.

So, this is how passion feels. It certainly is exhilarating.

And she had a distinct feeling this would *not* be the last time their paths crossed.

Claudia was looking forward to it.

Chapter 6

OLIVER PACED BACK AND forth in the study, waiting for Claudia Ellingford's arrival. Since their encounter in the alley, he had barely slept a wink for the past two nights. He would have to stay even more detached than usual when meeting with her today. It was his only protection from taking her into his arms and kissing her soundly. He flexed his hand as he could still feel her breast. Never had he been so—hard. When she had touched him, running her finger along his stiff and throbbing shaft—

The aching. The *yearning*.

The intense sensation had overtaken him, sending rolls of desire throughout his body, awakening every nerve ending, and stirring those hungry emotions to life.

What he had done was bold, rubbing against her, caressing her breast. And kissing her soft neck. What had compelled him? The danger they were in? The fact he was concealed under a disguise and free to act audaciously? For he would never behave that way as Viscount Tensbridge.

Oliver swiped a couple of books off the top of his desk in frustration. They clattered to the floor. When he glanced up, Dalton stood in the doorway with Claudia Ellingford next to him, one eyebrow cocked in question.

Damn it all.

"Miss Ellingford to see you, my lord. I will see that the tea tray is sent up," Dalton declared.

So much for staying detached; she looked lovely today, wearing a soft gray skirt, a matching short jacket, a small gray hat, and a white ruffled blouse. Her red hair was carefully pinned in place and swept up from her neck. That lovely neck Oliver wished to nuzzle and kiss again. But another attractive feature was her light hazel eyes, more green than brown—a perfect match for her glorious red hair.

"Please, take a seat, Miss Ellingford." He waved his arm toward the chair in front of the desk. Oliver swiftly sat, for arousal gripped him tight once again.

"Did you receive bad news, my lord?" she asked.

"What? Oh, the books. It is nothing of consequence. Tell me of your preliminary report." God, he sounded imperious.

Claudia reached into her case and brought out her notebook. "I followed your brother for four nights. All of them were spent in The Piggeries. Notting Dale. A slum area, if you were not aware, my lord."

"I am well aware as we discuss such things in Parliament. I have been told that clearances have already started in Notting Dale. There are plans for a mix of public and private housing to be completed by 1910." He sounded arrogant. But Oliver had to keep his distance, physically and emotionally.

"I will believe that about the housing when I see it, my lord. And isn't Tensbridge a courtesy title? Why would you be in Parliament?" she questioned. Claudia was polite and professional, and she wasn't holding his superior tone against him.

"I am not in the House of Lords. But since I'm the heir to the Earl of Carnstone, I am allowed to sit on a particular committee. Please continue."

"Your brother was in the company of Shinwell, Linton, and another man. I described the man to the Galways sisters, and they identified the man as Viscount Tolwood. The men attended an illegal dog fight, a pub, a gambling house, and a brothel. And that was just the first night."

Oliver expelled an exasperated breath in response.

"They stumbled home about one o'clock in the morning, and Tolwood took a hansom cab to his home, I assume," she continued, reading from her notes. "I started surveillance again at five o'clock the next afternoon. The place they are staying in was recently converted into flats, as many grand town houses have been of late. The residence belonged to a peer. It might have been Shinwell's father, but whoever owns it recently sold the property to the Central London Dwelling Company. I passed the information on to Miss Eleanora, and she stated Allenby would confirm the information."

It happened all over the city—prime real estate was grabbed up and turned into flats or rooming houses. It made sense with the overcrowding in various parts of London, but these companies were in it only for profit, not for any philanthropic reasons. These flats were not meant for those needing housing, like the homeless or working class looking for better accommodations. They were for the wealthy and no one else.

"Your brother and his flatmates are on the bottom floor." Claudia continued, "Easy for me to peer into the windows. There was a woman with them, I assume a prostitute, but who knows? Anyway, they shared her."

His brother was all in on the debauchery. "And you saw this?"

Claudia shrugged. "The draperies were open enough for me to peer in. After the woman departed, they drank. Copious amounts. Then, they returned to The Piggeries. I tracked them to the Black Moon pub, where they imbibed some more. Later in the evening, I followed them to a small shack. There were no signs on the building. They were only there for a few moments. Then they headed to Bangor Street, where the prostitutes congregate, and each had back-alley sex before returning to the flat."

His brother was a reckless, imprudent dolt—and he probably hadn't used any protection.

"The small shack in question," Claudia stated. "I discovered that it is a place to buy street-grade opium."

Oliver went very still. It was his grandmother's worst fear. Although the Pharmacy Act of 1868 controlled and registered the sale of certain poisons—of which opium was one—a trade still existed for those who did not wish to buy it from a chemist. The drug found outside an apothecary's control was also cheaper, not regulated, or of the best quality. Oliver had learned plenty from being a member of Hawkestone's caucus group.

"Where is this shack located?" Oliver asked.

"Why do you wish to know?"

Claudia Ellingford was maddingly inquisitive—a good trait for an investigator.

"To bring it to the attention of those in power."

"As if they are going to do anything about it. Very well, it is on Pottery Lane. It is a shack, more of a lean-to, next to the Black Moon pub."

"Are there opium dens in this Piggery area?" Oliver asked.

"They are in decline, even in the East End, but I assume there are dens in most sections of London. Most are by the dock area to service sailors. Anyway, allow me to give you more of my report. I peered through the windows in the rear of the house, and all I could see was half-eaten food and dishes everywhere, along with empty liquor bottles. A woman stopped in on the third day. I thought it might be another prostitute, but I observed her taking rubbish to the outside bin. They must have someone coming in to clean now and then."

"So, not living in complete filth, there's a mercy," Oliver murmured sarcastically.

"I have taken a few photographs during the day when there is light. But most of their activities are nocturnal. Do you wish me to continue with this surveillance, my lord?"

Dalton entered with the tea tray, setting it on the desk between them. There was also a plate of iced sugar biscuits. Dalton served the tea and then left them alone. Claudia poured milk into her tea, took the cup and saucer, and sat back. She sipped, watching him closely over the rim of the cup.

"Yes. Continue for now. My family wishes a thorough report over several days and perhaps a few weeks."

"Is this what is referred to as sowing those wild oats? Did you not do the same in your twenties, my lord?" The tug of a teasing smile pulled at the corner of her lovely lips.

"I am still *in* my twenties, Miss Ellingford. And no, I do not indulge in excessive immoralities. I live a more regulated life."

"I can well imagine," she murmured as she sipped her tea. "It is my experience that young men of means eventually run afoul of the law or, worse, the criminal element within slum areas."

"Precisely what I—and the family—wish to avoid. I assume there are gangs of thieves in this Notting Dale?"

Claudia reached for a biscuit. "Yes, my lord. And a ruthless rookery boss. Pottery Lane is not referred to as Cut-throat Lane for nothing." After consuming two biscuits, she flipped open her notebook to a fresh page, pencil in hand. "Now, tell me about your brother and your family. Do you have any siblings?"

"What has this to do with the case?"

She eyed him askance. "So I can ascertain your brother's character, calculate his next move, and how he will respond to certain circumstances."

"Fine. I am the oldest. Next comes two sisters, Lorene and Judith, and Bryan is the youngest. Yes, he is spoiled. My parents are the first to admit it. He has been mischievous his entire life, always getting into trouble. But mildly so, nothing like this. We are close-knit to a fault. I grew up surrounded by aunts, uncles, grandparents, great-grandparents, and multiple levels of cousins, as we all live within a three-to-ten-mile radius. We love and respect each other. To me, family is everything. That is why I and others in the family are concerned about Bryan."

CLAUDIA FELT THAT PESKY emotional lump forming in her throat again. She knew little of what Tensbridge spoke of, at least, the extensive, loving family aspect of it. She and her late mother were close; all they had was each other. But this? Claudia experienced a twinge of envy.

She pointed to the black armband. "I am sorry for your loss, my lord."

"Thank you. I lost my grandfather, the earl, and great-granduncle within ten days. Both of whom I admired greatly. They were the pillars of the family. I was particularly close to my grandfather. He was, in essence, my hero." Tensbridge's countenance softened, and she could see the sadness in those beautiful greenish-gray eyes of his. His heartfelt declaration also caused her heart to squeeze with empathy. And touch her in an unknown place.

Blast the man for making me feel.

"Is your brother attending university?" Claudia asked, wishing to change the subject.

"No. Bryan completed his studies this past spring. He has a common law degree from Cambridge, and the next step is to take his Postgraduate Certificate in Law. We had expected he would find work at a law firm as an apprentice before completing his studies, but he has not done so as yet. My brother is intelligent enough. He finished 10th in his class."

"Impressive. So not a dunderhead when it comes to education. However, lacking in basic common sense, am I correct?" Claudia observed.

"You have the right of it. My brother stopped by at ten this morning," Tensbridge continued gravely. "I told him that if he still wished to receive his allowance, he must check in every Friday. He looked the worse for wear, but I decided not to lecture him. Not at this juncture. Continue with the case, and when next we meet, I will require a layout of every place Bryan visited and any names of shady characters he has contact with on a continual basis."

Claudia bit back an exhalation. This would mean an extended period in The Piggeries. There was one man she loathed to cross paths with and the main reason she wore an elaborate disguise. A cruel criminal who placed his sticky fingers in every vice in the slum. A man who, for a short period, had taken up with her mother. Her mother had lived in fear, never knowing when his foul temper would explode. Her mother, Aileen, entered the relationship for monetary reasons only to keep a roof over their head (such as it was) and the wolf from the door. And as a sort of protection.

Jedidiah Danaher.

In reality, Jedi Danaher was worse than any hungry wolf. He stood as a beast in a class all his own. There was still a large Irish contingent in Notting Dale. Was Danaher still the rookery boss? Did he still own the Black Moon Pub? If there were any justice, Danaher would be dead already. How old would he be now, early to mid-forties? It was always hard to gauge his age, and Danaher never spoke of it. Chances are, he wasn't aware of his exact age anyway.

"Miss Ellingford?"

Claudia was pulled from her disturbing thoughts. "Sorry. Yes, I will try to discover any people your brother comes in contact with."

"Do not put yourself in danger. If there is not a safe way to collect these names, then by all means, dismiss the request."

"I will keep that in mind, my lord."

"Please call me Tensbridge. I am still not used to all this 'my lord' falderal."

"As you wish. The Duke of Allenby is making inquiries about Shinwell and Linton. I should have more to report the next time we meet. Shinwell is the heir apparent to his father, the Earl of Darrington. Do you know the earl at all?"

Tensbridge shook his head. "No. The Wollstonecrafts stay mostly near home in Kent. We do not socialize with London society except when necessary. My grandfather only traveled to the city when Parliament was in session. I imagine my father will do the same. I am only here because of the progressive caucus I am in. If only my brother's interest ran more to helping others than helping himself."

Progressive? How interesting. Her opinion of Tensbridge rose a notch. "Are there any other family members currently in the city that your brother might seek out besides your cousin, Garrett Wollstonecraft?"

Tensbridge shook his head. "No. My father and mother will arrive next month and stay at the Carnstone house near mine. And I believe another cousin will be traveling with them. Ronan Wollstonecraft. He is my Uncle Bennett's son and 26 years old. He, Rett, I, and a few cousins grew up together. We are close. Ronan will no doubt come to stay with me at some point."

"But your younger brother was not part of this tight-knit group?"

"No. Being five years younger, my brother did not fit in with our various adventures and revelries. Ronan's twin brother, Ryan, was also part of our group."

So Tensbridge was 27 years old. She thought him older, judging by the mature air he emanated. "Identical twin?" Claudia asked, caught up in the family narrative.

"No. My father and Uncle Bennett were twins, my grandfather and his brother, Riordan. None of them are identical. My parents did not have any twins."

Claudia peeked up from her notebook and smiled at Tensbridge. "You have quite the family tree. How lucky you are."

He raised an eyebrow as if trying to note the sarcasm in her statement, but he would find none. Tensbridge *was* blessed to have such a large, devoted family. And Claudia should not have commented on it. It made things too personal. Her smile disappeared as she continued to take notes.

"And you were not so fortunate?" Tensbridge asked softly.

"No. But I am not here to talk about me." She stood abruptly. "I should go. I have much to do and will continue the surveillance tonight."

Tensbridge was out of his chair in a flash, his movement so swift, it passed her sight as a wool suit blur. He took her hand, and that contact caused heat to wrap around her insides. What on earth was going on? Now, another man caused a physical reaction? It was so startling that Claudia pulled her hand from his as if she had been burned.

She took a step toward the door. "Shall I report back at the same time next week?" Her voice sounded cold to her own ears.

"Yes." The viscount stood stock-still with his hands clasped behind his back. His intense gaze never wavered. "Until next week. Dalton!"

The butler stepped into the room. "Yes, my lord?"

"See that Miss Ellingford catches a hansom cab to her destination."

Claudia headed toward the door with the butler.

"Good afternoon, Miss Ellingford."

Claudia stopped in her tracks. His farewell was spoken with a subdued, almost sensual tone. No coldness at all. She turned, met his heated gaze, and nodded. "Good afternoon, my lord."

Claudia had replied in the same soothing voice. What was she doing? Flirting? There was no time to think about her ill-thought-out response, so she rushed toward the door. As she followed Dalton through the front entrance, she laid her hand over her heart.

Hell's bells, it's pounding like mad.

Oh, this was not good. Not good at all.

Chapter 7

OLIVER CONSIDERED THE men sitting around the table. They were attending a meeting of The Rakes of St. Regent's Park in a secluded building on Albany Street. It was the first such gathering in over a month. Introductions between Rett and the rest of the group had already transpired. Now they were waiting for their president, Damon Cranston, the Duke of Chellenham, to call the meeting to order.

Across the table, Shinwell and Linton whispered together, casting glances at the other men. Shinwell stood. "Before we get to business, I wish to make a proposal."

"By all means," Damon remarked nonchalantly. "You have the floor."

"I do not care for the direction this gathering is taking. Charitable works? We are called *The Rakes*. Yet, at our last meeting, you proclaimed that this would be the main direction of the group going forward. It is not what this assemblage was founded on and is not why I joined. There is time enough when I am in my dotage to give to people in need. But for now, I want to pursue all the delights life has to offer."

A murmur of agreement came from a couple of the men.

"Honestly, this is all a crashing bore," Shinwell continued, his tone conceited. "You recently married men have suddenly become pillars of the community, steadfast and faithful. I thought a few of you would still indulge in amatory adventures. But no. You are all devoted husbands or husbands-to-be. Chellenham, your change of character boggles the mind. You were one of the most notorious rakes in this city—you and Watford. No one makes such a transformation in a matter of weeks or months. You are both living a lie."

Growls came from Damon and Watford, and Allenby laid his hand on Damon's arm to halt him from vaulting out of the chair and physically attacking Shinwell. Or so Oliver surmised, for Damon had a murderous look. The arrogant fool viscount was correct on one matter. It had been quite the conversion that had taken place in Damon. And Watford, too, for that matter. Oliver welcomed it. Falling in love could change a man. Who would have thought it? There was no doubt more to it than that, but it is Damon's business. And Watford's.

"I propose that the purportedly virtuous men form your own group and leave those of us who wish to be rakes to continue with the decades-old tradition," Shinwell concluded, giving them a self-righteous smile.

You could hear a pin drop in the cavernous room.

"*That* will not happen," Damon ground out. "If you and others wish to splinter off, have at it. The name remains with us."

Watford nodded in agreement. "As the last original founding member, I also say the name stays here. You have no claim on it. And do not endeavor to take it, as you do not want to cross me or any other here. We are not so staid as you believe."

"You only adopted the Rakes name recently. What do you care?" Shinwell shot back.

"Officially, that is true. But the sobriquet has existed for years. It stays with us," Watford bellowed.

"I do not see why we cannot do both," Gregory McFadden said. "There is more to life than never-ending debauchery. Especially in this enlightened age of industrialism and aestheticism." McFadden was a recent prospective member, a successful businessman with his fingers in numerous pies, including newspapers and railroads.

"Not in my life," Shinwell retorted. "What do I care about industrialism or the great unwashed of London, including snotty-nosed by-blows living on the streets? Really, Chellenham? A home for foundlings? And you will be taking in some of these bastards into your home? What a disgrace. But the bigger scandal is you claiming these brats as your siblings. You're as mad as a March hare."

This time, Allenby did not hold Damon back. The enraged duke was out of his chair, pushing Shinwell against the wall in the blink of an eye. Damon jammed his forearm into Shinwell's neck, causing the viscount to gasp and wheeze.

"Utter one more word of insult, and I will crush your windpipe. Gather your things and leave now. Never return." Damon stepped away, breathing hard. Oliver was shocked at Damon's sudden burst of implied violence but felt it warranted.

Shinwell coughed, rubbing his neck. "You *are* completely deranged. Come, Linton. Let us leave this pathetic group to their reformist lives."

Allenby turned toward Linton, who stood next to Shinwell. "Really, Rome?" he questioned his new stepbrother.

Linton shrugged. "I agree with Shin. I have better things to do with my time than raise money for orphans or whatever good deeds you have planned."

Viscount Tolwood stood.

Damon laughed cynically. "You always were a sniveling dog, always following others. Good riddance, Tolwood."

"I thought you were seeking a bride?" Asher Colborne, Baron Wenlock asked Tolwood. From what Oliver understood, Wenlock, Tolwood, Allenby, and Damon had known each other since their early days at school.

"Well, I am, Ash," Tolwood replied meekly. "But I say, why not have a little fun as I do?"

"McFadden?" Shinwell questioned.

McFadden brushed a piece of lint from his sleeve, imaginary or not. "I am not interested. I have a business reputation to protect and can do that well enough here. Besides, I don't like you, Shinwell. Not from our first meeting. You are a vain, self-seeking arse, and I want no part of you."

Well spoken. Oliver could not agree more.

Shinwell scowled. "Tensbridge? Considering your do-gooder family ties, I presume you will stay with these boring converts of pious philanthropism. You know, I have never seen you darken a brothel's door. I do not trust a man who doesn't indulge."

"And I don't trust a man who indulges too much," Oliver retorted, keeping the bulk of his anger under tight control. "My vices run more to gaming, not that it is your concern. I am staying here. And so is my cousin."

"But of course, he is," Shinwell barked cynically as he gathered his coat and hat. "Well, gentlemen. By all means, go forth and indulge in tedious charity work. I have organized an exclusive private party at The Velvet Vine tonight. If any of you change your minds, the bacchanalia starts at eight sharp." He gave the men a mocking bow. Then, turning on his heel, Shinwell swept from the room with Tolwood and Linton close behind him.

The door slammed.

Exclusive private party. Which meant an orgy of various delights, sexual and otherwise.

"First note of business, change the locks," Damon snapped irritably. "Second note: donate Tolwood, Linton, and Shinwell's recent membership fees to various charities."

"I concur," Watford snarled.

"Some of us have known Tolwood most of our lives. How many times had we protected him from bullies through the years, and he up and swans out of here following Shinwell? Of all men?" Wenlock exclaimed, shaking his head. "So much for loyalty."

"Are all the meetings this dramatic?" Rett asked as a footman entered the room, carrying a platter of sandwiches.

"Not quite," Allenby smirked. "Though the delivery of a severed leg last year certainly tops the list."

Rett's eyebrows arched skyward. Oliver would have to tell him the story later, as he had only recently learned of the episode. It is where Allenby met his duchess, Eleanora Galway, the co-owner of the Galway Investigative Agency.

"Thomas," Damon called out to the footman. "When you are done serving, I want you to rouse a locksmith and have him come immediately. I will pay the man extra. All the locks to this club must be replaced. Tonight."

"At once, Your Grace," the young man replied firmly.

When they were alone, Damon pushed the journal away. "It was bound to happen. Some of us *have* changed. But for others, the transformation began long before any of us fell in love. Well, perhaps not Watford."

The men chuckled.

"But as soon as he met Olivia, he fell hard. Love can be transformative," Allenby added.

"As the rest of you will someday discover," Wenlock said. "So, where does this leave us?"

"I indeed wish the main focus of this group to be philanthropic initiatives, but there is no reason why we cannot continue recommending various places for those who wish to indulge in whatever," Damon suggested. "Only please let us dispense with the grandiose bragging of one's conquests. It is tedious to the extreme, even when I did it."

The men laughed.

"I propose we dispense with titles," Wenlock proffered. "We are all friends here, first names only going forward when we are alone like this. And any new members who join must have the full approval of all the other members."

The Rakes pounded the table in agreement.

"And any prospective members, like Gregory, Rett, and Oliver, should be full members this very moment," Wenlock concluded.

Damon began to write in their club journal about the recent doings. Talk broke out among the men as the sandwich platters were passed around, along with coffee, tea, and the whiskey decanter.

Oliver tried to keep track of the conversation, but his mind wandered toward Shinwell's declaration about the revel in the East End. He would no doubt be taking Bryan to the brothel with him. Which meant Claudia would follow them. The Velvet Vine had a good reputation, although its neighborhood was not the best.

Would his brother be attending? He had to know. Right now. He should track them to see if they stay clear of danger. Oliver glanced at the clock. It was closing in on seven.

He stood abruptly. "Gentlemen, I have another appointment. I must take my leave. Rett, you stay and take copious notes. Tell the group about your idea of opening another free medical clinic within the Hornsby-Wollstonecraft initiative."

Rett blinked rapidly, then glowered. He was putting his cousin on the spot, as they had yet to discuss the idea at length. Oliver didn't wait for Rett's response, as he had already grabbed his coat and hat and halfway down the stairs.

THE SUN HAD STARTED to sink, causing rays to skitter across the clouds, casting an array of pink and purple colors in the sky. It was a rare but beautiful sunset. Claudia paid the hansom driver and jumped out of the cab.

Poplar High Street. The men couldn't be going to The Velvet Vine and Tackle, could they? Claudia had followed their cab to the East End from Notting Hill. She knew Shinwell and Linton attended a meeting on Albany Street because Tensbridge had sent a note to her informing her of that fact. So Claudia stayed in Notting Hill, watching the younger Wollstonecraft. Three men arrived at Notting Hill long enough to gather Bryan, so she followed behind in another hansom. Tonight, Claudia wore a wig of long flowing ebony locks and a putty nose. She slipped into the alley behind The Velvet Vine. Trying the door, she found it open, but before stepping across the threshold, she was met by a solid muscular wall.

Claudia looked up. "Colin, it's me. Mary O'Toole." She used her Irish accent.

The cook approached the door, wiping her hands on a tea towel. "That's Mary, sure as brass. Let her in."

Colin stepped aside, and Lily, the brothel's cook, smiled. "Look at you! I thought you were off on a new adventure?"

"I am in disguise."

"Well, it's convincing. That is quite the hook on that nose."

Claudia swept aside the tangled locks to show the full force of a convincing cosmetic scar. "I am following someone. Will Pan see me?"

"I'm sure he will. Colin, take Mary to his office, through the back way. I have to attend to my meat pies. It is for a private party."

No doubt the men she had followed will be attending.

"Ta, Lily. You are a dear."

Colin took her through the behind-the-wall walkway to Pan's office. "Stay here. Don't wander about," Colin grumbled.

"Aye."

The only one who knew of her real name was Pan. Even when she told her friends of her new opportunity—without revealing many details—she never mentioned her actual name or past. To their credit, they didn't ask. Claudia wanted to make a clean break from life on the streets and her Mary O'Toole persona. How ironic that she wound up back here.

Pan entered the room, showing no surprise at her appearance. No doubt Colin had already told him. "Claudia. Wonderful to see you. On a case?"

"I am," she answered, using her own voice. "I followed Shinwell and his party here. One of the men is my subject of interest. The eager puppy with the wavy brown hair."

Pan swept his arm toward the chair before his desk, inviting her to sit. "Shinwell and guests have been situated in one of the salons upstairs. I imagine the activities are already underway. And the eager puppy is with the group. Practically shaking with anticipation."

"I can well imagine. Is there any way to observe the goings on?" Pan had various voyeur rooms and strategic peek holes to ensure safety and observe the clientele to make sure they did not get out of hand with the sex workers in any way.

"Well, that would violate my customers' privacy, but Colin will watch the eager puppy, and I will send you a report to Cleveland Street. Will that suffice? They will be here all night, so there is no use hanging about for hours. I doubt they will go anywhere from here except home."

"Perhaps you have the right of it."

Pan clasped his hands and placed them on the desk. "Are you settling in? Your girls have been asking about you."

"They are hardly *my* girls," Claudia dismissed.

"Oh? Not from what they have told me. You were their protector, their guardian angel. You collected the money and saw that they were fed and had a roof over their heads most nights. And you kept none of the earnings for yourself. You stood up to any men who threatened them. Even cut a few."

"It was more than a few. I was, in essence, the ladies' procurer, their flesh peddler, their pimp. Let's not gloss it over. When I found myself alone at 16 years old, I soon learned there was strength in numbers. I surrounded myself with others in my situation. We managed to survive."

"And here you are within another group of women. The lady detectives. Are you protecting them, or are they protecting you?"

Pan hit a little too close to home. He always was an astute study of human character, its strengths and frailties. It is why he was an efficient manager in running successful brothels. As to his question, Claudia did not know the answer. That may be why she agreed to work for the investigative agency. In reality, she *did* move from one protective circle into another. Strength in numbers? Or maybe she needed the company of others more than she believed. To feel safe. Shielded.

What complete hogwash.

Claudia stood abruptly. "I must be off. I appreciate that you're sending me a report. Let me know if the eager puppy returns anytime, with others or alone."

"Bryan Wollstonecraft? Of course. I ask for names and references from all my customers. Shinwell claims the young man just joined the Rakes of St. Regent's Park."

"As far as I know, Wollstonecraft is not a part of the group unless that is a recent development."

"Interesting. I will look into that. As an aside, Colin informs me that a fancy carriage with no insignia on the door is parked on the street. It may be related to your case." Pan stood and came around the desk to face her. He gently clasped her hand. "Believe it or not, I care what happens to you. Make a friend of Olivia. You have much in common. Both of you could use a good friend."

Claudia laid her hand on top of Pan's, genuinely touched by his concern. "Olivia has already made overtures. We went shopping a few days ago and had tea at Lyon's. I am attending an afternoon tea at her house next week."

"Good. I'm delighted to hear that. Drop by and visit us when you are not on a case. Come for tea some afternoon and see how your girls are. You will be proud of them."

"I will." Then, Claudia did the strangest thing. She leaned in and kissed Pan on the cheek.

"Well. *That* I did not expect. A show of affection? You never cease to astonish me. Go through the rear entrance. The carriage is not far. Be careful."

Claudia released Pan's hand and made her way back to the rear of the building. Once in the kitchen, she came up to Lily. "Let the girls know I will visit soon, some afternoon for tea. Pan already made the invitation."

"Oh, they will be pleased to hear that, Mary. It's been a while since I made afternoon tea. Do let us know."

Claudia moved toward the door, then halted. "My real name is Claudia." She disappeared into the dark alley.

Peeking out onto the street, she located the carriage Pan had mentioned. It looked vaguely familiar. It was a landau often used by the well-to-do, a luxury carriage with a folding top. Like the one Oliver Wollstonecraft had arrived in for his meeting at Cleveland Street. It was black with silver trim and scrollwork, like this one. Standing in the shadows, she glanced up at the carriage driver. All in black, and his face remained in shadow. Claudia would lay coin Oliver Wollstonecraft sat inside.

Looking both ways on the empty street, she sprinted across the cobbles, grabbed the handle, opened the door, and slipped inside, sitting on the empty bench. Across from her and half hidden in the dark sat a well-dressed man in a long gray coat.

"Honestly, my lord, why even hire me to follow your brother if you will do the job yourself? Unless you are here to join the festivities at The Velvet Vine."

Chapter 8

IT TOOK A MOMENT TO realize the woman sitting across from him was Claudia Ellingford. What a convincing disguise.

"No, I am not here to join the doings inside," Oliver replied haughtily. "So, it was you I saw slink into the back alley."

"It is the requirement of my job, my lord. I can creep about with the best of them. And you didn't answer my question."

"I said to call me Tensbridge."

"Very well. Tensbridge, it is."

"As you know, The Rakes had a meeting earlier, and Shinwell proclaimed our taking on charitable enterprises was tedious, so he and two others walked out—no doubt to form their own social club. Before his overly dramatic departure, Shinwell stated that he had procured a private room for a party at The Velvet Vine, so I came to see if my brother was with them. I was about to depart when you jumped aboard. Now, how did *you* know about this brothel?"

"I am acquainted with the owner."

Oliver waited, but no further information was forthcoming. "And?"

"And nothing. The owner confirmed Bryan's identity. The owner will observe the doings and will send me a report tomorrow. You should know that Shinwell falsely represented himself as a member of your rake group. Claimed your brother as a member."

"Technically, Shinwell was still a prospective member when he made the arrangements, but we will have to say he is no longer affiliated with us."

Claudia scoffed. "Because you have a reputation to protect?"

"Yes, believe it or not. The club has been around for over twenty years, and the members treat anyone they come in contact with in a gentlemanly manner. We do not act as animals, always use protection when sex is involved, and always tip generously."

Claudia rolled her eyes. "Do you know how unsufferable that sounds? Allow me to explain. The misery of women did not register with the British government until the military started catching certain diseases that interfered with Great Britain's empire expansion. 'It's the prostitutes' fault!' So, multiple Contagious Diseases Acts were passed in the '60s. It allowed the government to stop, detain, and forcibly examine women for signs of venereal diseases. Women were held in hospitals for as long as the government decreed. Some of these women were not prostitutes, just poor women from the working class."

"The acts were repealed in '86. I agree it was a violation of privacy of the first order. Of basic human rights. What is your point?"

Claudia huffed and crossed her arms. "You wrap your club in a cloak of respectability when all you are doing is using women who have no other means of income or survival. Why don't you aristocrat types fight for women's rights in government? Voting? Equal pay? A woman's right to make decisions about her own body? Legalizing prostitution and making a safe environment for sex workers? It would go a long way to repair the damage of previous detestable laws."

"You are deeply passionate. And I concur with everything you said. It is why I do not seek out my vices in such a way. I am not your enemy when it comes to these important topics." Oliver paused. "And I apologize for sounding insufferable. It was not my intent."

Claudia's chest was rising and falling. She was clearly agitated. One could say this surveillance prompted her distress as if a mechanical switch had been flipped. And that had Oliver's protection instinct spiking with awareness.

"If this assignment is bringing up upsetting subject matter to you, past or present, I want you to remove yourself from this case. The last thing I wish is for you to be disturbed in any way," Oliver whispered compassionately.

Claudia flung off her wig, a few pins scattered across the seat beside her. She took a deep breath and exhaled. "It is my turn to apologize. I had no right to lecture you. You are one of the few wealthy men trying to foster some sort of change. I will keep my opinions to myself going forward."

"No. Speak your mind. I welcome it. I will pass on your concerns. Believe me, I, and others, will take it seriously."

She gave him a dubious look while removing the rest of the pins, and her red hair fell past her shoulders. The sight of it caused another aching wave of yearning to pass through him. *Damn it all.* He had to gain control of his desires. It was as if they had been freed from all restraints and what he would give to trail his hands through that crowning glory of blazing red hair.

"Well, thank you. That is something. But what do you hope to gain from gathering this information on your brother? It is obvious he's sinking lower into depravity with each passing day. What will you do, tie him to the roof of this carriage and take him back to Kent?"

Tensbridge shrugged. "If needs must. I had that exact thought myself. It appears that scenario may come to pass sooner than I imagined."

Claudia's disturbed expression changed to one of empathy. "You also should realize that some people cannot be helped—they travel a self-destructive path no matter what obstacles you try to place in their way. Restraining your brother may make him all the more determined."

"You may have the right of it, but what kind of man would I be if I stood aside and did nothing to assist my brother? The recently deceased earl—my grandfather—was a notorious rake in his younger years. My family initially cut off his allowance and tried to keep him home, but as you said, it made him all the more resolute. He had fallen so far that my family tore London apart trying to locate him. Uncle Garrett found him near death in an opium den, so the family committed him to a sanitorium. While there, my grandfather turned his life around. I must believe Bryan has it in him to do the same."

Oliver exhaled. "I promised my grandmother I would watch out for Bryan and not allow him to sink to my grandfather's youthful depths. I *cannot* allow him to sink. I just cannot do it."

WHY CLAUDIA OFFERED advice, she had no clue. But she had seen enough in Notting Dale and later in the East End to know that her statement was true. Tensbridge's revelations about his grandfather showed that even the elites encounter drama and difficulties, which she should try to remember. And why even care about this viscount and his family problems?

But she did care—slightly. Perhaps more than that. The sadness showing in his lovely eyes arrowed straight to her little-used heart. His passionately spoken words curled about it, causing it to thump like a drum in a soldier's march. Tensbridge unfurled something within her, what she could not say. It was a bizarre feeling, and Claudia disliked it. This man was an altruist. Thankfully, not a pious one. All the men in Claudia's life had been the exact opposite. Tensbridge was too good to be true, which raised all sorts of warnings. What exactly, she was not sure. Claudia had never met anyone like him before, and he fascinated her.

She gathered up her wig and the few pins. "Then I will do all I can to assist you in protecting your brother. I must go."

Tensbridge reached forward and clasped her hand. "Don't go. Not yet. At least allow me to give you a ride home. You have a room at Cleveland Street, correct? Allenby mentioned it."

His holding of her hand was not aggressive or restraining, but he held it gently and reverently like a man courting a woman.

Oh, how ridiculous.

But for the life of her, she could not pull it away. Tensbridge's hand was warm and strong, his fingers long and elegant, and his touch seared her skin.

Claudia met his gaze. "What *are* you doing?"

The viscount looked down at their joined hands. Neither of them wore gloves. "I have no earthly idea."

Finally, she pulled her hand away. "Don't do it again. You are a client at my place of employ, nothing more."

Tensbridge sat back in the shadows. He pounded on the window behind him. It slid open.

"Yes, my lord?"

"149 Cleveland Street, Kennedy, and hurry," Tensbridge demanded in a frosty tone.

"At once, my lord."

With a snap of the reins, they were off at a swift trot. The only sound was the horses' hooves clattering against the cobblestones. The inside of the carriage was awkwardly silent.

Her tone of voice and sharply spoken words were possibly too abrupt, but she had to end this growing attraction between them. A viscount, heir to an earl? It was utterly untenable. The fact that Olivia and the owners of the Galway Investigative Agency became involved with dukes was an anomaly.

Untenable. Anomaly.

Yes, she had a smattering of a good education before Whinstone pulled the plug for good on their comfortable life. The bitterness that she carried inside of her was not healthy. To taste the higher classes only to be kicked to the cobbles? It had left permanent scars on her soul. And it had killed her mother. The only person in this world that had loved her unconditionally.

But getting back to her attraction for Tensbridge. She did not think an heir to an earl was too good for her, far from it. Claudia believed she was respectable enough for any man, regardless of rank and wealth. But it wasn't Claudia's experience that wealthy men acted in a gentlemanly manner or spoke with empathy. Because of this, she had no interest in any man of the upper classes.

But Tensbridge was decidedly different.

Regardless, their lives would not mesh, not in any way. Life on the streets was a whole other kettle of fish. It was brutal, violent, and unrelenting. It had changed her. And in some ways, not for the better. Claudia should apologize, but it seemed it was all she had done to Tensbridge since they had met.

Nevertheless, she could not speak to offer that apology. How troubling to find she was on the edge of tears. Claudia gazed out the window, watching them travel along street after street. The carriage finally stopped. Claudia didn't wait for the driver. She opened the door and jumped down.

"Two o'clock Friday. I will expect your report."

Claudia did not reply. The words caught in her throat.

She ran for the front entrance and, once inside, slammed the door and leaned against it. And for the first time in ten years, the tears that had welled in her eyes spilled over, trailing down her flushed cheeks.

Chapter 9

FOUR DAYS HAD PASSED, and in that time, Oliver could not get Claudia Ellingford out of his mind. Tonight, he traveled to The Piggeries—or Potteries, whatever it was called—and two nights before that, in the East End. Oliver had no idea where his brother was or if Claudia followed him. She had been accurate about one fact: why hire her if he was going to be underfoot, shadowing her every move, either as the viscount or The Sentinel?

One thing that had stung: Claudia effectively shutting down their attraction. And it was mutual and indisputable. It stunned him how hurt he had been at her cold rebuke. Just as they grew closer, she withdrew, throwing up barriers. But he saw her struggling to hold in her emotions before she departed. Had there been a shimmer of unshed tears in her eyes, or was it his overactive imagination?

Yet, with The Sentinel, she was passion incarnate, taking his hand and laying it over her ample breast, rubbing against, touching, and giving him a raging erection that had taken hours to dissipate. Claudia Ellingford was indeed a maddening puzzle. One he yearned to unravel.

A commotion caught his hearing, multiple voices raised in high dudgeon. Running along the rooftops, Oliver ascertained the ruckus came from the next street. He jumped onto the stairs he had used before and, once on the cobbles, made his way along the road.

After turning the corner, he discovered four rough-looking thugs had surrounded a man. They tried to lay punches, but most were not landing as the tall man was swift and light on his feet. The victim of the attack, wearing a suit and a long wool coat, held his own but was clearly growing exhausted. The ruffians were gaining the upper hand.

Oliver thrust himself into the chaotic brawl, using his truncheon to ward off the attackers. His joining the fight only urged the ruffians to fight harder. He and the man being attacked managed to lay two of them low after spectacular roundhouse blows, but the others pushed forward, shouting expletives that would curl anyone's hair. One of the louts grabbed a hold of Oliver's mask, pulling it partway from his face. Oliver shoved the truncheon into the bully's middle, then swung upward with the stick to the man's chin. He dropped unconscious. The last man standing ran off, disappearing into one of the courtyards to points unknown.

"Viscount Tensbridge?" the man he had rescued whispered.

Damn it to hell.

Frustrated, Oliver pulled the mask back in place. He turned and glared at the man who looked vaguely familiar. Irritated, he grabbed the man's arm, pulling him away from the unconscious louts. Oliver stepped into a private alley in case the escaped thug still lurked about. He did not want the man to see him speak to this policeman. And the rescued fellow was indeed a copper.

"The man who ran off is wearing my hat," he observed wryly. "Detective Mitchell Simpson. We met at Damon Cranston, the Duke of Chellenham's engagement dinner. I recently transferred to the Lancaster Road station."

Damon's newly discovered older half-brother had just changed his name from Mitchell Evercreech. The man had attended the semi-formal dinner, looking somewhat uncomfortable and out of place, though Damon and Althea had greeted him warmly and went out of their way to introduce him to everyone. Standing here in the moonlight, he could see the slight resemblance to Damon. Oliver judged his height to be six feet and his hair more of a sandy shade than Damon's golden hue.

Oliver extended his hand, and the detective took it and shook it. "Simpson. I would appreciate your discretion in this matter."

"Of course, my lord, but I want to hear more. Let us get off the streets. Do you know of someplace private we can talk?"

Oliver released Simpson's hand and weighed his options. He could turn on his heel, disappear into the night, or trust this detective. Having a copper on his side would be beneficial. A detective who was situated at the nearby precinct. "Very well. Follow me, but this location must also stay secret."

He led Detective Simpson to an abandoned and condemned building scheduled for demolition on the first of next year. In the meantime, Oliver used it as a secret hideaway. By chance, he had discovered a concealed trap door on the floor of the large stone fireplace's hearth. In decades past, the space below ground must have been used to store illegal goods. He had found numerous smashed gin and French brandy bottles. From what Oliver could ascertain, it had not been used in many years.

The fireplace took up nearly one side of the room, and Oliver could almost stand upright in the hearth. Using a nearby iron rod, he propped open the ash-covered door and motioned for Simpson to climb down the narrow stone steps.

The policeman hesitated.

"This is not a trap, I assure you. We can trust each other," Oliver murmured.

Once below the stairs, Oliver lit the small gas lamp he had recently brought here, and muted lighting illuminated part of the cellar space. Then he secured the door. There was barely enough room for men of six feet in height to stand upright, but it would serve his purpose. The stone walls were sturdy enough and kept out most of the damp.

"My God," Simpson exclaimed. "You have quite the hideaway here, my lord."

It was not much to speak of, but he could come here for safety, take a break, or change his clothes. In another abandoned building situated nearby, he had located a few sticks of battered furniture and a pallet and brought them below. There was nothing here, however, that would reveal his identity.

He motioned to the rickety table and chairs. "Please sit." Oliver sat opposite and pulled off his mask, scarf, and floppy hat, sitting them in front of him.

Simpson continued to look about the area. "Damon told me of your recent bereavement. My condolences, my lord."

Ah. That's how the detective knew to call Oliver by his courtesy title. "Thank you. And call me Tensbridge."

"What's in the trunk, Tensbridge?"

"Clothes, a blanket, medical supplies, preserved meats, and other edibles. Water. Some coin. I plan for every situation. I have an area similar to this in the East End."

Simpson gave him a skeptical look. "You are a vigilante. You're an heir to an earl, correct? Why in hell would you be doing this? I am completely gobsmacked."

How to explain when he was not sure himself?

"I haven't examined it that closely. Do I have a self-absorbed fixation with hero worship? Does my ego need stroking by grateful strangers when I act the hero? Is my life so empty I need a constant diet of danger and excitement to feel anything at all?" Oliver paused, drumming his fingers on the table.

"Or maybe I see injustice in my worldview and want to do my part beyond sitting on committees and crafting laws that will take decades to pass. Perhaps I come from a family where service and duty are paramount attributes. My great-uncle was a teacher to underprivileged children and founded schools for those less fortunate. One of my cousins initiated a home for those with special needs, either physical or mental. Our family helped develop medical clinics in disadvantaged areas—also law clinics. My grandmother's family founded a sanitorium in Hertfordshire for those with various addictions. My grandfather went undercover in a cotton mill decades ago. His report helped change certain working conditions for women and children."

"If you don't mind me saying, Tensbridge, it appears you *have* given this much thought, and maybe your reasons are some of everything you mentioned," Simpson observed, his voice subdued. "As far as your family, they are storied and well-respected, to be certain. I have seen the places you have spoken of. The clinics and whatnot. But why this? To prevent crime? That is the job of the police."

Oliver grunted. "Right. In the nights I have been in Notting Dale, you are the first copper I have come across. And it is the same in the worst districts in the East End. You are aware there are parts of London the police will not enter. It has been that way for decades, possibly centuries."

Simpson shrugged. "I can't deny that, for it is a fact. That's why I ventured to this area, to see what it is about. My fellow officers said to stay away. I wanted to know why."

"It appears that you found out why. Who were those men?"

"The officers told me the man running this rookery is Jedidiah 'Jedi' Danaher. I've heard of him before—a low-level Irish thug who, through violent means, rose through the ranks to become the boss. Mind you, The Potteries are not what they were thirty years ago. Danaher has lost some of his power. But there are still enough people crammed into these streets, blind alleys, and courts to bend to his will. I assume those men are his; who is to know? This place also attracts vagrants. The way I walk and dress, they had me pegged for a copper or someone well off enough to rob. They were on me before I could walk the length of the street."

Oliver ran his fingers through his tangled hair. "I guess that is why the police do not venture forth in these areas. The Potteries are going to be cleared, and it has already started. Or so I have been told by men in the know. What will happen to Danaher then?"

"Like others of his ilk, he will slither away to some other dark expanse and continue with his thieving and violent ways. Like rookery bosses in St. Giles and other slums, they turn up like a bad penny elsewhere." Simpson exhaled. "You are aware this attack may be reported to Danaher. If he wasn't aware of your presence before, he will soon. And one of the men pulled aside your mask. He could identify you."

"All true. But it was dark, and there were no street lamps on that street. And I knocked him insensible seconds later. I doubt the ruffian got a good look. And the hoodlum that escaped? He wasn't even facing my way. He saw nothing. And where would anyone ever see me in the light of day? But I will remain vigilant and stay in the shadows."

"I made certain no one could see or hear when I quietly mentioned your name," Simpson stated. "I would never place you in harm's way."

"I appreciate that."

The men stared at each other briefly, taking in all they had said.

"Where do we go from here?" Oliver asked.

"I could demand that you stop this folly. But I can see by your tense and determined look that any warning from me would be fruitless. I propose we work together. There is a reason you're in this area. What is it?" Simpson asked, his gaze intense.

Simpson was astute. Oliver would give him that. "Before I answer, I want us to form a pact. We keep each other's secrets; we reveal any information we gather. We will be a team. Forget class and rank and all that nonsense. I am Oliver, and you are Mitchell. We work—together. However long it lasts. I call myself The Sentinel."

Simpson stared at Oliver for the longest time, mulling over the offer. It made Oliver respect the man even more.

"Pact it is—Oliver."

"My younger brother has fallen in with reprobate men of means. They have a flat in nearby Notting Hill. I hired The Galway Agency to keep track of him, and I observe his comings and goings occasionally. I also do what I can to assist those in need while here."

"Ah, Eleanora and Althea's agency. A good choice."

"I thought so. I will tell you something else I recently learned about The Piggeries. One London County Council's medical officer is drawing up a report on sanitary and health conditions. It will be the final nail in the coffin for a full-blown clearance."

Simpson nodded. "Good to know. This place has common lodging houses, some with two families in a room. The overcrowding is not sustainable. The infant mortality rate is horrendous. This place is crammed with loafers, beggars, tramps, thieves, and prostitutes. And murderers like Danaher. Ever read *Oliver Twist*?"

"Dickens? Of course."

"Well, Danaher is Bill Sikes—in the worst ways."

"As you say, good to know." Oliver must figure out how to pass this information to Claudia and keep his reckless younger brother out of the criminal's path.

"How do we keep in contact?"

Oliver rose and rifled through the trunk, locating a pencil and paper. After he sat, he scribbled out his address and handed it to Simpson. "My residence. Also, the address of The Rakes club I am in with your half-brother."

Simpson took the paper and stared at it. "And I am just to show up at your house?"

"Why not? We recently met at Chellenham's engagement dinner and struck up a friendship. No one in society will bat an eye, for the Wollstonecrafts are known to be eccentric."

"Yes, God forbid you become friends with a lowly police detective," Simpson replied drolly.

"It is how society would look at it, but not me or anyone I care about." Oliver shoved another piece of paper and the pencil toward the copper. "Give me your address—Mitchell."

The police scratched out the information. "I prefer Mitch." He handed the paper to Oliver. "But call me whatever you like."

"Westgate Terrance, Kensington? That is an impressive address."

Mitchell snorted. "Hardly. I am renting two rooms from a baronet's widow."

Oliver smiled. "A widow, you say?"

"She's 71 years old," Mitch barked.

Oliver laughed. "This may be the start of a fascinating friendship."

Mitchell chuckled. "Yes, so it seems. Again, I take it any appeal on my part to encourage you to give this up will fall on deaf ears?"

"I cannot. Not while my brother is in harm's way."

"Very well. I had best be off."

"You should leave the way we came in. Stay to the rear alley and off the main streets."

Mitchell Simpson nodded, shoved the paper in his pocket, and then took the stairs. Hesitating, he slowly lifted the trap door and silently ascended. Oliver waited several minutes, then changed his clothes. He kept appropriate working-class garments so he could blend in. Stuffing his Sentinel outfit in a burlap sack, he hoisted the bag over his shoulder, blew out the lantern, and took the stairs above.

Once out on the street, he casually strolled toward the outskirts of Notting Dale, where he could catch a hansom cab.

Standing at the head of an alley and about to cross the street, he heard a noise. A rustling sound behind stacked crates. It was probably a rat. They were everywhere in the city, so much so there were thousands of ratcatchers employed, even in the palace.

Then Oliver heard a pitiful meow. Moving aside one of the crates, a cat stared up at him. The sorrow-filled golden-green eyes pierced Oliver's heart.

He reached down and scooped up the cat, still a kitten, though an older one—and all fur and bones. From under the illumination of the street lamp, he could see the cat had longish hair, a fluffy tail, and a unique fur coloring mixture of tabby and calico.

Another mew, then a low trilling, as the cat rubbed against his face and started purring.

Well, that did it.

"It appears you are coming home with me."

Two solid and lasting friendships formed in Notting Dale that night, and Oliver welcomed them gladly.

Chapter 10

CLAUDIA RETURNED TO The Piggeries once again, as her subject was drinking in the Black Moon Pub with his companions in vice. They have been in there for over an hour, and hanging about the area any longer would draw suspicion. Tonight, she wore a messy, short brown wig, another fake nose, and a scar. The Galway sisters had a good mix of disguises, and Claudia found she enjoyed playing a role while undercover.

Pulling her tattered shawl tighter, she headed toward Bangor Street. It wouldn't hurt to converse with some of the prostitutes to ascertain the lay of the land. There were gas lamps on some of the streets, but only a few were lit. The muted illumination cast an unnerving glow across the cobbles. The fog was thick tonight, rolling along the roads like a creeping marauder. Finding a group of women standing at the head of an alley, she sidled up next to them.

Just as Claudia was about to speak, an older woman gave her a hard shove. "Hie off, this be our corner. You don't want Himself to find you."

"Who you on about?" Claudia said in a low voice, using her Irish accent. "Does Jaysus run this territory?"

"I wish it were Jesus and all, at least he were kind to whores. This bloke—you don't want to cross," the woman replied. "Now, sod off. Don't be hanging about here."

"Tell me who I should be lookin' out for," Claudia demanded.

The women scattered, disappearing into the shadows. They had skittered away so fearfully; Claudia knew the man they had been speaking about was heading toward her. Icy needles prickled all along her spine, causing the hairs on her neck to stand on end. Only one man caused this reaction of dread.

He grabbed her arm roughly. Standing directly behind her, he leaned in, his gin-soaked breath skimming across her exposed neck.

"Who are you, bitch, one o' mine?" he barked. The man spun her around, and Claudia came face-to-face with Jedi Danaher. It took all her inner fortitude not to react with disgust—or fear. Not that she exactly feared him. She never had, but she did not want to tremble before him. Enough people had done that, and no doubt still do.

"No, sir," Claudia replied in an even tone. "Just passin' through. I'll nip along sharpish. If you let me go."

Time had not been kind to Jedidiah Danaher. He looked older than his mid-forties, not that she knew his age. A large scar bisected his left brow, ending at his upper hairline. It was ugly, puckered, and mottled, as if someone had done a botched job on the stitching or the injury had not been appropriately treated. It was as if someone had laid the left side of his forehead open with a hatchet. Another scar, this one thin, began at the corner of his mouth and traveled partway down his neck. Yet, enough of the boyish handsomeness was still visible—on a face with empty, dead eyes and a cruel mouth—might appeal to certain women.

"You want work? You got the look of a whore." He brushed aside her hair with his free hand. "Not a complete hag," he rumbled as the tip of his finger ran along her cheek near the fake scar. Claudia silently prayed it stayed in place and that he didn't grab her hair or the wig would come loose or fall off. She remembered he liked to grasp the hair and pull, as he had done that to her mother.

"I ain't done much whorin'. I was a yanker some time back. Sir."

Jedi pushed her away. She will have bruises on that arm and no mistake. He was still a horrendous lout—and a miserable bastard.

"What the feck is a yanker?" he demanded, still looking her over.

"I pulled on cocks, yanked them—you know, friggin'—nothin' more." Claudia spoke the truth. When she and the girls needed extra money, Claudia would frig a man to completion for a few shillings. It had been disgusting work, but it was either that or starve. If there was one thing Claudia could claim from those horrible years on the street, it was that no man ever violated her. Or penetrated her. And no man ever will unless she allows it.

Certainly not *this* one.

At least Jedi never touched her during their eighteen months under his rule. Although he allowed them to stay in the pathetic two-room hovel at the end of a lane, he was rarely there.

Thank God.

The first night back in The Piggeries, Claudia sought out where she and her mother had lived. All she found was an empty lot.

"Well, go on, then. Yank it, bitch." He started to unbutton his trousers. "If you're good enough, you'll work for me right on this corner. Half of all earnings go to me. Protection and the like."

"I'm not lookin' for this kind o' work."

With the quickness of a predatory jungle cat, his meaty hand closed about her neck. "Then get gone, and don't return. This is my territory, yeah?" He squeezed, causing her to gasp.

"Yes, sir," she croaked as his fingers tightened further.

He released her, and Claudia turned to depart. Oh, how she was tempted to whip out her knife, stick it deep in his middle, and gut him like a fish from the Bethnal Green market. But Jedi grabbed her arm again, causing her to wince inwardly.

"I know you, I'm sure of it," he hissed dangerously in her ear. "And I will puzzle it out, no mistake. So don't show your face here again, yeah?"

"Yeah."

He freed her again, and instead of running, Claudia sauntered away with her head held high. In the distance, she heard a decided snarl, and Claudia smirked in response. Yes, she understood Jedi. The bully was quite put out that she hadn't cowered in his presence. But now she may be compromised from coming into this rookery again. The disguises will have to become more elaborate.

Seeing that horrid excuse for a man brought up old recollections that Claudia would rather forget. And she had a large enough stockpile of dreadful memories to haunt her dreams for the rest of her life without adding her time living in The Potteries. But she had learned it was best to face one's tribulations head-on.

Even so, she should wrap this case up right away.

OLIVER AWAITED CLAUDIA'S arrival for their Friday update. Bryan had shown up at ten that morning, looking as if he had just rolled out of bed. His clothes were wrinkled, and his appearance had deteriorated, with dark circles under his eyes and a decided pallor to his skin. He had answered Oliver's questions in a monotone, staying only ten minutes.

Oliver was tempted to withhold his reckless brother's allowance. Instead, he gave him half of the stipend. His brother had promised their father and grandmother that he would look into certain London law firms to find gainful employment. Bryan had done none of it. Next week, ultimatums would have to be made. That was something he was *not* looking forward to. Oliver had to remain cautious. If he demanded too much, his brother could effectively disappear into the bowels of London as his grandfather had done decades before. And London was far more significant population-wise than it had been in the 1840s.

Caramel, the cat he had adopted, was sleeping soundly on the cushion by the fireplace. Dalton initially had been horrified at the prospect. But after a bath and a feeding of sliced chicken, Caramel had captured the staff's hearts, including his unflappable butler. In less than a week, Caramel was right at home, following Oliver about the large residence as if she were a dog.

"Who's a pretty girl?" Oliver murmured.

Caramel raised her head and, through slitted eyes, blinked slowly at him. "Mur-reow?"

"Yes, you."

Rett entered the room, rolling his eyes. "Carrying on a conversation with your cat, once again?"

"And she understands every word."

Rett plopped down into a nearby chair. "Just don't bring home every stray you come across."

"As I have said many times, I cannot save everyone. I am aware of that fact, and my declaration also extends to animals. Besides, Caramel adopted *me*."

"Right." Rett glanced over at the cat, who was bathing before settling in to continue with her afternoon nap. "What is the update with Bryan? Is it worrisome?"

"Yes. Remember Shinwell and his private party at The Velvet Vine?" Rett nodded. "Well, Bryan attended." He informed his cousin of what he had observed and what Claudia had reported. Then he told Rett about Mitchell Simpson.

"Jesus, Oliver! A detective knows your identity? Why did you allow that?" Rett exclaimed.

"What do you suggest, that I murder him for knowing too much? He recognized me. I made a snap decision. Having a local detective in my confidence may prove to be fruitful. Besides, he is Damon's half-brother; I believe I can trust him."

"Just how many illegitimate siblings does Chellenham have?" Rett asked.

"Too many to count. Four of them, aged five to thirteen, are coming to live with Damon once he and Althea are married."

Rett whistled low in his throat. "It is certainly a strange group of men you have me involved with."

"But at their core, decent men. Have you given any further thought to joining my cause?" Oliver asked.

"To a small extent. I am still considering your proposal and—"

His butler, Dalton, entered the study. "Miss Ellingford, Your Grace."

The men stood and turned toward Claudia. She never failed to take his breath away. Her glorious red hair was swept up from her neck, and he yearned to see it tumbling down her shoulders. Oliver wanted to remove the pins himself and nuzzle her neck, kissing her soft skin as his hands tunneled through her silky hair. He willed away the sensual thoughts—for now.

"Miss Ellingford, may I introduce my cousin, Garrett Wollstonecraft. Rett, this is Miss Claudia Ellingford, an investigator with The Galway Agency."

Rett stepped forward and took her gloved hand, bending over it. "My pleasure, Miss Ellingford. I am actually a third cousin, twice removed, or is it a second cousin? We have lost track, so tangled are our family branches."

Claudia gave Rett a warm smile, and Oliver's heart squeezed with envy, for she had never given him such.

"It is a third cousin, Rett, as well you know," Oliver said through gritted teeth.

Rett released her hand. "True enough. My grandfather was half-brother to Oliver's great-grandfather. As I said, there are many tangled limbs. And on that note, I will take my leave and allow you to converse in peace."

"It was a pleasure to meet you," Claudia smiled, causing Oliver's envious annoyance to spike further.

His cousin bowed, then quit the room, closing the door behind him.

A tea tray sat on the small table by the settee. Oliver swept his arm toward the area where the sofa and two wing chairs were located near the fireplace. A small fire crackled in the hearth. It was the sixth of October, and a noticeable chill lingered in the air.

Claudia gave him a slight nod and headed toward one of the wing chairs. Oliver sat opposite. Again, she wore the gray wool skirt and jacket and carried a leather satchel. Once seated, she pulled off her kid gloves and laid them over the arm of the chair.

"Good afternoon, my lord."

So, it was going to be like this: formal and distant. There was no use calling Claudia on it.

Caramel meowed and rubbed against Claudia's wool skirt. She looked down at the cat, and her face lit up. It was the most astonishing thing. It enhanced her beauty if that were possible. "Oh, how adorable. So pretty! I wasn't aware that you had a cat."

"A recent event. I found the hungry kitty on the street, and she adopted me."

Claudia glanced up and caught his gaze. Was there a softening in her eyes, or was it his overeager imagination again? If so, he would gladly adopt fifty stray cats if only to see that warm and luminous expression. Claudia rubbed under the cat's chin for several moments, then, satisfied, Caramel headed toward her cushion and settled in.

"Would you mind pouring, Miss Ellingford?" Oliver kept his voice steady and his tone reserved. Hard to do since his insides quivered with desire. He wanted to pull her out of the chair, gather her in his arms, and kiss her until he ceased to breathe.

She sat the pouch at her feet. "Of course, my lord." Claudia went through the motions, passing him a cup of tea.

Oliver could not resist. Taking the saucer, he trailed his index finger along hers, watching closely for any reaction. It was subtle, but there, nonetheless. A slight flush to her cheek, and she did not pull her hand away for several moments. As for him, that subtle touch of skin against skin stirred the simmering embers into a full-on blaze.

Claudia sipped her tea, staring at him frankly as if she were about to mention their brief contact. Instead, she placed the cup on its saucer and opened her case, bringing forth a ream of papers. "I have the report from The Velvet Vine, my lord."

"Read it aloud. If you please."

THOUGH INITIALLY EAGER for the activities to begin, Bryan Wollstonecraft was told by his mates that he had to pass an initiation before joining the fray. One of the male sex workers would suck him off and bring him to completion. The young man balked, and an argument ensued, with punches being thrown. My men immediately entered the salon and broke up the fight. I informed the men that they were effectively banned from this establishment forthwith.

CLAUDIA LOOKED UP FROM the paper. Did she just say, "suck him off?" The image formed in his mind; only Claudia did so to *him*. And enthusiastically. He shook his head. This was not the time for erotic daydreams. Oliver would save that particular fantasy for later at night.

"Do you wish me to continue?" she asked, watching him closely.

"There is more?"

Claudia nodded.

"Then, by all means."

THE VISCOUNT DID NOT take it well. Shinwell broke furniture, cursed, and punched one of the male workers. I threw him out on his ear. The following morning, I received your note stating that Shinwell, Linton, and Tolwood were no longer part of The Rakes Club and that Bryan Wollstonecraft was never in the association. I must be more diligent in admitting certain people going forward. In that vein, I had one of my men (not included in the fight) follow Shinwell et al. to other brothels. They ultimately wound up at The Crowing Cock, in Spitalfields, and the four of them hired six females. They were there the rest of the night.

I have let it be known to the higher-class brothels that we are in contact with to shun Shinwell et al. in the future. Please pass on this information to Chellenham and The Rakes because Shinwell is still using their club to gain entry into various places of vice.

CLAUDIA FOLDED THE paper and tucked it into her satchel. Then, she passed him another form. It was a well-drawn map of the tangle of streets and lanes in the Notting Dale area. Various boxes were labeled, identifying places his brother had no doubt been.

"Honestly speaking, my lord, I cannot see this surveillance continuing. You have ample proof that your brother indulges in selective vices and the locations. Your brother and his flatmates have not ventured to the East End since that night. They have, however, hosted various entertainments in their flat. Tolwood was in attendance at the most recent gathering. I spoke to the landlord; he has already received complaints about the noise and has given them a warning. If they are evicted, you can bet they will find lodgings in less pristine settings."

"And the downward spiral will continue," Oliver said, frowning.

"Yes, it will persist. The young men spend much of their time at the Black Moon Pub, as I have learned some prostitutes use the rooms upstairs to conduct their business. The place next door? The shack? It has a small opium den in the rear. Out front? They sell tea and other goods."

"An opium den. 'Where one could buy oblivion, dens of horror where the memory of old sins could be destroyed by the madness of sins that were new.' Oliver Wilde."

"He is an author, correct? Is that from a book?" Claudia asked.

"Yes. *The Picture of Dorian Gray*. Wilde was just released from prison last May, where he served two years for gross indecency. I hear he is a shell of his former self and in poor health due to his incarceration." Oliver remained silent for several moments. "So, has Bryan partaken?"

"I had no way to gain access, my lord. But seeing his state when he emerged with the others, a burst of euphoria and the like, I can assume your brother indulged in something." Claudia picked up the cup and sipped her tea. "I can inform Eleanora Galway to finalize the bill."

"No."

Claudia arched an eyebrow at him. "No? My lord, I just told you there is nothing more I can do. Continuing with the surveillance will just be more of the same. And an added expense for you."

"I said before to call me Tensbridge. Give me two more weeks, and I will personally pay you a bonus. With the Galway sisters' permission, of course." Yes, he offered a bribe, but he really wanted further observation to ensure his brother did not run afoul of the rookery boss, Danaher. "A few weeks ago, I met the Duke of Chellenham's older half-brother. He is a detective at the Lancaster Road precinct. Perhaps he can give you information on the criminal element in the area. His name is Mitchell Simpson."

"I am already aware of the criminal element. The rookery boss tried to recruit me to be one of his girls working on Bangor Street. He was not best pleased when I turned him down. That is another reason I am not keen to return to The Piggeries. My disguises would have to be more intricate."

Jesus. She had a run-in with Danaher? "Then forget I even requested it. I do not want to place you in any danger."

Her mouth quirked. "I am in danger the moment I step foot into that area; anyone is. I can handle myself. In fact, I *will* continue for two more weeks. I will gain Eleanora's acceptance of the deal. And I agree to the bonus. However, it will be just between us. I will require twenty pounds. Is that satisfactory, Tensbridge? Shall we shake on it?"

God, she was fierce.

His admiration for her grew, as well as his desire.

He held out his hand across the table. "Then, it is a deal."

Chapter 11

WEARING HER RECENTLY purchased dark green silk taffeta tea gown, Claudia stood, teacup and saucer in hand, in the crowded morning room at the Watford town house. A large table was set up at the front of the chamber, covered by a white lace tablecloth. Upon it, silver urns holding coffee and tea, and platters of delicate sandwiches with questionable fillings, along with small frosted cakes, slices of seed cake, a Victoria sponge cake, and various biscuits, fruit, and cheese.

Olivia came to her side and affectionately squeezed her arm. "I think this is going well. I had more show up than I originally thought. The ladies are curious about Watford's choice of a wife. It is no doubt the reason for the high attendance."

"Then let them get a good look. You are stunningly beautiful." And Claudia meant it. Olivia particularly glowed today.

"Oh, thank you. I am so pleased you came. And as soon as you can fit me in, I want you to come for afternoon luncheon, just the two of us."

Claudia recalled Pan's advice: make a good friend of Olivia. She had to start somewhere, allowing people near. In truth, she missed her mother still, the close companionship, someone to confide in and share life's joys and disappointments. Logically speaking, how could one go through life without human interaction? For all her grand asseverations about keeping people at arms' length, it wasn't feasible. Claudia had been devastated by her mother's death and believed that not being hurt in the future meant remaining remote. But that was the reaction of a grieving 16-year-old girl. A decade had passed. As she observed earlier, perhaps Olivia was an excellent place to start—slow increments.

Smiling, she patted Olivia's hand. "I will, I promise."

"If it weren't considered unladylike, I would squeal with delight," Olivia replied, beaming. "I had best return to the serving table. As hostess, I am to pour, supposedly. Mingle, Claudia. Talk to people."

"I will try."

A woman was heading their way. Claudia guessed her to be in her late twenties.

"Here, I will make the introduction," Olivia whispered. More loudly, she said, "Baroness Addington. May I introduce my dear friend, Miss Claudia Ellingford? Claudia, Lady Corrine, who is the daughter of Viscount Rothley."

Claudia loathed these situations. Does one curtsey? Instead, Claudia inclined her head and gave a polite smile. "Lady Corrine. A pleasure to meet you." There. That wasn't so difficult.

"I am pleased to make your acquaintance, Miss Ellingford. The duchess tells me you are a private investigator."

"And I will leave you ladies to chat. I must dash." Olivia headed toward the table to resume her hostess duties. She gave Claudia a little wave before focusing on the women gathered around the tea buffet.

"It must be exciting work," Lady Corrine enthused.

Was this baroness mocking her? Claudia studied her closely. Attractive, of course, with the prerequisite complexion of an English rose to befit a viscount's daughter and baron's wife. Her look was earnest, and because of it, Claudia would attempt polite conversation.

"I have only been on the job a few weeks, but so far, it is exciting. I am enjoying it immensely."

"I have only been a baron's wife a few months, but so far, it is *not* exciting, nor am I enjoying it."

Claudia's eyes widened. She didn't expect that reply. What to say? "I am sorry to hear it, my lady."

"It is my fault," she sighed. "I agreed to the arrangement to benefit my family. If I were to call on you sometime soon, would you share a cup of tea with me? I need your advice, and I may need your services." She took Claudia's hand. "I truly admire you for living your life on your terms. Do you have a card?"

Good lord, Claudia couldn't believe the baroness's frankness. Pulling her hand away, Claudia reached into her reticule, fetched a card, and handed it to Lady Corrine, who quickly palmed it. "Leave word at Cleveland Street, and we will schedule an appointment."

"I will. Thank you, Miss Ellingford." The baroness gave her a sad smile and moved toward another group of ladies.

Perhaps Claudia should attend more of these soirées—a perfect way to drum up business. Were any of these society ladies happy? Well, a few, like the ones in her acquaintance. But they must be the exception to the rule.

As Claudia glanced about the room, her mind wandered to her conversation with Tensbridge yesterday. How mercenary of her to name a price for the bonus. And to not inform the Galway sisters? It did not sit well with Claudia. Her old instinct to grab any money she could to keep from starving remained deeply ingrained. To take advantage of the viscount's concern for his younger brother also did not sit well. When had she become so avaricious and selfish? Living on the streets could do that to a person, but it was no excuse. Her mother had brought her up better than that.

Claudia would inform the sisters of the particulars. She would *not* take the bonus money from Tensbridge, after all. But she would encourage the sisters to speak with Tensbridge and urge him to wrap up the case as soon as possible. There was nothing more she could discover.

Speaking of the Galways, Claudia had arrived with Eleanora, Althea—in her first public outing since her leg operation—and Edwina Callen. Olivia was busy greeting guests, and she and another woman Claudia had just met, Baroness Wenlock, were pouring the tea. Two maids stood nearby to clear away any dishes and replenish the platters. Olivia had whispered to her that Chastity Colborne, the baroness, had a past similar to theirs, living and surviving on the streets. How astounding. It shows you do not know about a person at first glance. She would do well to remember it.

Althea sat in a plush chair, her cane at her side, with Eleanora seeing to her every need. Edwina Callen came to stand beside Claudia.

"They are devoted to each other," Edwina whispered. "It makes me long for a sister. Do you have one?"

Claudia could see what Edwina meant. "No. No family at all." Except for her miserable stranger, soon-to-be-ex-duke father, currently rotting in prison.

"Your gown is absolutely gorgeous. I love the embroidered lilies on the decorative collar and the large lily down the right side," Edwina enthused.

Except for the tight, high neck, Claudia agreed. It reminded her of when she was a child and owned numerous pretty frocks. It was the last time she had worn anything so fine. "Your dress is lovely as well. The russet shade suits your coloring."

Edwina flushed with pleasure. Yes, try as Claudia might to remain distant, Edwina and Olivia were not having it. Edwina, in particular, had made a concerted effort to engage in conversation, often waiting for Claudia to return from her undercover assignments in Notting Dale. Edwina would make her a hot tea, assist in removing Claudia's disguise, and beg to hear all the details of

Claudia's night. Edwina had worn her down as she said she would. Claudia eventually welcomed the camaraderie. Who would have thought? She would welcome Olivia's as well. But back to this afternoon's tea gathering. One particular introduction had piqued Claudia's interest.

The Countess of Darrington. Shinwell's mother.

The older woman sat on the settee with another lady, the Duchess of Coldbridge, the Duke of Allenby's mother.

Claudia gently laid her hand on Edwina's arm. "I will return in a moment. Something regarding the case I am on."

"Of course," Edwina replied.

Claudia nonchalantly strode along the room's perimeter, nodding and smiling to a few women as she moved closer to the countess and duchess, who were speaking intimately. She grasped a sandwich on her way by and nibbled on it. Lord, how horrible, some sort of fish pâté with a thin slice of cucumber. Two things Claudia could claim: an acute sense of hearing and a sharp power of recall. And the excellent sense of smell.

Well, three things, then.

She stood with her back to the women, gazing out the window. She stood far enough away to not arouse suspicion but close enough to listen attentively.

"I do not know what to do, Christina," the countess sighed. "Troy has become impossible."

Troy Beckingham, Viscount Shinwell. The countess's son.

"I understand completely. Gerard is at a loss as to what to do about Rome. He will not listen to his father."

Romeo 'Rome' Linton, second son of the Duke of Coldbridge. Allenby's mother had recently married the duke. Yes, it was a good thing that she possessed an ordered mind, or she would need cards pinned on a board attached with colored strings to keep this all straight.

"At least Coldbridge takes an interest in his son. When I try to engage William, he merely waves my concerns away, claiming that Troy is acting in a typical manner for young bucks, as he calls them. 'I was one once,' he declared. He acts proud of Troy's shameful behavior. I cannot abide gossip, and already there is talk." The countess sighed. "If only Troy could be more like Paris, Romeo's older brother and heir. Such a gentleman, such an air of maturity."

"Yes, Paris is an ideal son—and stepson—and heir apparent, to be certain," the duchess replied. "Have you tried talking to Troy?"

"Yes. My son dismissed me out of hand and said I would not understand the pressures he is under as the heir and that he needs an outlet. He also said I was not to mention it again."

The duchess snorted. "That, my dear, is a rationalization if ever I heard one. You could have him followed. As you know, my son married the owner of an investigative agency."

"Yes, I could, but to what end?"

Exactly what Claudia had said to Tensbridge. After the information was gathered and presented to the client, it was up to the client to proceed. The agency's role concluded. And to follow Shinwell about? Claudia did not wish to do it, no matter the monetary inducement. From what she had observed, the viscount was a complete arse.

"I have something to tell you," the countess said, lowering her voice. Claudia stepped away. Sure enough, out of the corner of her eye, she saw the countess look around for anyone close by. Once the countess leaned in toward the duchess, Claudia returned to her previous spot by the window. "Years ago, I caught Troy with an older maid and a stable boy. They were having sex, the three of them. Troy was barely 15 years old, the stable boy not much older. The servants were dismissed immediately, but Troy received no punishment. William patted the boy on the back and said he was proud of him.

The time for discipline has come and gone. I believe my son is beyond all hope."

"Listen to me. You cannot say anything to anger your son," the duchess said firmly. "He is the heir, and once your husband passes, Troy could act resentful, denying you comforts. Remember, he will hold the purse strings. Your future will be in his hands."

"He will act that way, I know it," the countess replied crossly. "Then, I wash my hands of him. Act politely enough when I must be in his presence, but otherwise, avoid him at all costs."

"Etta!" the duchess exclaimed, clearly shocked.

"My niece, Celia, is married and lives near the Scotland border, so nothing keeps me here in London. You have no idea what I have had to endure. It has killed any regard I have for my son. He was a hellion from the moment he was born. Be glad Allenby is an honorable man, a worthy son. You are indeed fortunate. Treasure him. I will shed no more tears over mine. If Troy wishes to descend into debauched oblivion, so be it. He can sink. I will head to the country as soon as I can pack my trunks. And I may travel to Italy and places beyond when winter arrives."

"What about your husband?" the duchess asked.

"He can sink as well, although I believe he reached lower depths long ago. We have not been getting along for ages. We hardly speak, let alone anything else. I have no idea what he gets up to, and I no longer care."

Claudia headed toward Edwina. So, there will be no restraints on Shinwell, meaning he *will* sink and drag Linton and Bryan Wollstonecraft with him. The duchess will repeat this conversation to Coldbridge, and although Claudia never met the duke, she imagined he would not allow his son Rome to wallow much longer. She would relay this conversation to the Galways and to Tensbridge. It could likely convince him to close out the investigation and move forward.

Seeing Eleanora standing by the food table, Claudia hurried toward her. "May we speak alone?" she murmured.

Olivia must have heard, for she said, "Use the library. There is no one in there. Gideon is at his club with the rest of the members. Once out in the hallway, it is the third door on your right."

Claudia and Eleanora found the room with no trouble. Once inside, Claudia closed the door behind her. She immediately told Eleanora everything, including the bonus money Tensbridge offered and the conversation she had just overheard.

"Well. Twenty pounds?" Eleanora stated with annoyance in her voice.

"I *am* sorry. When one lives on the streets, any opportunity to make extra coinage takes priority over everything, including common sense. It will not happen again," Claudia declared sincerely. As she had observed earlier, this transition to a new life continued to be a bumpy ride.

"Very well. I accept your apology and appreciate your honesty. We allow bonuses from clients, of which the investigators receive twenty-five percent. The rest goes into the business. The amount you gave Tensbridge is not unheard of. The men paid a fifty-pound bonus on the Allenby case. But we wait until the client offers."

"Oh, he offered. I just named the amount."

Eleanora's mouth quirked. "In the future, let the client name the amount. As for the rest, you are correct. There is not much more we can do regarding this particular matter. Do it for one more week. Meanwhile, I will discuss it with Allenby and have him speak to Tensbridge. By the time you meet with him this coming Friday, we should be able to finalize it. Other clients are waiting."

Claudia exhaled, relieved. Closing out the case was prudent for the agency and herself. After this week's meeting, she could dismiss Tensbridge from her thoughts and nip that attraction in the bud.

"Speaking of other clients, I was approached by a possible customer. Baroness Addington. I would like to have a meeting with her."

"Addington? Oh, that's right. The old baron passed away recently. A distant cousin is now the baron. Did she say concerning what, exactly?"

"No, but judging by her conversation, I would say it concerns her husband."

Eleanora shook her head. "Ah. It wouldn't hurt to meet with her since you will be winding up this Tensbridge case. See it done and soon, and let me know what she wishes before we agree to anything."

"You do not want to be there? I thought you or Miss Sybil met with all potential patrons."

"I usually do, but I am seeing to my sister's recovery. And Sybil has enough to keep her busy. I would say you are more than capable of conducting an interview. Just be pleasant and accommodating."

Claudia smiled. "I will try my best."

One thing at a time, however. Claudia had Tensbridge's case to wrap up first. As she observed, it was best to move on and place any sparking interest in Tensbridge behind her. It was not wise on any level. Rubbing against and intimately touching a masked vigilante was one thing. He was anonymous, and she would probably never see him again. But a tall, handsome viscount with beautiful eyes and impressive shoulders, seemingly honorable and compassionate? '

No. Claudia could not allow it.

CLAUDIA WORE SO MUCH putty and grease paint that her face itched. There were dozens of pins holding the black wig in place. The hairpiece was braided, and she tucked it under the collar of her shabby dress. She kept to the shadows of the alley adjacent to the recently opened Avondale Park.

Wollstonecraft, his flatmates, and Tolwood were heading into the park, the former site of 'The Ocean,' the infamous pig slurry pond. The fact there was a park, complete with wildflowers, shrubberies, and benches, was hard to comprehend, but it meant that Tensbridge's information was correct. The council would initiate a clearance sooner rather than later. The common was located on the outer reaches of Notting Dale, closer to Kensington and Chelsea than the heart of the slum. Because of this, a uniformed copper patrolled nearby.

Since the men were loud and handing a bottle back and forth, the copper approached them and sent them from the property. Shinwell and the others did an about-face and stumbled toward an area called The Avernus (the gateway to hell, as one paper had recently called this section of The Piggeries). They had left their flat in this intoxicated condition, which meant they would be easy targets for Danaher's men if they were inclined to rob them. Danaher often permitted young men of means to arrive at their destination. It meant they would return and spend even more money on vices, which meant more currency in Danaher's pocket; at least, that had been his technique ten years ago.

Claudia kept to the shadows, well out of sight of anyone watching. There was a good deal of fog tonight, and overcast and cool. She should have worn something warmer.

The men ambled along William Street. They had never been in this section before. Claudia searched her memory. Was there a brothel nearby or other place of entertainment? So much had changed since she lived here. They were heading toward Pottery "Cut-throat" Lane. Not very prudent.

They rounded a corner and disappeared. Claudia halted. Could they know they were being followed? She had been so careful. Besides, the young men were clearly in their cups. Intent on puzzling this out, Claudia was not aware of someone stealthy approaching from her left. Before she could fully comprehend that the hairs on her neck were at full attention, the person grabbed her arm and whirled her around.

It was Danaher, and he had gripped the same arm as before, making her wince from the pain. She already had bruises from the night before last. Claudia kept her head down in case he saw any resemblance to her previous disguise or the girl she had been a decade ago. This street area lay in darkness due to the lack of lighted street lamps.

"Another strange bitch lurkin' about. Who the feck are you?" he snapped.

Claudia would not relive the scene of a few nights ago, so she gave a roundhouse blow that landed on his chin, sending Jedi down on one knee. About to reach for her knife, two men emerged from the darkened alley and seized her arms.

Danaher slowly stood, rubbing his chin. "Hit me, will you? Ugly sow." He punched her in the middle, knocking the breath out of her. Claudia doubled over from the impact. "Hold her upright. I'll teach her a lesson she won't soon forget."

But before Jedi Danaher could lay a further hand on her, someone dropped down from above and entered the fray. Still wheezing, Claudia slowly lifted her head. Although her vision was blurry, she could make out that The Sentinel had come to her rescue. He battered the men with his truncheon, moving with a predatory swiftness.

The two men released her and started to fight back, their fists flying toward the vigilante. It took all of Claudia's strength to remain upright. Her insides churned from the impact of the blow, and she felt nauseous and dizzy, fighting the bile crawling up her throat.

"You," Jedi growled, his full attention on The Sentinel. "My men told me of your interfering. Bloody bastard. This is *my* territory."

In the muted moonlight, she saw a flash of a blade. "Knife!" Claudia cried.

It alerted The Sentinel enough that he turned sideways. Although he missed a full-on deep thrust, it sliced through the layers of leather on his left side, and the vigilante grunted. How deep the cut was hard to tell. The Sentinel caught Danaher across the face with his truncheon, knocking Jedi to the cobbles before the ruffian could attack again.

The Sentinel turned to the other two men, battering them until they were unconscious. The vigilante laid his hand against his wound. Blood oozed between his gloved fingers. Shaking her head, trying to gain strength and clear the fuzziness from her mind, Claudia rushed to the vigilante's side. Taking her shawl, she bunched it up and held it to his gaping wound.

That few moments allowed Jedi Danaher to scramble to his feet. He grabbed her hair, and Claudia cried out with pain as the wig came away, along with hairpins and clusters of red hair. Jedi tossed the wig aside and spun her about.

"What the feck is this? Who are you? I only know one person with hair that shade. And she be dead. Unless—Claudia?"

Claudia pulled up her skirt. She would kill this man right here and now. He more than deserved it. All his evil deeds of the past? And no doubt the ones in his future. She would be saving others' lives if she ended his. But before she could grab her blade, The Sentinel bashed Jedi on the head, knocking him insensible. Danaher lay still. Was he unconscious? Claudia kicked him with her boot, and he didn't respond. It appeared so.

"No murder, not tonight. No time," the vigilante gasped. "Is the blood dripping on the cobbles?"

She glanced down. "No."

"Good. This way." He slipped his truncheon into his belt.

Claudia could hear distant shouts and loud clamor. They had to escape. However, it would only take seconds for a quick slice across the carotid artery. There was no time to debate the matter, for she sensed The Sentinel would disagree. And cold-blooded murder on a defenseless, unconscious man? It would not sit well with her, even if Danaher were the man in question.

Instead, she slipped the vigilante's arm about her shoulder, and they hurried off as quickly as possible. "Wouldn't it be easier to escape through the park? Toward Kensington?" Claudia pointed.

"There are not many exits out of Notting Dale; we will be caught. The smart move is to vanish right under his nose."

The Sentinel was correct once again. Danaher's men would locate them before they managed to leave Notting Dale. Moving swiftly through a maze of back lanes, they reached the rear courtyard of an abandoned house. The windows, which ones remained, were boarded up.

"In through those loose boards," he rasped, pointing to an entrance. "Check again to ensure I am not leaving a trail of blood. They will trace us if I am."

Under the subdued light of the moon, Claudia inspected the uneven ground. Then, up to his still-covered injury. "No blood." However, the shawl was soaked through.

Once inside, he motioned toward the large fireplace. "Use the iron bar. Open the trapdoor, there." He pointed to the floor of the hearth. The Sentinel's hand trembled. He was losing too much blood. Claudia did as he instructed. "Hide the bar in that pile of rubble," he muttered.

"Wait, there are no rats down there, I hope. I cannot stand them." That was an understatement. You don't live on the streets and not have to deal with rats. How many nights had Claudia slept in dubious dosshouses, lying awake all night because of the rustling and squeaking of rats in the darkness? She shuddered at the thought.

"No rats," he replied. "At least, none the last time I was here. Hurry. Let us get below."

Claudia assisted him down the narrow stone steps into complete darkness. He silently pulled the door shut using a piece of rope attached to the underside of the door. "Won't they see footprints above?" she whispered, holding him upright.

"No. I ensure there is little dust or dirt on the wood floors." He pulled away from her, and Claudia could hear him fumbling about. She listened to the strike of a match, and then muted lighting filled the area. The Sentinel had lit a small oil lamp.

"Won't they see the light through the floorboards?" she asked quietly.

"As best as I can make out, there are three layers of subfloor between the wooden slats and this cellar. Decades past, this was used as a storage area, probably for stolen goods. Quick, help me to the pallet. We have to halt the bleeding. In the trunk, there are medical supplies. And water. I hope you can stitch, miss."

Claudia opened the trunk and rummaged around, locating what she needed. "Yes, I can stitch wounds. Let us hope the cut is not too deep. Here, drink some water." Claudia kneeled next to The Sentinel. He pulled up his mask until it rested under his nose.

Leaning in with the glass bottle, Claudia studied the lower part of his face. It was familiar, with a sturdy jawline and a fine, sensual mouth where the lower lip was plumper than the upper. It may be one she made a study of. Why she thought that, Claudia had no idea.

Then she saw it. A mole—right above the man's upper lip.

It cannot be.

It cannot be *him*.

"Tensbridge?"

Chapter 12

OLIVER GROANED. WHY even wear a disguise if every blasted person he came across recognized him? Frustrated and racked with pain, he tore off the mask and hair scarf and tossed them aside. "What gave me away?"

"The mole above your upper lip. You disguised your voice well. I would never have guessed it was you." Claudia frowned. "Wait, that was you in that alley. When I—"

"We can discuss it later," he murmured. "Help me get this coat off. And the rest. I am not feeling well at all." Claudia assisted him in stripping away the layers until his torso was bare. With a grunt of discomfort, Oliver turned on his side. "How bad is it?"

Claudia pushed the lamp closer. Her fingers trailed along the slice in his skin. "It is not deep. But it is a long laceration, six inches or more. It's why it bled so profusely. It will take a while to stitch this closed."

"Then you had best get to it," he barked.

Claudia raised an eyebrow at his tone. "Steady on, my lord."

"Sorry. I am in considerable pain."

"Understandable. However, we should keep pressure on the wound until the bleeding subsides. At least, that is what I have heard is the proper response." Claudia refolded the shawl, tucking the blood-soaked portion of the garment at the bottom. She pressed it on his side, causing him to hiss through clenched teeth. "Let's give it about ten minutes."

"How did Danaher know your name?" he asked, watching her intently.

"He was involved with my mother years ago. It is a long, wretched story," she replied.

"We have plenty of time."

"How did *you* know Danaher's name?"

"The detective I mentioned. Simpson told me. That is why I wanted the surveillance to continue. I wanted to confirm Bryan did not cross paths with Jedidiah Danaher."

Claudia sighed. "It appears we have much to discuss. First, we have to tend to your wound." She pulled the shawl away and inspected it. "The blood flow is lessening. Good."

"Were you going to kill Danaher?" Oliver asked, his voice a husky whisper.

"If needs must. We were fighting for our lives. You should have let me finish Danaher before knocking him unconscious. He is a treacherous foe. Where is your dagger, by the way?"

"I did not bring it tonight; more's the pity. Have you killed before?"

"I have used my knife in self-defense situations. Did anyone I cut—bleed out? I never stuck around to find out."

Oliver gazed at her. She was a fighter and the most fascinating woman he had ever met.

"Have you killed anyone in your vigilante doings?" Claudia asked, meeting his concentrated regard.

"I haven't been doing it for that long. So, no. But who knows what circumstance may arise? Am I capable? I believe anyone is. But my first instinct is to avoid it at all costs. It would only anger and stir up the criminal element. And the police."

"You have a point. I can begin the stitching now. Please lower your leather trousers partway to give me ample space to work." Leaning close to the light, she efficiently threaded the needle and tied a knot at the end. "We are not working under the best conditions here. Infection may set in. Is there any alcohol I can use to sterilize the needle?"

He should have thought of that. But Oliver had not counted on hiding down here any length of time, let alone requiring no more than a stitch or two along with a plaster and gauze. But this? He could feel the cool, damp air against the open wound. This was more serious than he had planned for. "No. None." He unbuttoned his trousers with quaking hands and pulled them down far enough over his hip for her to work.

Claudia tore away a piece of her frayed skirt, soaked the material with water from the jar, then cleaned the wound. Then she pinched the injury closed between two fingers. "I know this is inappropriate considering the circumstances, but you are well put together, Tensbridge. Such muscular perfection." The needle slipped through his skin. "There, did the compliment lessen the impact?"

"Is that the only reason you gave it?" he rumbled.

"No. That is not the only reason. Who knew such potent masculinity resided under your stuffy wool suits?"

Oliver chuckled, then groaned. "Do not make me laugh. I work at it—staying in shape. One has to be able to fight, leap across roofs, and the like."

"You sat there in your study during our meetings, acting every inch the aloof aristocrat when you *knew* what we shared. The closeness, the touching—and rubbing against you."

He was growing aroused—in his condition, no less. "If you only knew how I wanted to vault across my desk, hold you in my arms, and kiss you senseless. Back you up against the wall, trail my hand under your skirt, and find the wetness therein."

The needle stilled, but she kept her head down. "I had a momentary lapse of judgment with your alter ego in that alley." Claudia continued with her stitching.

"With both of us in disguise, we felt safe enough to act on a mutual attraction. You never felt anything toward Tensbridge, then? I am not a vain man, but there was something—there. There still is."

"Did you just refer to yourself in the third person?"

"Yes, I suppose that happens when one has an alter ego. Allow me to correct that. You never felt anything toward *me*, then?"

"How long do we have to stay here?" Claudia asked as she continued to concentrate on sewing up his wound.

Changing the subject once again.

He would let it go for now, but they would soon address this. "We stay until tomorrow night. I would collapse if we tried to leave before sunrise."

The needle halted once again. "Tomorrow night? What about food? What about—normal bodily functions?"

"There is some food in the trunk, not much mind, so we must be prudent. Same with the water. And in the corner, there is a bucket we can use."

"God, how mortifying," Claudia mumbled as she quickened the pace of her sewing.

"Speaking of the bucket, you had best bring it here and hurry." Oliver retched, holding his hand over his mouth.

Claudia scrambled to her feet, located the container, and held it under his chin. He vomited, his insides roiled like mad. Oliver heaved until there was nothing else to bring up. He wiped his mouth with the back of his hand.

"Talk about mortifying," he croaked, his throat raw.

"You were in a vicious fight and seriously injured, Tensbridge. I feel like vomiting myself. Here, take another mouthful of water to clear the taste out of your mouth." She held the jar to his lips, and he took a sip. Rinsing his mouth, he spit into the bucket.

"Alone like this, call me Oliver—Claudia."

Placing the pail aside, she continued with her task. "Almost done, Oliver."

It took all his inner fortitude not to moan aloud at the sound of his name on her lovely lips. "I never asked how you are. That was quite the punch from Danaher."

"I will recover. There will be bruising, I've no doubt. It will match the ones on my arm."

"Show me."

Claudia pulled her sleeve up to her shoulder. The middle part of her arm was covered in brown and yellow bruises. Oliver could swear he saw a handprint where that monster had grabbed her.

"Is that from the other night? Danaher?" She nodded in response. The fury growing inside of him was disturbing. "I should have let you kill him," Oliver snarled.

"You have no say in whether I do or not. But you spoke sense. However, I have a distinct feeling there will be other opportunities."

Several minutes passed, and even though he had brought up the contents of his stomach, he still felt nauseous. Claudia was right. Though not a deep cut, it was still a severe wound. Oliver could only hope the blade did not nick his colon or kidney. Danaher's knife was no doubt filthy.

Claudia leaned in, took the thread between her teeth, and bit it. "There. Done. I hope the stitching holds. I am not a trained nurse. No blood is leaking through. For now." She laid a gauze over the wound, then wrapped a long strip around his middle to hold it in place and tied the ends. Claudia stood, taking the bucket to the far corner, and, finding a flat piece of wood, placed it over the top to cover it.

Then she returned to the trunk. "I thought I saw a blanket in here—ah. Found it." Taking his leather coat, waistcoat, and shirt, she folded them, making a pillow, and placed them behind his head.

"You should stay lying on your side and try to relax. Obviously, on the side *not* injured." Claudia covered him with the blanket.

"Not a nurse? You are certainly acting as one," he replied, pulling the trousers over his hips. "And I genuinely appreciate the care. Best we put out the lamp. We may need the oil." Oliver lifted part of the blanket. "Come here, in next to me. It will become colder tonight, and we must stay warm."

Claudia pursed her lips. "I am not sure that is wise."

"Because there is a mutual attraction?"

"Yes. We cannot act on it," Claudia whispered. Did Oliver hear regret in her voice?

"The condition I am in, I could not act on it even if I wanted to."

Claudia turned down the wick, and darkness descended. She did not move toward him. After several moments, she climbed onto the pallet and lay on her side, her back to him. Oliver laid the blanket over her and moved closer, laying his arm on her hip.

"Never mind that," he murmured, referring to his erection. "It is my permanent state whenever you are near."

Claudia laced her fingers through his and squeezed gently. "Try to sleep."

As if he could. How many nights had he dreamed of this since they met, having Claudia in his arms? As much as Oliver wanted to revel in her nearness and the feel of her soft curves, his eyes grew heavy, and sleep overtook him.

IT TOOK QUITE A WHILE before Claudia fell asleep. How long she slept, who knows? Oliver still breathed heavily next to her. She was lying with a man. Sharing a sleeping area was not as horrible as she thought. Oliver was warm, and his arm around her did not make her feel trapped. His potent presence calmed her rattled nerves. And what he had said earlier about vaulting over his desk and kissing her senseless? It had sent such a thrill of desire through her; she grew wet as he said.

But the biggest revelation?

Finding out Tensbridge—Oliver—was The Sentinel.

Hell's bells, never would she have guessed. Why would she even suspect it?

A viscount, heir to an earl? Why would he do it?

It must be an exciting story. But then, if Claudia asked him to tell it, he would want to hear of her past. She had never told anyone the entire horrid tale. To even speak of it would require a modicum of trust. For some reason, she felt it with Oliver.

But beyond that, they must escape. What to do? During their previous meeting, Oliver mentioned that the detective was at the Lancaster Road station. Perhaps she could slip out and enlist Simpson's assistance, have the coppers create a distraction enough to get Oliver to safety and a doctor's care. It was a notion worth contemplating.

Oliver stirred and coughed, then groaned. "Hell, I can hardly move. Can you take me over to the bucket? I have to urinate."

"As long as I don't have to hold your shaft for you."

Oliver chuckled low in his throat, then moaned. "I said don't make me laugh."

"I will bring the bucket to you. Can you get up on your knees?"

"If you help me."

Claudia fetched the bucket, knowing exactly where she had placed it previously. Already it reeked. How could they stay down in this stone cellar? The odor from their excretions will drive them out, if nothing else. Placing the bucket on the ground, she took Oliver's elbow and slowly assisted him in kneeling. He kept the groans low, but his distress was evident. He had been right; they would have never made it out of Notting Dale, especially with the faraway voices heading their way and growing ever closer. They were no doubt more of Danaher's men.

"Easy," she murmured. "The bucket is directly in front of you."

"Good." A long, steady stream filled her hearing, and then it ceased. "As you said, mortifying."

"We do what we have to survive, and—"

Noises from outside silenced her. They froze.

"What the feck, Billy. This be an abandoned buildin', has been for years. No one would come in here. It's ready to fall down."

"You 'eard 'imself, search every building and lean-to," another man replied.

They clomped about, their heavy tread reverberating through the cellar. Claudia's heart sped up as she fought a wave of fright. She must remain calm in this crisis and clear-headed.

"He also said he would rip out walls and floors. He's gone barmy. Havin' us look for a whore and some nutter in a mask. They're gone, I tell you."

"'imself says no. We 'ad men at every exit. No one left right after the attack."

"Who's to know? The prostitute and the nutter hid and slipped out hours later. Waste of time, this is. Come on. We got more to check on this street."

The voices and footsteps receded.

Claudia and Oliver did not move or speak for several minutes.

"You can take the bucket away. I'm done," Oliver whispered.

"Is it safe?"

"I do not know. Best we remain quiet."

Claudia helped Oliver lie on the pallet, then took the bucket to the corner and emptied her bladder. After covering it with the piece of wood, she made her way to Oliver. She laid her hand against his forehead. It felt warm. Not raging hot, but a slight fever, nonetheless.

She smoothed his hair. There were beads of sweat at his hairline. Claudia could feel him trembling.

"I think you have a bit of a fever. Let me find the water." She rummaged around on her hands and knees, feeling about for the bottle. At last, she located it. Growing worried, she helped Oliver sit up partway and brushed the bottle by his face. After removing the cover, he grabbed it with a shaky hand and drank. Once he laid flat, Claudia covered him with the blanket. Then she took a sip of the water.

"Talk to me," Oliver rasped. "Keep my mind off this pain. And the fever. Tell me about yourself."

"Why do you want to know anything about me?" Claudia whispered.

"Because I want to know you better."

"That is hardly an adequate answer."

"You fascinate me."

Claudia screwed the lid on the jar. Oliver also fascinated her, especially after discovering he was The Sentinel. What did it matter, here in the dark? If talking would ease his discomfort, she would do as he asked. "My mother was a courtesan, and my father is the disgraced and imprisoned Duke of Whinstone. Although I hear he will not be a duke much longer. I spent the early years of my life in comfort, living in a small flat on Eaton Place near Belgrave Square."

This was going to be a long night.

Chapter 13

OLIVER LISTENED ATTENTIVELY, concentrating on her words to forget his misery and the searing ache in his side. Whinstone? That loathsome excuse for a human being? Watford's cruel stepfather, who caused no amount of trouble leading to his incarceration? To begin her life at Eaton Place, only to be moved constantly to cheaper lodgings?

"The money stopped completely when I turned 12 years old, and, for a short period, my mother made money the only way she knew how." Claudia hesitated. "You are not shocked and disgusted?"

"Why would I be? Why would I judge anyone in a dire predicament?"

His answer must have satisfied her, for she continued, "Then, she met a man. By my thirteenth birthday, we lived with him in a small three-room flat in Vauxhall, within a cluster of boarding houses where manual laborers resided. Thankfully, William Murphy was not a cruel man. He was a sailor, away more than he was home. But when there, we were happy. William was more of a father to me than Whinstone ever was."

"I am glad for that," Oliver interjected quietly.

"William taught me how to defend myself. How to handle a knife, and where to cut to cause injury, either with a glancing slice or a fatal stab or evisceration. Regrettably, his ship sank off the Atlantic Ocean coast of Nova Scotia. There was no more money, but worst of all, no William coming home, his arms laden with parcels of food and gifts, or his laughing face greeting us each morning as he made us a hearty breakfast. Going shopping and for walks about the park, stopping for an orange ice or even vanilla bean ice cream."

Claudia gave a shuddering sigh. "I cried for his senseless loss. I cried for my poor mother. We were down to less than two pounds in coin, as William was due to make shore in a few weeks. How could we stay in that flat? We sold William's clothing and furnishings and found cheaper lodgings elsewhere. My mother was wracked with grief, for she absolutely loved William. He wasn't the most handsome of men, nor all that tall, but he was kind, generous, and loving. They had discussed marriage. I loved him, too. The thought of my heartbroken mother returning to the streets to earn coin twisted my insides."

"What did you do?" Oliver asked, genuinely moved by her story. To find contentment within a family formation to have it cruelly ripped away? Unfathomable.

Claudia remained silent.

"You *can* trust me," he urged gently. "I can sense you already do, to a point. Anything you say will not change my high opinion of you."

"High opinion? You do not know me at all," she replied matter-of-factly.

"Not completely accurate. You forget I know you as Tensbridge *and* The Sentinel. I observed your courage and determination—and how you labor at keeping people at a distance. Including me."

"Bringing people close is allowing vulnerability, a lesson I learned the hard way. *That* I cannot tolerate."

"You cried when you learned of William's death. That shows compassion, not weakness. And vulnerabilities show that we are human, capable of deep emotions."

Claudia snorted. "What does it matter? Any of it leaves a person defenseless. I will *not* put myself in that position. Not ever again." She paused. "Or so I try and tell myself."

Oliver wanted nothing more than to take her into his arms. But he remained on the pallet not only because of his injury but he did not wish to invade her space. "In my family, we show our affection readily. For one never knows when a certain day may be the last. Why have regrets over what was not done or said? Live and love to the fullest. ''Tis better to have loved and lost than never to have loved at all.'"

"Alfred Lord Tennyson. I do have some education. 'I am mistress of mine own self and mine own soul,' also from Tennyson. *I* am in charge of what happens to me. If I remain detached in certain situations, that is on *me*."

Oliver smiled in the darkness. Oh, he adored this woman. Of that, there was no doubt. "But you are not remaining disconnected with me. You are telling me of your past."

"Because you have been stabbed and are sick with a fever. I reckon that you will not remember most of it. How do you know I am even telling you the truth? I could be a consummate storyteller, weaving an overwrought fiction for your entertainment to keep your mind off your injury."

"But you are not," Oliver murmured. "I hear the sorrow in your voice. The anger when speaking of Whinstone. The regret and utter sadness when talking of your mother and William Murphy. It is sincere and deeply felt. I can ascertain that much. 'The shell must break before the bird can fly.'"

"Oh, please. No more Tennyson."

Oliver chuckled, then sobered. "Saying I am sorry for what you had to endure sounds futile, for I have no idea about any of it."

"Don't apologize for being raised in a loving and privileged home. Thank your lucky stars instead."

"Does that upbringing make me a dullard in your eyes? Women seem to prefer the brooding, tortured type."

"Brooding and tortured describes me, certainly not you. If I were to pick certain attributes preferable in a man, I would select stable, honorable, and confident. And a dullard? Come now, you are a vigilante! That gives you a wild and dangerous streak that is immensely appealing—to other women."

"But not to you?" Oliver asked softly.

"Perhaps to me. You are certainly a wonder."

A jolt of triumph raced through him. Oliver was about to speak, to tell her that she appealed to him in all ways when a scratching sound from above made Claudia grip his arm.

"Is it a rat?" she whispered worriedly.

He listened, and the sound moved away. "Do you detest rats because you came across them as your living quarters deteriorated? It is a silly question as no one likes rats."

Claudia shuddered as she removed her hand. "Nothing is worse than awakening to find a rat inches from your face, nibbling on crumbs from your stale bread, practically staring you in the eye."

"Well, I haven't heard any rats moving about here since we arrived. I believe we are fine for now. Do not sit over there in the dark. Come and lie next to me. It is cold in here, or is that just me?"

"It's a little chilly," she replied.

He could feel her slide in next to him. Claudia lay on her side, facing him. Gratified that she was near, Oliver placed the blanket over her. "So, I ask again, what did you do next after William died tragically?"

With a sigh of resignation, she continued. "I thought I might do what my mother had done when in desperate difficulties, what many women did and, horribly, what many girls had to do and still do to survive. But what did I know of pleasing men? So, I resorted to a little thieving—a wheel of cheese here, a loaf of bread there.

We managed, living frugally on the few coins we had left, making plans to find other employment. Perhaps in a factory or mill. But my mother became seriously ill before we could carry the plan out. I swallowed my pride and went to the home Whinstone shared with his wife, the previous Duchess of Watford. To ask for money for my mother."

"What happened?"

"He was home and refused to see me. I was physically removed from the property and told never to return."

Oliver frowned. "Miserable bastard, but there is a part you have left out. Danaher factors in here somewhere, does he not?"

Claudia exhaled shakily. "I am exhausted. Let us sleep some more. Then we have to make plans for escaping. No one knows we are here."

"That is not exactly true. Simpson knows of this place."

Claudia laid a hand on his forehead. "You are still not well. Your fever could worsen. We cannot stay. You heard those men. Danaher will tear The Piggeries apart just because he can. And yes, Danaher fits into my story, but I cannot manage revealing it now."

Oliver took her hand away from his forehead and squeezed it gently. "Then, later."

"And you will tell me about The Sentinel?" she whispered.

"Yes, whatever you wish to know." He leaned in as much as he was able and kissed her forehead. He was still holding her hand when he fell asleep.

OLIVER AWOKE ABRUPTLY as Claudia gently shook him. "Are you well? You were groaning in your sleep. Are you in pain?"

Is he? God, his mouth was dry as a crust. "Water," he croaked.

He could hear Claudia searching in the dark for the water jug. She cursed when it fell over. Thankfully, it had a screw top so none could leak out.

"Found it. Should I light the lamp?" Claudia whispered.

"No. We must save the oil." Oliver tried to sit up, and a roll of pain tore through his side. Another thing he neglected to pack in his medical kit was willow bark or even that new aspirin powder Doctor Drew Hornsby told him about. Again, he never imagined being stuck down here for hours or days.

Claudia came in close. "Just lift your head; do not try to sit upright."

He felt the rim of the jar touch his cheek and turned his head to drink. Oliver took two large swallows and then pushed the container away.

"Take some more," Claudia urged.

"No. I'm fine."

"I wonder how much time has passed," Claudia mused as she screwed the top on the jar. "I napped more than slept."

"I kept you awake. I do apologize."

"It is understandable, considering your injury. You never answered me. Are you in pain?"

"It is not so bad if I lay still. It comes and goes. I ache all over, though, probably from the slight fever. I do not feel any worse, so that is a good sign. But who knows, I am not well versed in medical matters."

"You should try and sleep some more. It is good for recovery, or so I've read."

"I am wide awake now."

"Our absence must have been noticed, or it will come the dawn. The Galway Agency knows I am in Notting Dale. Will they contact the police? Will your cousin raise the alarm? Or perhaps your lady fair wonders why you never arrived for your rendezvous."

Oliver smiled. "Are you asking if I am attached to anyone, intimately speaking?"

Claudia remained silent for several moments. "I suppose I am. I am merely curious."

Right. So much for Claudia's declaration of keeping people at a distance. "I have never been involved seriously with anyone. Ever."

"Wait. What? Are you saying what I think you are saying?"

Oliver heard the genuine shock in her voice. "That I am a virgin viscount? It is true."

Claudia snorted. "You are having me on. In my many experiences in the East End, I could not turn around on the street or in the pub and not brush up against some toff out for cheap thrills."

Oliver stayed silent. What possessed him to reveal such a personal fact? It slipped out—must be the slight fever addling his mind. Well, perhaps not. Claudia had shared so much; it was only fair he reciprocated.

"Oh," Claudia said with a subdued tone. "It's true, then. Not that there is anything wrong with that, not at all. But why? I thought all those with wealth and titles indulged—and frequently."

"They do. I *am* a member of The Rakes of St. Regent's Park."

Claudia chuckled. "You joined as a cover."

"Partly. I also thought it best to align myself with powerful men. If I were to move forward with my vigilante plan, I wanted to know where the worst of the vice is to be had. For that is where the underprivileged are forgotten and ignored."

"That is certainly the case. Did you take a vow of celibacy?"

Was Claudia mocking him? Seeing he was ill, it was hard to judge, but he heard no sarcasm or scorn in her tone. She sounded genuinely inquisitive.

"No. I have had singular encounters with a few women. We gave each other sexual release. I just did not take the final step. As far as the peerage goes, perhaps I am old-fashioned. I believe it a deeply intimate act and not one I want to share with someone I hardly know." Oliver paused. "Now that I say it aloud, it sounds peculiar. Why give a woman oral or touching pleasure but not go the rest of the way? I cannot explain it adequately. I want it to be with someone special."

"I-I think the same. You may not believe this, but in ten years living on the street, I never—not all the way."

"Forgive the personal question, but in what way?"

Claudia sighed. "On the rare occasion we were desperate for money, I frigged men to completion. Are you disgusted now?"

"No. I have seen enough on the streets over the past several months to understand the desperation you are speaking of. I condemn no one, most of all—you."

"I was not a prostitute in the strictest sense. I fell in with a group of women, and despite my young age, I became their protector, procurer, cash carrier—their pimp. They called me their captain, and I suppose I was, for I collected the money and, in wielding my knife, protected them on more than one occasion. I secured us at least one hot meal daily and a roof over our heads when possible. But it was precarious—our safety and our lives—from day to day."

"I can see you in that role," Oliver murmured, his heart aching for what she had to endure. "As a captain or leader. It suits you."

"Keeping the gangs at bay was difficult and a constant struggle. The women looked to me, but I never let them close. Not really. What does it say about me that at the first opportunity, I turned from them, eager for a fresh start?"

"There is more to it than that. There is part of your story you haven't disclosed as yet."

"And why *am* I telling you all this?" Claudia cried, clearly agitated. "Because I am scared, cold, hungry, and find myself in involuntary proximity and a dangerous situation with someone under normal circumstances, I would never share a conversation, let alone confide my horrid past."

"Because I am a viscount? You would never let that stop you."

Claudia sighed again. "Oliver, where would our paths ever cross in a social situation?"

"At our mutual acquaintances' gatherings. This isn't 1806, where everything is strict decorum occurring in ballrooms or other restrictive and monitored settings. Times have changed."

Claudia snorted. "Not that much."

"No, it has. Perhaps there is some truth in what you say for certain elites, but not any I know. Beyond that, you cared for the women under your protection. You kept them safe. In a way, *you* acted as a vigilante, like me. Not a pimp. Don't ever think that." Oliver exhaled, growing more fatigued by the moment. "I wish I could see your expression. I will wager emotions wreak havoc over you, and you fight it diligently." Oliver started coughing.

"Enough for now," Claudia urged. "You must sleep some more. We both must."

Oliver brushed his fingers by her cheek. "I was correct. Tears. You feel things deeply, Claudia Ellingford. There is no need to hide it. Not with me."

"You don't know me—"

"Oh, but I want to know—every depth, every dark corner, and crevice, every aspect of your life, along with your hopes and dreams. All of you, Claudia, every inch of your skin..."

He was too exhausted to form any further words. His eyelids fluttered shut, but he did not fall asleep right away. Oliver lay perfectly still, trying to will away the waves of aches and torrents of pain rippling through him. Finally, he started to drift into a troubled sleep.

"Oh, I feel," Claudia whispered, "I was attracted to you as the viscount and the Sentinel. But I must fight it. However, you make it so blasted difficult—"

Oliver wasn't sure if Claudia spoke those words or if it was all a dream. But he fell into a deep slumber with a hopeful smile on his face.

Chapter 14

"WAKE UP!" CLAUDIA CRIED. She shook Oliver once again. At least this time, he groaned. How much time had passed? He trembled all over. The fever was at its zenith. "Here, take more water."

"Food first," he croaked as he placed a box of matches in her hand. "Light the lamp to my left."

Claudia slowly crawled toward the area he indicated, ensuring she didn't knock it over. Feeling for the shade, she lifted it off, struck the match, and lit the wick. A dim light filled the area. Blinking, her eyes adjusting, she made her way to the trunk. "What food?"

"Oat biscuits. Dried beef. It is in the tins. Some cheese, too."

Claudia found clothes in the trunk. Garments a laborer would wear. She could use them to travel to the police precinct. The seeds of a plan began to take root. But Oliver must be attended to first. Starving, her stomach growling loudly, she pulled the tins out of the trunk.

"Can you sit up now, do you think?" she asked.

"No. Give me a piece of the dried beef, and I will chew on that. And some cheese."

After seeing to Oliver, Claudia wasted no time in feeding herself. After sipping some water, she assisted Oliver in taking a drink. "Listen. I have to make a run for it. To get help."

Oliver started coughing and pushed the bottle away. "No. It's too dangerous."

"At least let me peek to see if it is day or night."

Reluctantly, he nodded.

Claudia quietly stepped toward the trap door. She hesitated, listening for any voices or movement above. There was none. After climbing the steps, she crouched down and gradually lifted the door. A beam of sunlight poured through a gap in the boarded-up windows and spread across the wood floor. It was hard to know if it was morning or afternoon, as she was not well-versed in the positions of the sun to tell time.

After lowering the door, she returned to Oliver. There was still food clasped in his hand. *That is not a good sign.* Taking advantage of the slight illumination, Claudia lifted the gauze and peered at his wound. It was angry-looking and slightly red. But there was no blood or pus. *There's a mercy.*

"Tell me about Danaher," he asked, his voice husky.

"I will if you eat some more. Here, have some cheese." Claudia broke off a piece and held it to his lips.

"You strike a hard bargain."

"Perhaps, but you must keep up your strength. Eat, Oliver." He took the proffered cheese, and when he chewed and swallowed, she held the dried beef before him. "Eat a little, and I will continue my tale of woe. But why you wish to hear more of it, I do not understand."

"As I said earlier, to know you better," he replied gravely between bites. "To comprehend what makes you tick."

His emotionally spoken words about wanting to explore every part of her, including her skin, still played over and over in her mind. Could he be fascinated by her alone, or was it because they were in a cramped hiding place, facing danger? Claudia would never forget what he said, for it touched her heart. But dredging up the past was playing havoc with her emotions.

"Make me tick? I am hardly a clock sitting on a mantel," she sniffed.

"Nor would I wish you to be. Not all men wish to control and bully women. That is not your experience, but decent, honorable men are out there. Like William."

Right. Not her experience was correct. Except for William, as he said. "And you are one?" Claudia asked softly.

"Yes, I believe I am. I *know* I am. But we all have flaws. No one is faultless."

"That is an accurate statement." Seeing that he had finished the beef, she gave him an oat biscuit. Claudia had come this far and might as well continue. "Danaher is definitely not an honorable man. My mother and I were down to our last few shillings. We heard there were abandoned row houses and lean-tos in Notting Dale that many squatters used. We headed there. Just our blasted luck, we chose one of the shacks Danaher had laid claim to. He and his men bustled in and told us to shove off. But then Jedi had a good look at my mother. Even beaten down by poverty, grief, and the beginnings of her illness, she was still beautiful."

"Like you," Oliver whispered.

Claudia blushed, and somewhere deep inside, she was pleased. So much for keeping her emotions guarded. Around Oliver Wollstonecraft, it became more difficult the longer she was with him. Face it, she was hiding nothing now. Her soul was laid bare. Regarding her mother, she had been much more attractive than Claudia could ever hope to be. Still, she appreciated Oliver's comment and committed it to memory with all the other lovely things he had said.

"We had the same red hair, although hers was a shade darker than mine. My mother made a deal with Danaher. We could stay in the hovel, and he would pay her a flat weekly sum. My mother agreed to be available for his animal lust whenever the mood struck him. I was also part of the deal. I was to be left alone and protected from Danaher and anyone else. To our astonishment, he agreed to the terms."

"And were you left alone?"

"Yes. Everyone knew we were under Danaher's protection; they took a wide berth when I went to the market to buy food. Some of the grocers gave us free bread and the like. We existed—barely. It was no life at all. And because we lived in a shack, rain and wind often seeped in. And the cold. We had plenty of firewood, but it never helped with the permanent chill my mother had to endure."

"What did she have, the illness you spoke of?"

"Consumption, or tuberculosis, whatever it is called now. And it slowly and insidiously consumed her. She hid her failing health as much as she could from Danaher. He was not all that observant at the best of times, at least as far as anyone in distress. For what did he care about? Nothing at all. Only his own comforts—or maybe not even that."

"Watching your mother fade away must have been difficult," Oliver said solemnly.

"Oh, yes. My mother was my companion and friend. There were only sixteen years between us. About a week before she died, she took my hand and made me promise that as soon as she passed, I must escape Notting Dale before Danaher found out. My mother did not trust him to leave me alone. How could I abandon her in that awful shack? I had already gone to Whinstone, so there was no other option."

Revealing this part of her life was more challenging than Claudia imagined. It stirred up complicated emotions long buried. Feelings she believed would never surface again. Guilt, grief, fear of the unknown. Resentment. And unwavering love and sacrifice. Mix that with her turbulent emotions toward Oliver, and she wondered if she could ever hide her feelings again. How disturbing.

"Wait," Oliver said. "Whinstone became involved with your mother when she was sixteen?"

"The age of consent was thirteen at the time. It was raised to sixteen in '85. Not that Whinstone cared about any of that. Yes, I know the laws regarding this. My mother made certain Danaher understood them as far as I was concerned."

"Where were your mother's parents in all this?"

"My mother never talked about her past much, though she revealed that her detestable father sold her to Whinstone in lieu of a debt. I thought such a loathsome act was illegal."

"It has been—for many decades. But it is still done in secret. Your mother enduring such a fate fills me with rage. The injustice of it all."

"Me as well. When my mother tried to locate her parents one afternoon shortly after her father handed her over to Whinstone, she discovered they had moved. No forwarding address."

Oliver cursed under his breath.

"Why should this surprise you? Women are treated as possessions, as are children. Regardless of recent changes in the laws," Claudia stated. "More needs to be done."

"I shouldn't be astonished, but it angers me, nonetheless. But this isn't about me or my feelings on the matter. You and your mother deserved a better life. So does anyone in such circumstances. But nothing ever seems to change, regardless of a few good men in Parliament trying to eke out fair laws for all. It is disheartening. So, what happened to you after your mother passed away?"

Swallowing hard, she dashed a tear from her cheek. "Leaving was the hardest thing I had ever done. My mother managed to save a few shillings. I used that to find my way to the East End. I have no idea what happened to my mother. I told the neighbor that she had died and to call the authorities. Mrs. Bridle was trustworthy enough. I watched as she headed toward the Lancaster Police Station, so I left."

"We can discover where your mother is buried. Since '37, all records have been kept by the state, not churches, as in the past. There will be an account of her death and burial."

"I've never told anyone this," Claudia whispered. "Thank you for not judging my past."

"I would never do that, not for you or anyone."

Oliver's empathy comforted her. His words reverberated with emotion, giving her the courage to reveal her past and expose the never-healed wounds. "I have felt alone since her death."

"It appears you are as lonely as I am."

Claudia's mouth dropped open in shock. "You? Lonely? You have a large and loving family, friends from your group, and probably more besides. You are not speaking sense. Your fever is starting to affect you, which is worrying."

Oliver shook his head. "It is not my fever talking. Being alone is more of a physical state. Lonely is feeling alone in a crowd. My doctor friend told me that feeling that way is caused by a fear of intimacy. At least, that is one of the reasons. What he said gave me pause, for it describes me more than I realized. He also mentioned trauma, but that aspect doesn't define me. Although it fits you, does it not? You have been dealing with trauma for much of your life."

Blast the man for seeing inside her. Her lower lip trembled as she tried to hold back the intense emotions sweeping through her. Claudia took a shuddering breath.

Oliver held out his hand. "Come, let me hold you."

Oh, how tempting.

This susceptibility was blasted annoying, but on another level, sharing her past turned out to be cathartic. It felt like part of a crushing weight had been lifted from her. Against her better judgment, she crawled next to Oliver as if they were two spoons in a drawer. Claudia drew in another quivering breath, then exhaled.

"It is all right, Claudia. You can cry. Do not hold it in any longer. I have you. I will hold you close for as long as you wish. What little strength I have at the moment—is yours."

And with those softly-spoken, compassionate words, Claudia let the tears come.

Chapter 15

OLIVER WAS NOT WELL. He might not have a raging fever, but he felt queasy, his muscles ached. The tiny bits of food he had consumed churned in his stomach like a ship caught in a storm. They must have been down here over twelve hours, perhaps closing in on eighteen or twenty-four hours. It was difficult to tell.

If the knife cut had nicked his colon or kidney, he would be dead by now. But it was apparent the injury developed a minor infection. And it would worsen if they did not escape their hiding place. What did he know of medical matters? Next to nothing. Oliver drew conclusions from books and articles he had read. There is no basis in fact.

Holding Claudia in his arms made him forget his wound and all it entailed, at least temporarily. She had cried quietly until she fell asleep. Oliver smoothed her hair from her forehead until she stirred. Her story had touched him deeply, and he understood there was more to it. What transpired once she escaped to the East End? How did she meet up with her group of ladies? Is that where she met the owner of The Velvet Vine?

Whatever the rest of her story, it was up to her to share it. Oliver would not pester her. But one conclusion he came to: Oliver wanted to see more of her, be with her. Smitten is a word that came to mind. Infatuated. Enamored. Whatever adjective fit, he felt it.

Claudia yawned and snuggled closer, causing his erection to harden further. He was injured and feeling nauseous, yet still aroused. The intimacy they had shared, all in the dark confines of a stone cellar, was part of it. His attraction toward her was not only physical—far from it. When they finally escaped, would that closeness continue in the world above ground? Oliver wanted it to endure—and grow.

"Why be The Sentinel?" she asked softly.

"Detective Simpson recently asked the same question." Oliver repeated what he had told the detective and the man's succinct response.

"I think the detective is right. It is a little of all your thoughts on the matter."

"Yes. It certainly isn't any particular incident; it was more of seeing and hearing what occurs in the slums. While attending university, my family volunteers at one of the family initiative clinics, either medical or legal. It certainly opened my eyes. I decided I wanted to be of more help than a few hours a week in a free clinic. So, I made a study of vigilantes, not that there is written history, but they have been part of oral history for centuries."

Oliver chuckled. "Or maybe it is just a song or ballad passed down, like Robin Hood, which may or may not be fiction. But in asking around, I heard tales of 'phantoms and certain highwaymen' through the recent decades in London. They were more prevalent before the Metropolitan Police was formed in '29. Not so much now. I'm young and fit, why not use it for good? There is time enough to sit in smoky rooms at Westminster and craft laws. I wanted to make a difference—now."

"That is all fascinating, and what you just described and what you told the detective—is all part of it. It makes me admire you all the more. But perhaps boredom may be an inducement as well."

Oliver frowned. "That makes me sound shallow, that the other reasons are trifling."

"They are far from trifling. In fact, I believe you wish to do good more than anything. That is obvious. But you cannot deny those with money, title, and power become jaded easily."

Claudia wasn't wrong on that score. How many times had The Rakes of St. Regent's Park sat around the table, expounding on the tedium of their lives? Couldn't boredom be the primary motive for their group in the first place? They were rather arrogant, but most of them were peers, after all. Egotistical thoughts were part of the makeup. And having no purpose in life.

"Perhaps your brother is bored," Claudia continued. "Instead of focusing his restless energy on doing something worthwhile, he internalized."

"Internalized? I have never heard it put that way."

"I don't know why I said that. I do not think it is even a proper word. But it fits. You said your brother was spoiled. Bryan chose a self-seeking path despite his affectionate upbringing and fine examples of altruistic family members. How to coax him from that route may be daunting."

Daunting, indeed.

The family may have to hold an intervention. Another generation of Wollstonecrafts cloistered away at the sanitorium? It may come to that. Could it be a familial weakness passed through the generations? Could such personality quirks or traits be passed on?

"You said before your grandfather was and is your hero. That in his youth, he suffered an opium addiction."

How interesting her question mirrored his thoughts. "Yes, as I said, he turned his life around. He went undercover in a cotton mill as a supervisor, and all the information he gathered assisted in crafting better labor laws for women and children toiling under hazardous circumstances. He met my grandmother, a nurse, at the sanitorium and later at the mill. It is a love story for the ages."

"So you are The Sentinel for that reason as well. To be like your grandfather, who you admire and love. To honor his memory."

Yes, that also could be another motivation. Oliver hadn't made the connection before, but it fit. Aidan Wollstonecraft was and still is his hero, as Claudia said. His sudden death hit the family hard. It was the first time Oliver had seen his father break down and sob uncontrollably.

"I spoke in jest about tying your brother to the roof of the carriage and taking him to Kent," Claudia said, tearing him from his thoughts. "But you may have to do exactly that. And soon. I overheard a conversation at Olivia's afternoon tea."

Claudia told of Shinwell's mother washing her hands of him. That he had been a hellion since birth. Yes, he would sink—and take Bryan with him. Perhaps Oliver should approach the Duke of Coldbridge. He was Christian, the Duke of Allenby's stepfather, and a decent sort. The duke wanted to ensure that his second son, Rome, did not become collateral damage along with Bryan—something to consider if he ever gets out of this quandary.

"Drastic action may be the ultimate outcome. As soon as we are out of this predicament, I will talk with Allenby about how to approach his stepfather, Coldbridge, regarding his son's involvement with Shinwell." It was becoming increasingly difficult to keep up with the conversation, but Oliver remained determined to do it to keep his mind off the rolling waves of pain coiling through him.

"How long do you plan to keep it up? Being The Sentinel," Claudia asked, bringing him back to the present conversation again.

"I have not given it much thought. As long as I am physically capable of doing so. I am trying to recruit my cousin to join. And I probably should not have revealed that. I will keep it up until I satisfy whatever empty part inside of me urged me to take this up in the first place. I thought it prudent to remain anonymous, and this seemed like the perfect solution."

"Why all the leather?"

"It makes for ease of movement. I saw a photograph of men in the wilds of the American West wearing leather vests, long coats called dusters, and leather coverings over their trousers. I paid a saddle maker good money to craft a similar outfit I designed."

"How clever. And it is smart to stay anonymous. And if your cousin joins you, that secret is also safe with me. Are there any other reasons for doing this?" Claudia asked, wholly absorbed in their conversation.

"Well, as I mentioned, I help people in real time. It is infinitely more satisfying than working on legislation that may take years. I try not to obsess over it, for I cannot help everyone. Oh—Christ!" Oliver yelled, biting his lip. The pain that trundled through him caused his vision to blur.

Claudia sat upright. "No more conversation. You need help *now*. I have been working on a plan. Hear me out," she whispered as she laid the blanket over him, tucking it under his chin. "I will change into those laborer clothes in the trunk and head to the police precinct and locate Simpson. I will ask him to do a raid in The Piggeries, inspect houses and the like, and even arrest a few of Danaher's men, make a real show of it. Simpson and two constables will enter this building, and two will walk out. One of them will be *you*."

"How?"

"Simpson can smuggle in a uniform for you to change into. It means you must walk out as if you are *not* injured. As for the uniformed copper, he can slip out and join another group of constables."

"Danaher's men might be watching the rear of the courtyard; they may catch you before you can even put this plan into motion. And it is a good one."

She is utterly magnificent.

Especially when her beautiful hazel eyes sparkled with excitement and interest.

"Thank you. Perhaps I should wait until the sun goes down, but it is best I go now. As I said earlier, you can bet others have noticed that we have been missing all night. I am sure your servants and your cousin are aware, and so are Edwina Callen and The Galway Agency."

"Then, I am obliged to marry you since we have been alone all night," he smiled shakily.

Claudia gave him a dubious look. "You are jesting, surely."

"If this were 1806, society would insist. My honor as a gentleman would brook no argument. Also, and more importantly, your reputation must be protected."

Claudia chuckled. "Now I know you are kidding. I have no reputation to protect."

Still, why in hell had he mentioned it? It must be the fever. Somewhere, deep inside of him, that germination of an idea, silly or not, took a foothold in his mind.

"Let's be serious," Claudia stated firmly. "Perhaps family and acquaintances have coppers looking for us right now. They all know I have been to Notting Dale, and so does your cousin. This would be the logical place to look. I have to try and get assistance. You require immediate medical attention."

"What if Danaher and his men apprehend you? Perhaps we should just stay put. Simpson knows of this hiding place."

Claudia shook her head. "But Simpson doesn't know that we are missing."

Oliver's mind was in a whirl, his thoughts jumbled. "He doesn't know—yet. I told Rett about Simpson. Maybe he will seek out the detective."

"That is a big if. And it may take more time than we can spare."

The flame in the oil lamp flickered. Oliver cast a glance toward it. "There is only a little oil left."

"All the more reason for me to leave. There is hardly any food or water remaining. We cannot stay down here any longer." Not waiting for his reply, Claudia tore off her tattered gown and tossed it aside. Wearing nothing but a thin chemise and frayed drawers, his heart hitched at her luscious curves. Strapped to her thigh was her knife, tucked away in its holder. He moaned at the glorious sight of her.

"Are you in pain?"

"Of a sort," Oliver croaked, growing aroused. "Is it wrong of me to admire your beauty again, but most of all, your courage?"

Her look softened. "No, it's not wrong. I am quite gratified that you find me attractive."

"Is it reciprocated?" Be damned if he sounded emotionally susceptible.

She dropped to her knees before him, cupping his face with her hands. "Oh, yes. It most definitely is." Claudia leaned in and kissed him. That touch of her lips, the warmth and softness, gave Oliver a brief spurt of energy. He hungrily devoured her mouth, his tongue slipping in and tangling with hers. She froze momentarily at the ferociousness of his kiss but then dove in, giving everything back and more.

Oliver had kissed his share of young ladies. But this? Beyond all his expectations. Earth-shattering. Utterly splendid. He tunneled his fingers through her glorious hair, which was as silky as he had imagined. Moaning, he took the kiss deeper, eager to taste her sweetness. A soft sigh escaped the corner of her mouth as she moved her hands into his hair, gently grabbing fistfuls while she enthusiastically kissed him in return. Passion existed deep within Claudia. Of that, there was no doubt. He wanted more, oh so much more. Then, as if a puncture had deflated a balloon, Oliver fell back on the pallet, weakness overtaking him.

"Hell's bells," she murmured, brushing her finger across her swollen lips.

"Indeed. We have much more to explore," Oliver rasped faintly.

Claudia plopped down next to him, pulling him into her arms. His head rested against her breast, and her heart thumped madly, in tune with his. Her fingers tangled in the lock of hair falling across his forehead. Her soothing touch cooled his fevered brow—and aroused him to the point of pain. No other woman ever affected him like this.

"That may not be wise."

Disappointment shot through him. "I think we make a formidable, splendid match. We would be foolish not to pursue it."

Claudia kissed his forehead, then gently pushed him aside and stood. She frowned as she collected the garments from the trunk. "What happened down here and what was said, it is best it stays here. You know that."

Oliver knew nothing of the sort but had no strength to argue the point.

She turned away, removing the knife holder, then pulled on the trousers and rolled up the cuffs. Claudia tore off the chemise, wrapped it around her chest, and hurriedly dressed in the flannel shirt and wool coat. Tying her hair in a knot, she tucked it up under the workman's peaked cap. She then pulled up the trouser leg and strapped on the knife holder.

"I am about seven inches over five feet, tall enough to pass for the height of most men. Once outside, I'll smudge dirt on my face and hands." Claudia faced him. "How do I look?"

"Eminently kissable."

Claudia crossed her arms and huffed. "You are incorrigible. You are not going to let this go, are you?"

"About the solid and lasting bond forming between us? No, I will not let it go. You should know it now: I can be a stubborn bloke." Oliver paused. "If anything were to happen to you—don't go. Do not leave me." Now, he certainly sounded pitiable, but Oliver was more afraid of her well-being than his selfish needs.

"I know these streets. I lived in this area for close to two years. Danaher and his men will not catch me." Then she gave him a teasing wink. "I promise I will be careful."

"Listen. Simpson may not be at the station, as he mentioned working night shifts. He is staying in rented rooms not far from here. Go there first." He gave Claudia the address. "Say The Sentinel sent you."

Claudia picked up the near-empty water jug and placed it in his shaking hands. "Be prudent with the water." Then she handed him a tin. "There is a little cheese and a biscuit left. Please nibble at it. You must keep your strength up. I will return, I promise." She brought over the bucket to him. "Do you need to urinate?"

"I can manage," he croaked. "Douse the lamp before you go."

She did, and darkness covered them like a cloak.

"Make certain the coppers clear this place out. There should be no clues left as to our identities," Oliver croaked. His throat was killing him, and fatigue was again rolling over him.

"Yes. Of course." Claudia took a step toward the stairs. Then halted. "If anything were to happen to *you*—please stay safe." Then she ran back to him and kissed him hard on the lips. She was gone before he could muster any semblance of stamina to kiss her in return.

EDWINA CALLEN PACED back and forth in the Duke of Chellenham's drawing room. Althea sat beside her duke fiancé on the sofa, her bandaged leg resting on a pillowed stool.

"I have only known Claudia briefly, but she would not stay out all night and the next morning without sending word. Miss Althea, you made that stipulation quite clear in our training," Edwina declared.

"Yes, I certainly did. Always let others know where you are," Althea replied. "What has Claudia told you?"

"I last saw her at afternoon tea yesterday. She mentioned she was about to head to Notting Dale to follow her subject. She always returned around one or two in the morning on previous nights. Sometimes, I waited up for her. Last night, I was too tired and went to bed around half past eleven. When I arose in the morning, I saw her door was shut and assumed she was sleeping late as she had been since accepting this case." Edwina wrung her hands in agitation. "Oh, if only I had checked earlier!"

Althea could not help but be worried. This is the first time someone from their agency has not checked in. "Her subject is Bryan Wollstonecraft, Viscount Tensbridge's younger brother, correct?"

Yes, it is," Edwina replied.

"I should head to Oliver's and see if he knows anything," Damon interjected.

Althea held out her hand, and Damon took it and squeezed it assuredly. What would she have done without this beautiful man by her side these past weeks? He was with her every step of the way during her operation and continued recovery. When the kindly Doctor Stevenson initially told her that she might have to use the cane for a few years, Damon held her as she cried out her crushing disappointment. Thankfully, that feeling passed, for many had it worse off.

Damon had reassured her that all would be well and that she could continue with her investigative agency. And so far, that had come to pass. Althea felt more robust each day and eager to begin her new life, blending being a duchess with her professional life. It would be a challenge, but one she happily accepted.

And Damon's much younger half-siblings coming to live with them after their marriage? Althea looked forward to that, too.

Damon had already hired a governess and a nurse to assist. The future looked bright, indeed. But back to the matter at hand.

"Yes, by all means, go to Oliver's. I will go with Edwina to Cleveland Street. We will meet you there."

Damon kissed her forehead, then headed into the hall, shouting for the butler and footmen.

Althea's brows knotted in worry. Claudia's first solo case, what if she had run afoul of some nefarious criminals? The agency never had any dealings with Notting Dale before. Perhaps they should have canvassed the area more thoroughly before sending in a novice.

Enough doubting.

The young woman was confident, capable, and resourceful if Althea gained anything from her initial interview and subsequent dealings with Claudia Ellingford.

Hopefully, there will be a logical explanation for her absence.

Althea stood, leaning on her cane for assistance. "Come, Edwina. We will locate her. Let us go to Cleveland Street and start the investigation."

Nothing will happen to Claudia, not while Althea drew breath.

Chapter 16

CLAUDIA CROUCHED IN a cluster of overgrown shrubs on the vacant lot next to the dilapidated house they had hidden in. She hadn't been able to travel far, for the streets were loaded with Danaher's men. The sycophants were easy to spot; they all had the same slack-jawed, brutish looks. At this rate, she will never make it to Westgate Terrace in Kensington.

Does she dare saunter right past them and hope her disguise is convincing enough to fool the poorly-educated hoodlums in thrall to Danaher? There may be no choice. The word no doubt tore through the streets that Danaher was looking for two people, with a reward offered for any information. Claudia couldn't linger here. Oliver needed medical assistance.

Yes, Oliver.

That searing kiss. Claudia had felt it straight to her toes, and her heart acted like it wanted to burst from her chest. And for her to hold him close and kiss him again before she departed? Not wise. She was supposed to be dead inside. Apparently, she responded to passion like every other human. It was a normal reaction, nothing else. Undoubtedly, deeper emotions have been engaged. But Claudia refused to believe it.

Oliver said he wanted more. Perhaps she should take what he offered. Then, she could move on with this annoying, unrelenting desire out of her system. *Sex.* The concept wasn't abhorrent to her, even though she had seen it used as a tool for men to get what they wanted, like holding power and ownership over women. Claudia was capable of looking after herself. She did not need a man for protection.

But being held in Oliver's arms was a revelation. He exuded such warmth and comfort; it was easy to see how women could succumb to such a luxury. But more importantly, what was more astounding than her physical attraction to him was that she had shared so much, and he had done the same. Outside of her mother, she never allowed anyone to see her vulnerability. And because of all that, Claudia could never use Oliver to slake her now-awakened desire and toss him aside. She felt terrible for even considering it. Remaining vigilant of her rampant feelings would be one of her top priorities. If that were even possible.

The first order of business is to be free of this chaos.

Seeing a fleeting opening, she emerged from the shrubs and headed toward the Kensington area. Slouching, she rammed her hands in her coat pocket and sauntered like she had seen many poor working men do: a shuffling gait of absolute weariness. Claudia had rubbed dirt on her face, hands, and neck, hoping that would serve as an adequate disguise.

"Here! You, there. Stop!" a voice called out.

Two men hurried toward her. "Who are you, and why are you here?" One man growled. They both held cudgels in their meaty fists, ready to strike at one wrong answer.

"Higgins, be my name," Claudia said with a low rumble. "I work at Hammersmith City Railway. Why you be askin'? What's the to-do? I just be cuttin' through to get to me room."

"Where?" the taller man yelled.

"'Tis yonder, o'er on Talbot Road."

One of the men flared his nostrils and stepped in reverse, for Claudia had not only smeared dirt on her face and hands but horse manure as well. "How come we've never seen you afore this?"

"I just got the job and took the room. Why?" Claudia shot back.

"And what's your job at the railway?" The other man asked, his eyes narrowed in suspicion.

Claudia scratched her head under her cap. "I shovel what they tell me. Coal. Dirt. Horse shite. Today it be shite."

The men moved farther away, disgusted looks on their faces. "Don't cut through here again, you follow? And wash, for Jaysus's sake."

As if they couldn't use a thorough cleaning as well. Claudia touched her forelock and shuffled off. Once she rounded the corner, she stopped, holding her hand over her rapidly beating heart. One hurdle completed. Westgate Terrace in Kensington was not that far. There was a communal water pump near the new Avondale Park, if memory serves. Hopefully, it wasn't removed during construction.

Because of the deadly, mid-century cholera outbreaks, most common water areas were dismantled when discovered as the source of the epidemics. Claudia would have to wash some of this muck from her, or she would be run out of Kensington by the coppers. Best to stay in disguise, Claudia couldn't allow her red hair to be seen at all. Who knows what people were watching?

Taking a deep breath, then exhaling, she continued her shuffling pace toward the pump.

JEDIDIAH DANAHER WAS a lot of things; patient was not one of them. He had been roaming the cluster of streets within Notting Dale since he had come face-to-face with Claudia Ellingford. He knew it was her—no mistaking that red hair. Why was she dressed that way, and why return? Jedi had to find her. Why? No one runs from him after all he has done for her. Giving her a roof over her head and food on the table. Claudia *owed* him. And he would see that she repaid him—one way or the other. And that way was information. Claudia knew about this vigilante; he was sure of it.

As Jedi sauntered through the streets, his thoughts turned to the past. Claudia was long gone by the time he had learned of Aileen's death. He had his men ask about it, and he could have expanded his search, but Jedi had moved on to other pursuits and no longer lamented the loss in income. Jedi knew that the then 16-year-old girl was untouched. He had grand plans to auction her off to rich toffs and, thereafter, use her as his top prostitute for exclusive clients.

But that all went by the wayside when she had done a runner. The girl was shrewder than he had thought. Jedi knew Aileen was sick, though the stupid woman tried to conceal it. He didn't care. As long as she satisfied his intermittent sexual needs between her coughing jags, that is all that mattered.

Why waste his time looking for that termagant when he had other pressing concerns? Like that masked nutter acting a hero, or the fact more and more rooming houses were being pulled down and people evicted. Jedi had experienced clearances firsthand in St. Giles and, later, in the Seven Dials. Although he only had a few years of education, he was shrewd enough to realize he would soon have to shove off and find another place to do his business.

But until then, this was his home, his kingdom. Jedi was the boss, and no one attacked him or his men. He couldn't allow it to stand. He rounded the corner to see two of his men standing close together, sharing a cigarette. A fat lot of good they were, too busy seeing to their comforts than watching the street. Jedi marched toward them and grabbed the shorter one by the scruff of the neck.

"You bleedin' bastard. You're supposed to be at the other end of the road, not here gossipin' and smokin' like a couple o'fishwives. Who's been by here?"

The man cringed. "Sorry, sir. Won't happen again."

Jedi pushed the man away and spat. "Too right, it won't."

The taller man dropped the cigarette and ground it out with his boot. "Only one man. He said he worked for Hammersmith Railway. He were filthy and stunk and said he shovels horseshit and the like. I told him to wash."

Jedi stood before John Birch, who had been with him for years, as if these two pillocks didn't need a thorough scrub-down. One luxury Jedi indulged in, taking baths as often as possible.

Inches from the man's face, he snarled, "And how do you know you were talkin' to a man? I told you the woman wore a disguise. Did you ask him to pull out his cock to prove he was a railwayman worker?"

"N-n-no, sir," Birch stuttered.

Jedi grabbed Birch's bollocks, squeezing hard. "Then you should have done this." He twisted, and Birch shrieked, tears running from his eyes. "You follow? Which direction did this worker go?"

Still screaming, Birch could not reply, so the shorter man, whose name Jedi couldn't be bothered to remember, pointed toward Avondale Park.

"He went that way, sir. Said he has a room over on Talbot Road."

Jedi released Birch, who dropped to the ground, curled into a ball, and whimpered loudly. Jedi kicked him for good measure. "Worthless shite. Get on your feet. And do your feckin' job. Check the men more thoroughly. Bring any strange women to me. And if that shite-smelling railway boyo reappears, I want to see him, too. You follow?"

The shorter man assisted Birch in standing. They both nodded vigorously, withering under his murderous glare.

Disgusted, Jedi strode away. He should have cut their throats and be done with it. But then he'd have to replace them. Finding loyal men of a certain age with the required criminal proclivities was becoming more challenging.

As he rounded the corner, Jedi stopped short. Standing by the ancient water pump was—someone. The man Birch had encountered? The person was dressed in laborer clothes, alternating working the pump and washing his face and hands. Birch had told the man to get clean, and he was doing that very thing. The laborer wore an oversized peaked cap pulled low over his eyes. Jedi couldn't see his face or what color his hair might be.

Only one way to be sure.

Jedi sprinted across the lane toward the laborer but froze when he spotted a uniformed copper. The constable banged his stick on the pump, shouting at the laborer. Then, the overbearing policeman grabbed the railway worker by the arm and pulled him along the path through the park.

Feck it all.

The coppers mostly stayed out of The Piggeries, but with this new park and more respectable houses growing ever closer to his kingdom, things were changing—and not for the better. Waiting a few minutes, Jedi crossed the road and entered the park.

"Here, what's all this, then?"

No mistaking *that* query. Jedi turned to face a tall policeman, not the same one that ran off the railway laborer. Bloody coppers were everywhere.

"Just takin' a stroll, guv."

"Well, you can stroll back to The Piggeries where you belong, Danaher. Oh, aye, I know who you are. Shove off, you Irish scum. Or I'll take you to the station and charge you with lurking and loitering."

Jedi growled low in his throat. If this were under the cover of night, he'd have taken this copper and spilled his innards all over these fine, new cobblestones. Angry and frustrated, Jedi Danaher headed in the direction from whence he came. Leaning against a street lamp, he folded his arms. Jedi had the distinct feeling this railway worker would be back this way again. And when he did, Jedi would be here to check him over.

For something wasn't quite right.

The loose-fitting clothes, the slender build, it could be a man, but it also could be Claudia. And if it *was* Claudia, where was the masked man? Jedi had caught him with his knife. He was convinced of it. They were holed up somewhere, licking their wounds—with Claudia in disguise to seek help. Or maybe she escaped because the masked nutter had bled out and cocked up his toes. Jedi had to know.

Regardless, he would keep watch. In this particular instant, he would be patient.

And get satisfaction, one way or the other.

Chapter 17

CLAUDIA STOOD BEFORE the house Detective Simpson lived in. How to work this? God knows if she was followed. She did her best to avoid suspicion. While standing at the water pump, however, Claudia had the distinct feeling someone was watching her every move. Perhaps it was a blessing that copper had grabbed her arm and escorted her out of the park.

Regardless, she was here now. Claudia tugged the bell, and a woman, obviously a maid considering the white apron and cap, answered the door.

"Deliveries are around the rear," the older woman bellowed. The maid tried to close the door, but Claudia stuck her boot across the threshold.

"Detective Simpson, is he in? It is a matter of utmost importance that I see him. It concerns a significant case." Claudia spoke in her own voice. "I am in disguise. I work for The Galway Investigative Agency."

The maid arched a dubious eyebrow. "Do you have a card?"

Claudia fought back her frustration. Losing her temper would not be prudent. "No, because I am in disguise. I need to speak to him right away."

"He's not here."

Oh, no.

"Did he go to the police station on Lancaster Road?" she asked, disheartened.

"I have no idea. The detective rents rooms here. I am not his keeper. He comes and goes as he pleases. A boy brought a note earlier. I had to wake Mr. Simpson out of a dead sleep. He dressed and left right away."

Hell's bells.

"Do you still have the note?"

The maid blew out an exasperated breath. "No, I never read it. I gave it to Mr. Simpson. Take your foot out of the door."

"Please, I need to leave a message for the detective."

The maid pushed on the door, attempting in vain to close it. Claudia winced from the pain of the heavy oak door slamming against the side of her booted foot.

"Hannah. Show the woman into the foyer."

The maid stood aside, opening the door wide. An older woman, elegantly dressed in an afternoon tea gown, stood in the vestibule. She looked to be in her mid-sixties or a little older. Her blonde and gray hair was carefully arranged in an upswept style. "I am Lady Ainsworth, and this is my home. What is the meaning of this?"

Claudia turned to the maid. "Please close the door."

The lady nodded, and the maid fastened the lock.

Claudia tore off her cap, and some red hair tumbled to her shoulders. "My lady, I am Claudia Ellingford of The Galway Investigative Agency. May I please leave a note for Detective Simpson? After, I will go to his police station and not bother you again. I would not be here if it weren't an urgent matter regarding a case I am working on for a viscount. Detective Simpson offered his assistance."

"James." Lady Ainsworth motioned toward a tall, muscular footman. "Take Miss Ellingford into the morning room and allow her to write a note. Then escort her out through the rear entrance." Lady Ainsworth pivoted to meet Claudia's gaze. "In case you were followed here."

"Yes. Very shrewd, my lady."

"I have my moments. I will ensure your missive is given to Detective Simpson, but it may be some hours before he returns. Mitchell keeps ungodly hours. I will place footmen at the front and rear entrances and ask them to bring the detective to me immediately. When he returns." Lady Ainsworth examined her. "Perhaps a change of clothes? To throw off any scent?"

Claudia couldn't help but grin. Though she had washed, there no doubt was still an equine odor lingering about. "I believe we could use you at our agency, my lady."

The older woman looked pleased at the compliment. "Tosh. I am a voracious reader, especially the works of Arthur Conan Doyle. Moreover, you have brought a little excitement to this widow's dull day. Which clothes do you prefer? Male? Female?"

Claudia had heard of the author, but as with Oscar Wilde, she had no time these past years to purchase any books, let alone read them. "It should be clothes similar to these, my lady. It makes it easier to move about certain streets."

"Hannah, find some clothes for Miss Ellingford. James, escort Miss Ellingford to my desk in the morning room. You will find paper in the top drawer. Can we bring you tea or food, my dear?"

"Thank you for the kindness, but I must dash as soon as possible."

"Promise you will come for a visit soon. I want to hear all about this case you are working on. We will have afternoon tea."

Claudia smiled, for she genuinely liked Lady Ainsworth. "I will."

Claudia was hustled into a small but lovely morning room decorated in sunny shades, from the white French provincial furniture to the yellow rose wallpaper. The footman gathered pen, ink, and paper, then stood aside, hands clasped behind his back.

What to write?

DETECTIVE SIMPSON,

I work for The Galway Investigative Agency. O.W. needs assistance at once. He sent me to find you, for he has been seriously injured and is taking refuge at the place you were recently made aware of. It will be difficult to extract him, for the surrounding area is being watched. Vigilantly. I suggest the following: as soon as the sun sets, move into the site with as many uniformed police officers as you can muster. Create a distraction, even arrest some of the men in question. Enter the building with two policemen, smuggling in a uniform for O.W. He will walk out with you. Two uniformed coppers in, two out. The other police officer can slip out the rear. Please remove anything that could identify him.

CLAUDIA HESITATED. What to do next? Head back to Notting Dale? She must. Oliver's life depended on it. She couldn't stay here in Lady Ainsworth's lovely morning room drinking tea and eating cakes. The thought of Oliver alone in that chilly cellar made her heart ache. She would *not* abandon him, alone and shivering in the darkness. Injured, feverish, and hungry.

I WILL HEAD TOWARD the Lancaster Police Station, hoping to find you there. If I cannot locate you, I will head to Cleveland Street and enlist the assistance of The Galway Agency. C. Ellingford

SHE SHOULD SEND A NOTE to Cleveland Street. Evidently, her absence would have been noticed by now, as well as Oliver's absence. Claudia glanced at the clock on the mantel. Half past two. Could Oliver hold on until dusk? Perhaps she should go to Cleveland Street first, then to the police station.

Hell's bells, her mind twirled about in all directions.

Calm yourself.

Logic dictated that finding Simpson and enlisting his help must take priority over everything. Taking a deep breath and exhaling, Claudia pulled blank paper from the drawer. But logic did not always win out. Not when she was so worried about Oliver.

I AM WELL. O.W. NEEDS assistance. I left a note for Detective Simpson with Lady Ainsworth, 9 Westgate Terrance. O.W. needs him. Now. Please find him. Important: follow my instructions in Simpson's note. I will come to Cleveland Street soon. C. E.

CLAUDIA FOLDED THE note in half and wrote the Cleveland Street address. "Can you please deliver this letter to either Eleanora or Althea Galway? It *is* imperative. The address is on the outside of the note."

James took the message. "I will, miss."

Hannah entered the room with a pile of clothes. "My lady says to take your pick. They belong to the gardener and his son."

"Thank you." She folded the Simpson note. "This is for the detective. Please tell him it is urgent."

James stepped outside while she changed. The clothes were not the best fit, but they would do. She kept the peaked cap as it hid her face and hair better than the hat in the heap of garments.

Lady Ainsworth knocked and entered the room. She handed Claudia a burlap sack. "Inside are various foods a laborer might carry. Ham sandwiches, oat biscuits, cheese, and the like. Along with a jug of tea. You will also find a small pocket knife with a serrated blade. Hopefully, you will not need to use it. James will escort you out through the rear courtyard. Make use of the water closet in the hall before you leave. Take care, my dear."

A second knife may be helpful. "You have thought of everything. Thank you. I will return for a visit soon, I promise."

Lady Ainsworth smiled. "I look forward to it."

With a final thank you and after using the water closet, Claudia slipped out the rear entrance into a large, fenced yard filled with the remains of some September flowers, dahlias, and sunflowers, specifically. Once she located the gate, she exited onto the street and hurried along the walkway.

Starving, she reached into the sack and found one of the parchment-wrapped sandwiches and quickly ate it. A little voice kept nagging in her thoughts to go to Cleveland Street instead of the police station, but that would only waste valuable time. Locating Simpson was her top priority. Only Simpson knew of Oliver's vigilante persona; she must protect that.

Besides, running into a random police station wearing man's laborer clothes and demanding assistance would get her kicked to the cobbles. Dressing as a fine lady would have garnered even more attention, so this costume was wise, for she had dealt with enough coppers over the years to know how they react with either guise. Although the Galway Agency could convince the Met Police to offer help sooner. What to do?

She glanced over her shoulder at the burlap sack. There was a slim chance she could slip this food to Oliver before heading to the police station. If there were none of Danaher's men about. It was a reckless idea but one worth considering. It would be hours until any rescue could be achieved. There was no food or water left. He was in a weakened condition; he'd never make it to sundown. As she surmised earlier, logic was hard to pin down in certain circumstances.

Especially in this case. Claudia had grown to care for Oliver in a short period. Claudia was worried sick over him all alone in that dark place. His comfort overrode every other consideration. What if he took a turn for the worse? He needed food to keep up his strength to combat the infection until they could extract him and get him proper medical assistance.

She *must* see to him. Right now.

Instead of traveling directly through Avondale Park, she took another circuitous route, cutting through a street filled with rubble, wood piles, and caravans. A dog barked loudly when she rounded the corner. Claudia froze. Luckily, the animal was tied to a post. She continued on her way, zigzagging through back alleys, hiding when she heard voices. Danaher's men were still about, but she eluded them.

Holding her breath, she hurried past the bramble shrubs she had hidden in previously and darted across the walkway into the rear of the house Oliver hid.

Hell's bells, I've done it.

Without time to further congratulate herself, Claudia quietly moved aside the loose boards and slipped inside. It was hard to tell if there were fresh footprints, for the wood floors were primarily clear of dirt and dust. Which, in itself, should be suspicious. But she understood why Oliver kept it swept clean. The iron bar was precisely where she had left it. Standing perfectly still, she listened.

There was no noise from below, and the street remained quiet. Once she opened the trap door, she concealed the bar again.

Claudia started down the steps. "It's me," she whispered. Slowly, she closed the door and was engulfed in complete darkness. "Oliver!"

A soft groan came from the general area she had left him. With shuffling steps and taking great care not to knock anything over, she found him. Without thinking, she dropped the burlap sack and immediately gathered him close. He was still alive. Excitedly, she kissed his face all over, and when she found his lips, she stopped there and kissed him deeply. Oh, the taste of him, so enticing. Like a sweet, decadent dessert.

At first, Oliver did not respond.

But when Claudia took the kiss deeper, tangling her tongue with his, it was as if a burst of energy ignited within him. He felt around in the dark and cupped her face, tilting her head slightly to return the enthusiasm. Their tongues interlaced again, and they explored every inch of their mouths. Her insides trembled as if a flutter of butterflies had been let loose. Kissing this man for hours was tempting, but she must keep her senses.

Oliver pulled away. "Why did you come back?"

"I brought food. Simpson wasn't home, but I left a detailed note of my plan. I also sent a note to Cleveland Street asking them to find Simpson and collect the message I left with Lady Ainsworth. It's after three o'clock. I couldn't leave you here for hours without food or drink."

Crawling on her knees, she felt around for the burlap sack and thrust it into his hands. "Sandwiches, tea, and biscuits. How is your wound? Damn, I can't check it." Claudia laid her hand against his forehead. It felt clammy. "Still a slight fever. Where is the blanket?"

"It's to my right. I kicked it off. I am hot one moment and cold the next. I ache all over. The pain that tears through me when I make the slightest move—how am I going to walk out of here?" he whispered, frustration clear in his voice. "What do I smell?"

"I had to smear dirt and horse manure on my hands and face to enhance the disguise. I washed most of it off. You should stay sitting up so you can eat," Claudia replied. "Let me help you. Then I have to leave."

"What? No!" he hissed. "Why?"

"I have to locate Simpson. I am going to the police station. We cannot rely on notes being delivered. I *must* find him right away."

Oliver grasped her wrist. "You will be caught. You have been fortunate so far, but I've heard numerous voices outside since you left. I also could hear noises like someone ripping down walls in nearby structures."

"All the more reason for me to find the detective immediately." Claudia took his hand and kissed it. "I will not abandon you to fate. I must keep trying. And thank you for not lecturing me for bringing you food."

"I would never second guess anything you do. I have complete confidence in your abilities."

Claudia smiled in the dark. A man not judging her? How rare and welcome. "We could try and make a run for it right now, but the chance of being caught is far too great. Hopefully, with this food and added rest, you will be strong enough to walk out with Simpson later."

"You are maddingly stubborn," Oliver murmured, "But I understand your reasoning and agree. I would not get far without collapsing if we were to try now." He paused. "You are so fierce. So utterly lovely. And what we have said and done is most decidedly *not* staying here. You have captured me in all ways."

What could she say to that? Nothing, except kiss him once again. She wished to stay and kiss him all over, especially across that enticing knot of muscles across his abdomen, and perhaps lower.

Such wicked thoughts in such a circumstance, but Claudia couldn't help it. Another lingering, deep kiss, and then she reluctantly pulled away. Reaching for the sack, she grabbed the food and the jug of tea, pushing them into his hands. "Keep up your strength. Stay well. Stay alive. I *will* get you out of here. I promise, even if it takes my last breath." Oliver wanted and needed Simpson, and Claudia would locate him if she had to tear the city apart.

"Be careful," he replied, squeezing her hand. "When we get out of this, I am taking you out to dinner."

Dinner? Why? To what end? Realistically, there could be nothing between them beyond this fleeting mutual attraction and regard. Oliver's standing in society was not the reason. Claudia always believed she was good enough for any man, regardless of title or station, but also thought herself incapable of a long-term intimate relationship and commitment. It was not something she longed for or gave much thought to.

And there was certainly no time to consider it now.

Claudia kissed his feverish forehead and replied, "Yes, we will go to dinner." Anything to keep him calm. "Promise me you will eat everything."

"I will," Oliver rasped. "Stay safe. Do not agree to dinner just to placate me."

Claudia stayed silent.

"Ah. You agreed to appease me. Forget dinner, then. Instead, agree that we will see each other after this perilous situation concludes."

"What, courting?" she stated incredulously. Oliver couldn't be serious.

"Yes, why not? It is what I desire. I desire *you*. But only agree because that is what *you* want."

"I do not know what I want," Claudia whispered miserably. Her emotions churned, swirling in disarray.

Oliver gently took her hand and kissed it. "Then we will figure it out together. Go now before I kiss you again."

Claudia patted his hand, released it, then moved forward, arms in front of her, feeling for the wall. Waiting and listening, she heard nothing but complete silence and gradually opened the trap door. A small beam of light crawled across the cache's dirt floor, illuminating Oliver. He gazed at her with such yearning it caused her breath to catch in her throat.

He is so beautiful, inside and out.

First, she blew him a kiss, then gave him a trembling smile. Her insides were in knots, not only from this hazardous situation but also from Oliver and her jumbled feelings. But there was no mistake. She harbored feelings for him, and they grew more profound the more she was with him.

Once her eyes adjusted to the change in lighting, she ascended.

The Lancaster Road station was more than a few streets away. This wouldn't be easy. But, as she had assured Oliver before, she knew this area. The general layout was the same as ten years ago. She must head northeast, through Silchester Road, if she remembered correctly.

Stealthily, Claudia made her way through alleys and courtyards, avoiding Danaher's men. A sense of relief overcame her, for she was almost out of Notting Dale. All she had to do was stay on Talbot Road and continue in a northeasterly direction. If her plan fell into place, they could be safely away from this horrid area in a few hours. Oliver needed a doctor's care. That is what kept her moving forward and gave her courage.

A voice wafted out of the nearby alley. "Horseshite. I know that smell anywhere. Take him."

Another man grabbed her arms and held them tight. *No!* Not when she was so close. Claudia must stay calm and talk her way out of this.

The man stepped out of the shadows, and her heart sank.

Danaher.

He whipped the peaked cap from her head. "Claudia. Welcome home."

Chapter 18

DANAHER'S LAIR LEFT much to be desired for a rookery boss's hideaway. There were only a few chairs and a table located in the lean-to. But then, Danaher always had more than one place to scurry away to—like that rat he is.

Claudia took a moment to reflect that returning to Notting Dale to bring Oliver food was not the wisest choice. Her heart overrode all common sense. There was no use admonishing herself over it now as more immediate issues lay before her.

A tall young man shoved her toward one of the chairs. "Sit."

"Good lookin', ain't he?" Danaher chortled roughly. "He's mine, so it's said. I'm bringin' him along, like."

Claudia turned to give the young man a thorough inspection. He was darkly handsome with wavy black hair. He appeared to be around twenty years old. No doubt Danaher had the same look when at that stage. "Run, lad. Get as far away from this man as you can."

Danaher gave her a clout across the head. "No one asked you."

Fair enough.

"Why take me? What do you care about me or what I'm doing?" Claudia asked.

"I don't bloody care. Well, I did for a bit, for I had plans for you. And you mucked that up good and proper. Cost me good money."

So, her mother had been correct in her assumption of Danaher. He would have put Claudia to work on the streets. She wound up on the streets anyway, but it had been on *her* terms, *her* control. A vast distinction from being under this monster's thumb—and her mother had known it. So did Claudia, even at age sixteen.

"Anyways, I want that masked nutter," Danaher continued. "Give him to me, and you'll come to no harm."

Claudia barked a caustic laugh. "Right. Don't forget, I know you. You will pass me around to your men like I was a frosted cake on a silver tray. I've seen you do it before."

Danaher stood closer, looming over her. "Have you, now? You were always sneakin' about. Stickin' your nose in. And you still are. Why are you in my territory?"

How much information to give him? Could she stall him enough until the sun set and the Met Police arrived? That is if Simpson got her note. The Galway Agency would not just shrug off her absence. They would first go to Oliver's and, in finding him missing, work out a search strategy. If her note arrives at Cleveland Street, they will locate that letter at Simpson's. There were many moving parts, but Claudia believed those mechanisms would click into place. Eventually.

"To watch you and plan my revenge," she replied sarcastically.

"Give over. For what? I didn't kill your mother," Danaher snapped.

"You didn't help her, either. A doctor, medicine, a better place to stay. You did none of it."

Danaher grunted. "Why should I? Besides, it were obvious she were dyin'. Nothin' I could do. I ask again, why're you here?"

It was best to keep him talking and reveal enough truth to gain his interest and perhaps a sliver of trust. If memory served, Danaher could tell when people lied. "I am an investigator for a detective agency."

"She's a copper!" the young man exclaimed.

"Jaysus, Cillian. Agency, not police. Besides, there ain't any women coppers on the streets."

"Not yet," Claudia muttered under her breath. "But there will be one day."

Danaher growled in response and turned his attention back to Claudia. "Again, why're you here in my territory?"

"A well-to-do client hired me to follow someone. He's in with a bad crowd. They come here to partake in the various vices available. I am merely noting what the young man is up to and where. That is all."

Danaher cocked one eyebrow, the one not bisected by that awful scar. He shrewdly turned over her words in his brain, ascertaining if she expressed the truth. "That's why you wore costumes and the like. To make sure you'd blend in."

"Yes, and I also didn't want to run into *you*. Bad memories and all that."

Danaher gave her another swat across the head, harder this time, enough that a burst of stars danced in her vision. "I gave you and your sick mother a roof over your head. And firewood. And shillings, besides. So, aye. I helped her."

"As I said, not enough to make a difference. And my mother paid for that pittance many times over, and you know it," Claudia spat. "You must realize your time as a rookery boss over these dwindling streets is ending. Soon, you will have power over no one at all. Still notching your kills with ace tattoos on your arm?"

Danaher chuckled cruelly. "Aye. Your mother must have told you that. I'll be startin' on the other arm soon enough. Don't tempt me to add you and all." His eyes narrowed as he assessed her closely. "You always were a clever girl with your snobby way of talkin'. I like that. You challenge me. We'd make a good team. In all ways."

Claudia inwardly cringed. "Not a chance."

"As I said, you owe me."

"No, I don't—and you know it. You don't care about me. You never did. How did it all go wrong for you? When you were a child. Abandoned on the streets, I imagine. How else to survive except by thieving and whoring? I will bet you did both to prevail. Haven't we all? How many rich toffs paid for you?"

Danaher's scowl turned thunderous. Provoking him may not be the soundest plan, but she must stall for time. Claudia continued, "You were a pretty boy with all that curling black hair and light blue eyes. Any humanity you had at birth—and I doubt it was much—was pounded out of you through the years, one way or another. Bent over rubbish bins in dark alleys for a three-shilling fu—"

Danaher had his hands around her throat, cutting off her words and her breath. "You mewlin' bitch. Judgin' by your foul words, you've been livin' on the streets and all. You know exactly 'tis all about. There's a cost. You will pay."

Cillian grabbed his father's arm. "Don't harm her. You need information—about the vigilante. And why slay good merchandise? Look at her. She'll bring a pretty penny. Those tits alone are worth gold. Your original instincts were right on that."

The mention of money stayed his hands, and he released them from around her neck. They had removed her coat, and the loose wool shirt buttons were undone halfway down, showing her breasts all but spilling out of the top of the tightly wound chemise she had wrapped around her chest.

Claudia gasped and wheezed, trying to catch her breath. She hit a little too close to home. She knew nothing of Danaher's past, but what she described was a tragic tale for many people in such circumstances—male or female of whatever age. Claudia cast her glance toward Cillian. He had some education, perhaps a mother or other family members who loved him. Why was he here with Danaher? Young and impressionable? Or just plain stupid?

"Gold?" Danaher said, looking at his son.

"Aye. We keep this termagant locked in a room. Charge top fees. Let those toffs have a go, two or three at a time. Think of the money. Gold sovereigns in our pockets."

Danaher pinched his son's cheek, then gave it a playful slap. "Oh, aye. You're mine, sure as brass. Good lad." Jedi turned his attention to her once again. "I'll think on it."

The thought of being locked in a room to serve men caused her stomach to lurch. For many years, that exact scenario made up the bulk of her nightmares. The young man was more like his father than Claudia initially believed. Apple falling, tree, however the saying goes.

"Wait. That were you with the brown hair and the scar. The yanker. I knew you were familiar." Danaher took a step closer. "Is that what *you* did to survive? Pull on cocks for a shilling or two?"

"So what if I did? We all do things to stay alive. As well, you know." God, her voice was hoarse. Danaher really would have killed her.

"And now you're an investigator. Or so you say."

"I'm telling the truth. I'm good at my job. I fooled you. I'm not after you or yours, so let me go. I can finish the investigation, and I'll never return here again. You have my word."

Danaher laughed. "You have brass; I'll give you that."

"My fellow investigators will go to the police if you keep me here too long. They know I'm in Notting Dale," Claudia continued. "This place will be overrun with coppers before you know it."

Danaher chuckled again. "Clever girl. You see, regardless of what me son says and suggests, I'm not interested in you. You were right about that. Tell me about the vigilante, and I'll consider lettin' you go. All I want to know about is the masked nutter. You follow? I know what he is and how he stepped into a family dispute. He beat a man unconscious because Charlie wanted what he was entitled to."

"The laundry woman had every right to keep her hard-earned money to provide for her children. Not hand it over to her lay-about husband to spend in your pub. Yes, I witnessed the episode. It is where I first came across The Sentinel." That is not entirely correct, as she met Oliver's alter ego in the East End, but Claudia wasn't planning to tell Danaher everything, and not necessarily the complete facts. Giving Danaher the name of the vigilante would persuade him even more that she was telling the truth. *Her* version of the truth.

"So, that's his name, bloody stupid if you ask me. That washerwoman wouldn't tell me. She won't be ironin' clothes for a long time. I broke her arm, see. And I'll do the same to you and all. Yeah?"

That poor woman. Claudia will find where the ironer lives and compensate her for her trouble. Oliver would contribute as well if they got out of this difficulty. "I don't know who he is."

"Don't make me out to be a pillock. Charlie told me this Sentinel ran off with a woman. It was you."

Claudia shrugged. "He hid me from those angry men and then left. We didn't even talk. I never saw him again. Until the other night."

"Aye. Comin' to *your* rescue. How convenient, that. I cut him good. Is he dead? I think not, or you wouldn't still be runnin' around these streets. You got him hidden away. Eh? Going for help? Or did you already? Was that you, the shite-smellin' railway bloke? I think so."

"I don't know what you're on about," Claudia sniffed.

"I smell a faint odor of shite. It *was* you. And I can prove it. Cillian, bring Birch and that other gobshite."

Blast it.

There had not been much of the putty and grease paint left on her face when encountering those imbeciles earlier, but there may have been enough to cast a cloud of doubt. Plus, she was wearing different clothes now.

Cillian wasn't gone long, and two men meandered into the room behind him. One was tall and slender, the other short and squat. Already, Claudia could smell the fear off of them. Fear of Danaher. Which means they will tell him what he wants to hear.

"Take a good look. Is this the railway boyo?" Danaher demanded.

"He didn't have no red hair," the short one declared.

"We didn't see his hair, eejit. And he was wearing different clothes," the taller one said.

"He didn't have no titties, either, but this bloke does," the short one snapped.

"Look at the face," Danaher snarled.

The two men glared at her. One was about to speak when another man rushed into the room.

"There be coppers everywhere! They brought wagons and are swarmin' all over, enterin' every house. We got to leave!"

Claudia fought hard to keep the relief from outwardly showing, but inside? She felt like crying from the release of pent-up emotion. She glanced at the table, where her knife lay beside her cap. Cillian, however, had *not* found Lady Ainsworth's pocketknife hidden in the lining of her overcoat. But the coat was on the back of her chair. Could she reach it in time before they swarmed her?

Danaher growled. "Birch, you come with me. You, Shorty, stay with Cillian and watch this one. I'll be back." Danaher and Birch slipped out the rear entrance.

Raised voices could be heard now, along with police whistles and an almighty clamor.

"He won't be back. Danaher's done a runner," Claudia said, her voice still raw. "Saving his own skin. Leaving his son behind is typical.

If you two were smart, you'd do the same. Make a run for it before it's too late."

"Shut your gob!" Cillian yelled.

Claudia wasn't tied to the chair, so she hurriedly ran through escape scenarios. Meanwhile, the short hoodlum rubbed his hands together, clearly agitated. He paced about, peering out through the covered window through a gap in the boards.

Taking advantage of his distraction, Claudia jumped to her feet, grabbed the chair, and swung it about, crashing it down on Shorty's head. She gave another swing, and the man fell to the ground, unconscious. The coat fell to the floor at her feet.

Cillian ran toward her, and she twirled around in a circle, catching him on the side of the head with the chair, although Danaher's son stayed upright. The wood must have been rotten, for the chair splintered apart, jagged wooden pieces flying in all directions. Cillian was knocked senseless long enough that she was able to grab the knife from the coat.

She brandished it in front of her. "Come near me, and I will slice you open from stem to stern. I am capable."

Cillian wiped the blood from the corner of his mouth and shook his head as if to clear it. "Oh, aye. I've no doubt." He reached into his coat pocket and brought out a knife about the same size as hers. "But you heard Himself; you ain't leaving here."

"Oh, I am."

"Don't try it. I don't fancy being in a knife fight with a woman, but don't think I won't do it."

"And damage the merchandise?" Claudia sneered.

The raised voices drew nearer. Claudia wasn't waiting for Cillian to make the first move. Kill Danaher's son? That wouldn't be smart. But she could disable him. Lay a vicious gash on his pretty face if she could get near enough, or a few stabs to his side or back, enough to damage muscles and tendons.

Claudia shouted and lunged toward him, and the blade made contact with the side of his face near the hairline. But Cillian also managed a slice, catching her left side in almost the exact area Oliver had been cut. She grunted, but as she raised her knife for another possible lunge, her legs gave out just as three policemen burst through the door.

Cillian immediately rushed through the rear entrance, and one of the policemen gave chase.

"Detective Simpson," she managed to croak. "He's looking for me." At least, she hoped so.

"Miss Ellingford?"

"Yes."

They took her arms and brought her to her feet, and she cried out in pain. "Please, the coat, hat, knife, and holder. Bring them."

Then darkness covered her like a cloak.

Chapter 19

OLIVER COULD HEAR THE tumult above, rushing footsteps, cursing, police whistles, and shouting. Had Claudia's ingenious plan come to fruition? It appeared so.

He lay, weak and wounded, wondering how to leave this hiding place. Partaking of the sandwich, tea, and biscuits helped, and the food was not roiling in his stomach, another promising sign. Could the sustenance provide the temporary strength needed to leave here walking upright?

Lying in a dark cellar gave one plenty to ruminate over. Such as acting as a vigilante was not quite the clever idea he had initially thought. But Oliver wouldn't change anything, for it allowed him to come to Claudia's rescue, briefly making him feel like a hero. But then Claudia rescued him in return, nursed his wound, and even returned to check on him. She kissed him soundly more than once. And held him close, soothing his brow. She must care for him on some level.

Where was Claudia now? Was she safe?

He was worried sick about her. Who knows how Danaher would react if he came across her? That clamor extended to the floor above. Oliver held his breath as booted footsteps headed in his direction. The door opened.

"It's Mitchell Simpson."

Oliver released the breath he held. "Down here."

"Hell, there's no light," Mitchell growled.

"The oil burned out long ago. Follow my voice."

"Stilton, give me your lantern. And remain on your guard. No one is to enter this building. Knock them unconscious with your truncheon if needs must. Understand?"

"Yes, Sergeant."

A light beam filled the cellar's interior as Mitchell closed the trapdoor behind him. "Stilton is a good man; I trust him to stay quiet. I haven't told him the particulars, nor does he know your identity. I said you were a trusted informant trapped and hiding from Danaher."

"Clever. You never mentioned you are a Detective Sergeant."

"A recent development." Mitchell laid the lantern on the floor and held a sack aloft once he faced Oliver. "I have a police uniform here. I believe it will fit. Do you need assistance?"

"Yes, Danaher sliced me on my left side. I'm not sure I can walk out of here without drawing attention. But what of Claudia Ellingford? Did you speak to her? She found you at the station?"

"Er, not exactly."

Oliver's blood ran cold. "What do you mean?"

"Once I obtained the note she left at my residence, I immediately sought out The Galway Agency. They also received a message, but neither of us has seen Miss Ellingford."

"Damn!" Oliver hissed through clenched teeth. "Help me get dressed. We have to find her. She's dressed as a laborer."

"You need medical assistance."

Oliver grunted as he sat upright. "I managed to get this far without dying. Another few hours will not matter." Mitchell assisted him in standing. "I am not leaving here without her. End. Of."

"End of what?"

"Any further discussion."

With great difficulty, they managed to fit the uniform on Oliver, with Mitchell buttoning the tunic and placing the belt around

Oliver's waist. He handed the helmet to Oliver. "Wear it low over your eyes, and walk close to me, lean on me if needed. The carriage is out front. We must approach it from the rear since the front entrance is nailed shut. Can you walk that far?"

"I have no choice. Gather up everything you can and place it in your sack. Smash the oil lantern. Upend the furniture. And I hate to say it, but there is a bucket that will have to be disposed of."

"So that is what I smell."

"What can I say? I've been down here for hours. It is nearby; do not knock it over."

Oliver watched Mitchell methodically carrying out his suggestions, gathering up bits of clothing and remnants from the trunk. With a swift kick, the detective smashed the oil lantern and splintered the table and chairs into kindling. Slinging the heavy sack over his shoulder, he picked up the bucket and headed toward the trap door.

"Stilton!" Mitchell shouted.

A face peered in the doorway above. "Yes, sir?"

"Take this bucket and dump the contents into the weeds, then toss the bucket. Here is the lantern as well. Wait for us outside."

Stilton took the bucket and lantern and disappeared. Darkness enveloped them.

"The poor man," Oliver muttered.

"He'll get over it. Take my arm, and I will assist you up the stairs. We can take our time. Save your strength for your walk outdoors."

Oliver took Mitchell's arm, and they slowly ascended the narrow stairs.

"After we locate Miss Ellingford, I will take you to the hospital," Mitchell said.

"No. I have a physician I trust implicitly. He is one of our family doctors. Doctor Drew Hornsby is the son of Viscount Hawkestone. If I cannot see to it, make sure you have my staff call him in, for you are to take me to my home, along with Miss Ellingford. You have the address. Promise me, Mitchell."

"You are a stubborn sod. I promise to take you and Miss Ellingford to your house and see to it Doctor Hornsby is called. Isn't the oldest son to a viscount a baron or lord of something? I can't keep it all straight."

Once above the stairs, Mitchell closed the trap door and hid the iron rod. Retaking Oliver's arm, they shuffled toward the rear entrance.

"Drew Hornsby is the adopted son of the viscount. So, no honorary or courtesy titles," Oliver replied quietly.

Mitchell snorted. "That bloody figures. Here we are at the door. Steel yourself and walk close to me. Try to keep your back and shoulders straight. Here we go."

The cool air hit Oliver, and he inhaled deeply, savoring it. The atmosphere in his hideaway had grown oppressive and foul as each hour ticked by. A sharp pang tore through his left side, and he grunted softly. Each step forward was searing agony. But Oliver held his head high. He nearly moaned with relief at the sight of the carriage.

All around him, chaos reigned. Policemen tackled men fleeing the scene. Others were loaded into a large carriage built for transporting numerous people.

"We are picking up as many as we can, and if we are lucky, Danaher will be among the throng," Mitchell murmured. "But I have my doubts. He is as slippery as an eel. You're doing brilliantly. We are at the carriage. You enter it first, and I will be close behind to ensure you do not collapse."

Oliver was ready to do that very thing. Biting his lip, he placed his booted foot on the first rung of the metal steps. A fierce jolt of pain tore through him at the effort, but he managed to climb inside the conveyance, where he promptly flopped onto the bench seat. Mitchell tossed the sack inside and followed it, slamming the door.

Mitchell stuck his head out the window. "Stilton. Climb up and sit with the coachman. Tell him to drive around the area. Be on the lookout for a woman dressed as a laborer. How tall is she?" Mitchell asked Oliver.

"Six or seven inches over five feet, or thereabouts, and she has red hair," Oliver ground out between the waves of discomfort.

"Did you hear that, Stilton?"

"Yes, Sergeant," Stilton replied.

The carriage was underway, and Mitchell propped Oliver up far enough that he could gaze out the window. Oliver looked out one side, Mitchell the other. How many minutes passed? Oliver had no clue. They must find Claudia. Oliver wouldn't rest until they located her.

"Is that her?" Mitchell yelled, pointing out the window.

There was no mistaking the red hair. Two policemen were holding Claudia up by her arms. "Yes." The relief that tore through Oliver was unfathomable, indeed. All he wanted to do was hold her tight to his heart. The carriage pulled over to the side of the road before Mitchell could even ask the driver to do so.

Commotion swirled around him, not only from locating Claudia but also from other policemen amassing men and parading them toward the awaiting enclosed wagons. Oliver could scarcely determine what was happening since his mind reeled. The door opened, and the policemen assisted Claudia inside.

"She is in and out of consciousness, Sergeant," one of the policemen stated to Mitchell. "We found her in one of the shacks. She's been injured. Sliced on the left side."

God, same as me.

"Put her there," Mitchell said. The policemen laid Claudia across Oliver's lap, along with her coat and knife holder. "Now go assist the others in gathering this scum off the streets. Keep them all at the station until I return. Stilton, go with them."

"Right away, sir," the policeman answered as he jumped from the bench seat.

After the coppers departed, Mitchell gave Oliver's address to the driver, and they were off at a brisk canter.

Oliver gently pushed aside a tangle of red hair from her face. "Claudia."

There was no response.

He glanced down at the seeping wound. "We need to place pressure on it."

Mitchell took the wool scarf from around his neck and balled it up. He handed it to Oliver, who placed it against Claudia's side, holding it tight.

"Claudia!"

This time, her eyelids fluttered, and she looked up. "My lord?"

Thank Christ.

He smiled at her calling him 'my lord.' "We are on our way to my place. This is Detective Sergeant Mitchell Simpson. He got me out as per your instructions. And now we have found you."

"Oliver insisted that we not leave here until we had you. He was most adamant," Mitchell interjected.

Claudia swung her gaze back to Oliver. "You did?" she whispered.

"Yes. I would never leave you behind," Oliver replied fiercely. "Not. Ever."

"When all is settled down, I need to hear the story of what transpired from both of you," Mitchell said.

"One thing at a time," Oliver answered as he stroked Claudia's face. All Oliver cared about? Seeing Claudia well. If anything had happened to her— "Are you injured beyond this stab wound?" Oliver asked worriedly.

"No. A few slaps. Nothing more," Claudia rasped weakly.

Thank God for that. Yes, they would hear the rest of the story. And if Danaher were the cause of her injuries, Oliver would see to it that he paid—with his very life.

Oliver continued to stroke her cheek and hair. "We found you. That is all that matters. I was bereft to hear you hadn't turned up. I—" He spoke in an emotional rush, his heart exposed. Oliver glanced up at Mitchell, who had an eyebrow raised at Oliver's passionate tone.

To hell with someone listening in.

"If anything had happened to you, I would have broken into pieces. I would be a complete wreck," Oliver continued, looking down at Claudia. "You are safe. I have you."

Claudia took his hand and squeezed. "Oh, Oliver," she whispered, her voice raw. Her emotions hovered at the surface, ready to spill over. He could see it.

He leaned in closer, as much as his injury would allow. "I want you in my arms, always. I am falling for you, Claudia Ellingford. I am absolutely smitten. You have captured my heart."

Claudia closed her eyes and took a shuddering breath. A lone tear escaped and trailed down her pale cheek.

Oliver continued to hold her, caressing her hair. He understood if she spoke, Claudia would lose control. In light of that, he would not say any more here.

Forget pain. Forget the fever and other aches.

Claudia was safe and in his arms. That is all that mattered.

Chapter 20

JEDI DANAHER STOOD in the underground cache one of his men found soon after the coppers had departed. How many of his men had been seized? The Met Police wasted no time clearing The Piggeries, leaving mayhem in their wake.

It smelled down here, beyond the dampness and mold. The odor was a distinct mixture of body excretions and sweat as if one or more had been hiding here. This must be where that Sentinel bloke and Claudia had holed up, separately or simultaneously.

Jedi kicked at the broken glass of the oil lamp. He could see clearly as he had one of his few remaining men fetch two lanterns. The trunk was empty, but he found biscuit crumbs in a small tin. How is it that he never knew of this place?

Voices were raised above him, and someone was descending the stairs. His son stood before him, holding a dirty cloth against his cheek.

"You bloody well left me there!" Cillian yelled.

"Too right. It's every man for himself; the sooner you learn that, the better. Did a copper cut you? Or was it that wee girl?"

"She may have got a slice in, but so did I. Before I could do more, coppers burst in. I had to leg it. I heard from Charlie that she was bundled into a police wagon. We can find out where they went and—"

Jedi held up his hand. "Do you think I give a flying shite about Claudia Ellingford? If I had any use for her, I would have tracked her down years ago. I only wanted her to find out about this vigilante, The Sentinel. *Him*, I want. And he got away."

"That bitch cut me!"

Jedi grabbed the cloth held against Cillian's cheek and pulled it from the wound. "Quit your whinging. It's no more than a wee scratch. Mewling like a babe, you are. Hear me; I brought you into the fold because you serve a purpose. If I wanted *you*, I would have sought you out long before now. Remember that. I don't give a toss about you or your hag of a mother. Never did."

"You're a miserable bastard," Cillian sneered.

"Aye, I am that—a bastard in every sense of the word. Here's something you don't know about me. I am the illegitimate son of a baron. I had proper schooling for a few years and a decent life. That way of talking I do out on the street? It's put on. I exaggerate it. Everything changed when my mother died. I was alone, living on the streets, as Claudia said."

Cillian gaped at him as if deciding to believe what Jedi had revealed. "Why didn't you go to the baron? Why live on the streets?"

"Feck him and his backhanded charity. I make my own way. I still do. Get your face stitched up, but get it done properly by a competent surgeon. You want the scar to be barely visible. I learned that the hard way." Jedi reached into his pocket and flipped his son a gold sovereign. "See Surgeon Bellows on Talbot Road. Tell him Danaher sent you."

Cillian turned away to leave, but Jedi grabbed his arm and turned him roughly about until they were face-to-face. "You repeat anything I said down here, and I'll finish the job that wee girl started. You'll be tripping over your guts, you follow?"

"Yeah, I follow. What you told me puts a lot into perspective. See? I had some schooling and all."

"You've got a smart mouth on you. You're mine, all right. Sure as brass. Meet me at the hideout at The Black Moon when you are done being doctored."

His son gave him a brisk nod, then disappeared upstairs.

What possessed Jedi to reveal that? It was not like him. Maybe he wanted to see his son's reaction to the revelation. Not that it mattered. Jedi only had two meetings with his biological father; one right after Jedi's mother died and another eleven years ago.

That first meeting, the baron had the then twelve-year-old Jedi brought before him.

"I CAN'T TAKE YOU IN," the baron stated emotionlessly. "I have a wife and son. But I know of a place that can find you a good home or a place to work. An acquaintance of mine sponsors the foundation. It's called Chellenhome. I will not pay any more money to see to your care. I cannot have you in my life. This will be the last time we meet."

THE ANGER AND LOATHING that tore through Jedi at that moment had been potent. It was his first thought of murder, and even at age twelve, he nearly carried it out as he eyed the nearby fireplace poker.

"TO HELL WITH YOUR CHARITY. I'll make my own way. But I'll be back. You'll never know when I will turn up. And you will offer assistance then. I'd have to be in a low place to come crawling back to you. But know that I might. Because you owe me."

OR WORDS TO THAT EFFECT. Jedi reached that low point about a decade ago as he had barely escaped the Seven Dials with his life. He sought out his father and discovered the baron had lost his only son in a drowning accident some years before, and his lady wife had died shortly after that. It had given Jedi perverse pleasure to see the grief still etched on his father's aging face. Jedi offered no false sympathy. Baron Addington silently handed Jedi the two hundred pounds he had demanded, then closed the door in Jedi's face. That money allowed Jedi to take a foothold and ultimately take authority over The Piggeries. He might have to seek out the baron again if things take a turn.

But first, to locate this Sentinel bloke. No interlopers, whatever their motives, would take away his kingdom.

A FLURRY OF ACTIVITY ensued once the carriage arrived at the Tensbridge town house. Dusk gave them enough cover to take Oliver and Claudia through the rear entrance.

"Wait," Oliver rasped. "Place Miss Ellingford in the connecting room next to mine."

Oliver didn't remember much after that. Damon and Rett were there with Althea and Miss Callen. He could hear many conversations in the back of his mind as he slipped in and out of various depths of sleep. He never felt so exhausted.

A firm hand on the shoulder shook him awake. "Your lordship."

Doctor Drew Hornsby. There was no mistaking the clear blue eyes and the golden-tawny hair. Drew's spectacles sat low on his nose.

"Claudia?" Oliver rasped.

"I saw to her wound. She is resting comfortably. There is no initial sign of infection. You, on the other hand, will need a longer recovery."

"I am not surprised," Oliver mumbled.

"I cleaned and restitched the wound, applied camphor, and wrapped it loosely."

Oliver glanced downward. He was bare-chested, and the doctor had neatly placed a large plaster with gauze on his side.

"You have a slight fever, so I prepared a mixture of willow bark and meadowsweet. You must drink it, and it is best mixed with tea." Doctor Hornsby pushed his glasses further up his nose. "Perhaps someday, the scientists will develop a medication to fight infections, but until then, we must work with what we have. I have also left a small amount of laudanum for any pain. Just a drop in your tea will also assist in sleeping. You will recover, but rest is needed more than anything."

"Thank you, Drew."

"I will return tomorrow afternoon, and hopefully, I can obtain some aspirin powder. No food tonight, just sleep. In the morning, a light breakfast. I have conveyed complete instructions for your dietary needs to your kitchen for the next few days. Miss Ellingford as well."

Relief tore through Oliver, sending his emotions in all directions. The urge to cry, not only from exhaustion but from the news Claudia was not seriously hurt, nearly overtook him.

"Is DS Simpson still here?"

"Yes, along with the Duke of Chellenham. You may speak to them, but only briefly."

The young doctor patted his shoulder and departed. A few moments later, the men entered the room. Oliver held out his hand, and Mitchell clasped it, squeezing it briefly before he released it.

Damon then took it. "My God, Oliver. I assume there is an explanation for this? Althea has a theory—"

Oliver laughed, but it came out as a rough bark. "I am sure she does. You can speak in front of Mitchell."

"Are you this vigilante that came to our aid weeks ago? Outside The Savoy?" Damon asked as he released Oliver's hand and stepped back.

"Yes."

"Jesus," Damon whistled.

"Tell no one, except Althea."

"Agreed. I will keep your secret, as will Althea. Rest, my friend. I will return in a day or so." Damon turned toward his half-brother. "Mitchell. Look after him."

"I will."

Damon quit the room.

"Well, my lord." Mitchell then gave him a quirky smile. "Quite the adventure."

Oliver wearily chuckled.

"Your cousin says he will visit with you tomorrow. Your cat is also impatient to see you."

Oliver nodded, his eyelids growing heavy.

"I will return tomorrow afternoon. Hopefully, you and Miss Ellingford can tell me what occurred. Meanwhile, I will head to the station to see what guttersnipes we scooped up and if Danaher is among the multitude." Mitchell patted his shoulder, then quietly left the room.

Fatigue eddied all around him, sinking deep into his bones. Just as he was about to slip into a deep slumber, the springs dipped slightly as if someone had crawled in next to him.

"Claudia?"

"Shh. I want to stay here with you for a while. Do you mind?"

Mind? His heart leaped with joy. "Not at all," Oliver rasped. "As I said, I want you in my arms—for always."

Claudia sighed deeply, which Oliver had learned meant she did not want to discuss what he had just said.

"I am too wound up to sleep and refuse to take any laudanum. I've seen what overuse can do. Besides, I needed to know if you are well."

"And to seek comfort? For I could use it myself."

She came in close on his uninjured side, and he placed his arm about her until she laid her head on his shoulder. "Yes," she whispered. "Exactly that."

Claudia, lying in his arms, felt—perfect. Absolutely perfect.

"What about your injury?" Oliver murmured.

"A little more than a scratch. I am fine." She kissed his cheek. "Go to sleep. I will watch over you."

"For the rest of our lives?" he replied drowsily.

Oliver didn't hear her reply, for he had fallen asleep.

Chapter 21

CLAUDIA LAY IN BED, watching the sun peek over the grand buildings across the street. She slept an hour here and there, but it wasn't the deep, restful sleep needed to recover. The activities of the past forty-eight hours still churned about in her mind. Laying aside the danger they had faced, what was still hard to grasp was that Oliver—was the Sentinel.

Claudia believed him to be a stuffy, bored aristocrat when he was anything but. How fascinating, such complicated layers. When he spoke, 'For the rest of our lives,' it momentarily chilled her heart but also caused its beat to speed up due to the wave of absolute bliss that inundated her. Yes, Oliver caused a great deal of confusion within.

His candid, emotional confession in the carriage became even more intense after she had been rescued. Smitten? Falling for her? Captured his heart? Those heartfelt words yielded a tumult within her, prompting her trepidation to spike.

But oh, those words.

They arrowed straight to her heart, causing it to practically burst from her chest. If only she could be as open and honest as Oliver—confident of his feelings with a clear understanding of how to deal with them and verbalize them. Claudia had yet to learn how to do it. She felt utterly flummoxed.

Bitterness and cynicism made her believe no man was worth her attention or affection. Claudia had accepted she would be alone for the rest of her life and planned accordingly. How does she reconcile her low opinion of men in general, particularly wealthy ones, with the near perfection of Oliver Wollstonecraft?

Very well, he wasn't faultless. No one is. His hero—what to call it? —obsession? No, that did not fit. Perhaps a preoccupation or fixation? Blast it; it all meant the same thing, and Claudia wasn't exactly sure if it was a negative or positive.

The door facing the hallway burst open, and a woman carrying a tray entered the room.

"Baroness Addington?" The woman she had met at Olivia's tea party?

"The very one." She placed the tray on the sideboard and moved to close the connecting door. "The viscount is still sleeping. We do not want to disturb him." The baroness turned to face her. "Do you need assistance sitting upright? I have brought you a little breakfast. And it is very little, oatmeal and toast, as per Doctor Hornsby's orders."

"I can manage." Claudia gingerly sat upright, her gaze never leaving the baroness, who quickly snatched the tray and placed it on Claudia's lap.

"I suppose you are wondering why I am here," Lady Corrine stated as she pulled a chair over to Claudia's bedside and sat on it. "I was with Althea Galway yesterday when Detective Simpson arrived to give the news of finding you and the viscount." Lady Corrine waved her hand. "It is not my business to know what occurred. But I offered my services. I am a trained nurse."

A baroness, a trained nurse?

"Please excuse what must be my shocked expression."

Lady Corrine chuckled lightly. "I am a member of the Royal British Nurses' Association. For nearly ten years, I nursed in a workhouse infirmary until I agreed to an arranged marriage to the new baron because my family needed the money. So, here I am. In a loveless marriage, I am trying to find a way to make myself useful again. Too much information?"

"No, not at all. I am impressed." Claudia picked up the mug of tea and sipped it. "I am sorry to hear that your marriage is not, er—"

"Ideal? I had no illusions going in. After all, I am thirty years of age. Why he pursued me of all women, who knows? I never asked him."

"Wait, aren't you the daughter of Viscount Rothley? Perhaps that was the reason."

The baroness pushed the plate with the toast closer to Claudia. "I managed to smuggle a bit of jam out of the kitchen for you." Lady Corrine lifted the napkin to show a small ramekin dish. "Raspberry preserves."

"Oh, thank you." Ravenous, Claudia dipped her spoon into the jam and slathered it on her toast. "I have to ask, why would a viscount's daughter become a nurse?"

"Money. Pure and simple. Or at least it is one of the reasons. My family has no money at all. My younger brother—the heir to this underprivileged viscountcy—also works. He is a vice president at a bank. I saw a way to clean the debt slate and give my family a new start. The old baron had a lot of money tucked away in the bank. Scads of it. It worked out all around."

Claudia frowned. Why is it always the women that had to make sacrifices? Why didn't her brother marry money? Whatever the explanation, it was none of her business. "Except for you, my lady."

"Well, it is what it is. Now, tell me about Detective Sergeant Simpson. What do you know about him?"

Claudia watched Lady Corrine closely. Asking about the detective? Why? "I only met him briefly yesterday. I know next to nothing about him. Oliver, I mean, the viscount, respects him. I have no idea if he is married. Is that what you wanted to know, my lady?"

A slow smile curved about the baroness's lips. "Why, yes. I am merely curious." She exhaled. "Oh, drat it all. He caught my attention. Hardly proper for a newly married woman, but I am not dead."

Claudia laughed. "I liked you from the moment we met."

"It is the same for me. Now, I am here to examine your wound, then you must sleep. Which I believe you will since you drank my tea concoction. Do not worry. There are no opiates in the tea; it is cat mint and chamomile. It will help you relax. I assumed you haven't slept much."

"No, I haven't." For many reasons, including the enticing viscount next door.

Lady Corrine stood and removed the tray, then lifted Claudia's nightgown. Carefully pulling the plasters and gauze aside, she examined the wound. "What skilled stitching. You will hardly have a scar." She lightly touched all around the injury. "No swelling and no seepage or signs of infection. You should be up on your feet in a matter of days." The baroness placed the plaster back in place.

"And the viscount?"

"Doctor Hornsby says there is a slight, lingering infection, but the viscount is fighting it. He may be abed for a week or maybe less, for he seems fit enough. Sleep works wonders. And you should try to do that very thing. Doctor Hornsby will arrive later this afternoon, but his examinations must wait. I surmise the viscount will sleep for hours, and so will you." Lady Corrine assisted Claudia in lying flat, brought the quilt under her chin, and removed the tray from Claudia's lap.

"You are an excellent nurse, my lady," Claudia smiled. "Thank you for the care."

"You are entirely welcome. Try and sleep now." Lady Corrine slipped out of the room, closing the door softly. Claudia's eyes grew heavy, and at last, sleep overtook her.

WHEN OLIVER NEXT AWAKENED, he found Doctor Drew Hornsby examining his injury.

"I hope I haven't disturbed you," the young doctor said as he placed a fresh piece of gauze on the wound. He then sniffed the old gauze. "Good. No signs of putrid pus, blood, or infection."

"There's a mercy."

"You have slept nearly around the clock, my lord. Another good sign. In fact, when I stopped by yesterday afternoon, you were still napping."

"How long have I been sleeping? I recall awakening more than once. I couldn't tell whether it was day or night. I have lost all track of time."

"It is the morning of the next day, my lord. We thought it best to allow you to slumber when you could. Dalton was close by, I assume."

"Yes. I remember my butler bringing me toast at one point. Drew, call me Oliver. You don't have to slip in the occasional 'my lord.' We have known each other since we were boys."

"That we have. When dealing with patients, automatically using the title is a habit." The doctor placed his hand on Oliver's forehead. "Barely even warm. You are making a remarkable recovery, Oliver. But you will still have to stay in bed for a few days. You are on the mend enough to have more than oatmeal and toast. I will inform the cook to make you eggs, ham, or bacon, whichever you prefer."

"Can I have both?"

Drew chuckled. "Another good sign."

"And Claudia—Miss Ellingford?"

"She is sleeping. Baroness Addington said Miss Ellingford did not get much sleep the first night. But she brought her breakfast early this morning, and Miss Ellingford is napping now after sleeping most of yesterday."

"Baroness?"

Drew explained that the recently married baroness had close to ten years of nursing experience and the particulars of her offering to assist.

"I am surprised but also thankful for the aid."

"I will come again tomorrow morning. Continued bed rest."

"Whatever you say, Drew. I will follow your orders. I don't believe I can do much except sit upright today, at any rate."

Drew placed his stethoscope in his case and closed it. "And you should sit upright. It speeds up the recovery process. Now, your cousin awaits an audience along with your feline companion. It has been quite a chore keeping your cat out of your room. Rest and eat. And sleep when you can."

The doctor no sooner opened the door to depart when Caramel tore into the room and jumped on Oliver's bed. Purring loudly, she sought out Oliver's hand, and he scratched under her chin. Turning twice counter-clockwise, the feline settled in beside him, then sighed contentedly.

Rett chuckled. "The cat spent hours outside your room as if holding a vigil. Believe it or not, I woke this morning to find her napping at the foot of my bed. Blasted cat hair everywhere."

"She's accepted you as a friend. Here, help me sit up. I am tired of lying flat like an invalid, although I still feel like one."

Rett held out his arm, and Oliver gripped it tight as Rett pulled him forward in a sitting position. Then, his cousin fluffed up his pillows. "Comfortable?"

Oliver gritted his teeth. "Not really. But this will do."

Rett sat on the chair by the bed. "Well. What happened?"

"If you don't mind, can you wait until DS Simpson arrives? I don't want to tell the tale more than once."

"Fair enough. About Bryan."

Oliver slapped his forehead. Good God, he hadn't given his wayward brother a single thought these past days. Who knows what sort of chicanery Bryan has engaged in? "He completely slipped my mind. What day is it? I have lost all track."

"Understandable. Today is Sunday, and it is half past ten. Bryan arrived Friday morning at the appointed time. I told him you were not feeling well even though I had no idea where you were. I also was a little more forward with him than you have been. I grabbed him by his collar and shook him a bit, maybe tossed him across the room—"

"Jesus, Rett!"

"He is a spoiled, miserable excuse of a man, and I told him so. I also said he was hurting this family with his reckless, selfish behavior. I reiterated that your father will be here in less than two weeks, and he had better clean up his act, or there will be hell to pay."

"Well said. It is all true. I think there was a similar scene between our grandfathers back in the day. I take it Bryan did not take kindly to the roughhouse and the harsh words."

Rett crossed his arms. "History doomed to repeat itself and all that? How ironic. And no, Bryan bloody well didn't like the reprimand. I will not repeat what he said, but he angered me enough that I decided to follow him. He returned to his flat, so I took a page from The Galway Agency's book and fashioned a disguise. I borrowed the gardener's work clothes. Not that they fit all that well; the trouser legs only came to my shins, but it served the purpose. Early that evening, I returned to the flat to witness quite the scene."

It was that moment Dalton, the butler, brought in a tray. "Your breakfast, my lord, and when I heard Mister Rett was in the room with you, I brought extra food and tea."

Rett rubbed his hands together. "Well met, Dalton. I can take it from here."

Once the butler placed the tray on Oliver's lap, he bowed and quit the room, closing the door behind him.

Rett poured them tea. "Do you wish me to cut your ham for you?" he teased.

"No, just get on with the story."

Rett swiped a piece of crispy bacon from the plate, popped it in his mouth, chewed, then swallowed. "A man showed up in a fancy carriage with two footmen. A tall, formidable man with gray at the temples. They basically kicked the door in. I moved as close to the place as I dared. There was a great deal of shouting, and from what I could tell, the Duke of Coldbridge arrived to extricate his son from the flat."

After the afternoon tea at Watford's, the Duchess of Coldbridge must have relayed the conversation about Shinwell and, knowing his son was staying with the viscount, took matters into his own hands. The duke was decent and would not want his son, Rome Linton, involved in multiple depraved acts with Viscount Shinwell and Bryan. Good for Coldbridge.

Oliver ate some of the ham and egg and washed it down with a gulp of tea. "And did he? Extricate him?"

Rett reached for more bacon, placing it and hunks of cheese on a plate. "Oh, yes. The duke literally dragged Linton out by the hair. I saw Bryan and that loudmouth miscreant, Shinwell. Shinwell staggered about, hurling insults at the duke, until one of the muscular footmen punched him in the midsection, bringing Shinwell to his knees."

"Good. Shinwell is a lout and a despicable excuse for a human. Should we do the same? Kick the door in and drag Bryan out by the hair? Maybe we should have done that when I first learned of his debauched activities."

Rett sipped his tea. "And then what? Keep him here, tied to a chair in the attic or cellar?"

Oliver took another forkful of scrambled eggs. "Perhaps we should. I will be recovering for a few days, as will Claudia. There is no one to watch him—unless you wish to continue."

Rett scoffed. "I will not be his observer, though I enjoyed being in disguise. It is my opinion that Bryan should learn from his mistakes. On that, I agree with your father—to an extent. I have a better idea. We can enlist your friend, Detective Simpson, not in his official capacity as a detective but as an authoritative force. We gather together a few of the men from The Rakes, maybe muscular footmen of our own, and storm the place. Chellenham would assist, and Allenby. Watford and Wenlock, too, if needed."

"I haven't known Detective Simpson all that long. That is quite the favor I would be asking. The men in our group are one thing—"

"Then let's make Simpson part of the club. He is Chellenham's half-brother and, by all accounts, an honorable man. Having a member of the police within our membership is a prudent move."

Rett smiled, satisfied with his suggestion, and bit into his toast with gusto.

Mitchell in their group? Why not, indeed?

Chapter 22

WHEN CLAUDIA AWOKE from her nap, she was assisted by the baroness into Oliver's room and into a wing chair placed by his bed. Lady Addington put a wool blanket across her lap. Also in the room was Detective Simpson and Oliver's cousin, Rett Wollstonecraft. They sat at a small table facing them.

"I will leave you alone. Claudia, I will see to your luncheon," Lady Corinne smiled.

"Thank you, my lady."

The Baroness and Detective Simpson locked glances. Claudia surmised a mutual interest since they gazed at each other longer than was polite. How interesting.

Once the baroness closed the door, Oliver began his narrative, starting with coming to her assistance and taking refuge in the underground cache. Claudia picked up the story, explaining her plan and how Danaher had found her and brought her to one of his hideouts. How the police arrived, her brief knife fight with his son, and the fact he would have a recent scar on his face.

Detective Simpson took notes. "Unfortunately, Danaher was not among those arrested, nor is anyone matching the description of his son. You said the son's name is Cillian?" Claudia nodded. "Can you describe the other men in the room, Miss Ellingford?"

"One was tall, thin, with sparse black hair. Danaher called him Birch. The other one he called Shorty. He is of small stature, no more than four or five inches over five feet, with longish brown hair to the collar. His left cheek is covered in pockmarks."

"I believe we have Shorty in custody. Good. A place to start," Detective Simpson stated.

Oliver's cousin, Rett, told of his doings in watching Bryan Wollstonecraft.

"Which brings us to a suggestion I heartily agree with," Oliver interjected. "I would like it if you joined our group."

The detective cocked an eyebrow. "The Rakes of St. Regent's Park? Why?"

"Your brother runs it—"

"Half-brother," Simpson interrupted.

"But a brother, nonetheless," Oliver stated firmly. "The club *is* a brotherhood of sorts, and we do good works."

"And you wish to have a copper in the assembly? I have no wealth or title, and everyone within your membership has one or the other or both."

"Then it is high time that changed," Rett declared. "I put your name forward to Oliver, why not, indeed? Yes, it is to the club's advantage to have a member of the police, not that we would do anything that would require you to hush anything up. But you know of Oliver's alter ego and could assist in protecting him. Plus, Oliver speaks highly of you."

"I know Damon will be pleased," Oliver added.

"And Olivia," Claudia stated. "When we met for shopping and tea, she mentioned how thrilled she was to find an older *and* a younger brother. She particularly wishes to know *you* better."

"Admit it," Oliver smiled. "You like us. You also want siblings, or why else attend Damon and Althea's engagement party?"

The detective grumbled, then shrugged. "I will think about it. I assume there is a reason you wish me to join beyond what you have mentioned."

"There is," Rett replied. "It concerns Oliver's younger brother, the one I followed." Rett relayed the plan.

The detective frowned. "If this is why you wish for me to join your enclave, then I pass. The police are not to be used as your personal revenge squad. As it is, I have no legal leg to stand on to keep Danaher's men in prison. The inspector accepted my explanation of a crime deterrent, but I must release them in two days. Except this Shorty, and I will need a formal report on record with you, Miss Ellingford."

"Please, call me Claudia. And I will lodge a formal complaint. Shorty was in the room when Danaher kept me against my will. The henchman tried to impede my escape." She gave the detective a warm smile. "I understand your hesitancy to assist with the extraction plan, but do not let that stop you from joining the group—Mitchell."

The detective growled low in his throat. "I will consider the proposal. But leave me out of your schemes. Now, tell me everything again, Claudia. When I return to the station, I will inform the inspector I have just cause to keep this Shorty person for further interrogation with the possibility of charges."

"I will tell you this: Shorty is frightened of Danaher, and he will never reveal his rookery boss's whereabouts," Claudia said. "If he even knows."

"Maybe. But the prospect of serving time in Newgate Prison can loosen tongues," Mitchell replied.

"Here is something else you should know about Danaher. When I lived in Notting Dale, I heard him mention to my mother he had one or two coppers that fed him information. Policemen from the Lancaster station. Does he still? I would not be surprised. You may want to be careful in your dealings and keep important information to yourself or a few trusted men."

Mitchell snorted. "I haven't been there long enough to figure out who to fully trust or not, but I will heed your warning."

After Claudia repeated what occurred in the shack, Mitchell tucked his notebook away and stood. "You are correct. I want siblings and a brotherhood, I suppose. But I will say again, leave me out of your legal gray area machinations. Understand?" Mitchell stated this matter-of-factly, not gruffly.

"As you say," Oliver replied.

"I will return tomorrow with an update." With a nod, Mitchell departed.

"Stubborn bugger," Rett smiled.

"Easy enough for us to say. Mitchell does have a career to protect," Oliver replied.

"And with that, I am off," Rett declared. "I will leave you both to rest until luncheon. I must say, you both look better than when you first arrived."

Once they were alone, Claudia was not sure what to say. Pragmatically speaking, she should nip this growing attraction in the bud. She had been dealing with this internal struggle from almost the moment she met him. Frankly, all this hand-wringing was tedious. She needed time and space to think this through. But whatever conclusion she came to, Claudia did not want to hurt Oliver for the world.

"You should get some rest," she offered gently.

"I have slept enough. Why not stay here with me?" Oliver patted the bed.

"Listen, whatever you think transpired when we were trapped in that cache—you know it cannot continue above ground in the real world. Because of our peril, we may have said things in the heat of the moment. I am not interested in anything—serious. And it is not you. I do not want attachments with anyone." So much for not hurting him. The words tumbled out before she had a chance to stop them.

"We shared more than our pasts and our secrets. You know it," Oliver whispered.

"What we shared was a dangerous situation, fraught with stress and trauma. That brings people together—for a short period. But it doesn't mean there is any depth or permanency to it. We clung to each other in the darkness. That is all."

"You are trying to distance yourself from the emotions I have stirred inside you. You are trying to distance yourself from *me*. What I said to you in the carriage has you scared witless."

Claudia stood, taking a sharp breath from the pain that tore through her side. She turned toward the window because tears shimmered in her eyes, and she did not want Oliver to see that he spoke the truth. Claudia *was* trying to distance herself. And hell's bells, she *is* scared.

"Close the draperies," he asked softly. "Then come and lay next to me. Let me hold you as I did when we were alone in the cache. As I did the other night."

For the life of her, Claudia could not refuse him. After closing the window coverings, darkness blanketed the room, and she climbed onto the bed, taking care of her injury. Once he laid on his side, Oliver shifted and gathered her into his arms. They fit together perfectly, like teaspoons in a pantry drawer.

It is not that Claudia felt protected in his arms (as she was more than capable of defending herself), though there was an aspect of that. It was the warmth Oliver radiated, the comfort that gave her such a feeling of serenity, a quietness of her troubled soul.

No, there was something else.

It was the *heat*.

Oliver made her nerve endings crackle with life. He stirred her dormant desire with the slightest touch of his hand or by pulling her close to all that tall, broad masculinity. All Oliver had to do was walk into the room, for that matter. Not only was he handsome, but he also had a kind face and a good soul. Unlike her, he was not troubled, which made him all the more appealing to Claudia. She had enough damage for both of them. His vigilante bent gave all that perfection a ragged, wild edge. Claudia liked that, too. Very much.

In conclusion, Oliver was everything she could hope for in a man. If she wanted one. Claudia may never find a rare gem like this again. What to do?

"It is more than clinging to one another in the dark," he murmured, bringing her out of her confusing thoughts. Oliver's fingers stroked her flushed cheek. "A bond has formed between us, and we will regret it the rest of our lives if we do not explore what is occurring. I want you. I need you. And as I said in the carriage, I am most definitely falling for you."

Oliver rolled his hips, and there was no mistaking his hot and hard arousal against her backside. A soft moan escaped her lips before she could tamp it down.

Drat the man!

"Although you are more than capable of handling yourself, I yearn to protect you," he continued, nuzzling her neck.

Claudia understood, for she felt the same about protecting him. "I am not in any danger. Danaher does not want me. As I told Mitchell, he only wanted to know about you—The Sentinel. You are a threat to him and his empire. He sees himself as a king, and you imperil his domain. I know the man; he will not quit until he discovers your identity."

"Then we must remain vigilant and stay close to one another. I am tempted to seek Danaher out and beat him to within an inch of his life for threatening, striking you, and holding you against your will. Perhaps I will—once I recover."

"He could have done far worse. As I said, I was a means to an end." Without thinking, Claudia cuddled in closer. "He may already know I am here as the carriage could have been followed. Danaher probably has men watching the police station. This is far from over. If I stay close to you, I could put you at risk. He knows I work for a detective agency; discovering which one wouldn't take much effort. He could have me followed from there."

"All the more reason you should stay here—with me, beyond our recovery. There is strength in numbers. And we are more substantial together."

Claudia sighed. "I never should have told him I was following a member of the upper classes. Now, he will question every rich nob that goes into Notting Dale."

"True. Did anyone ever tell you that you sigh a great deal?" Oliver teased as he kissed her forehead.

"Yes, my mother. She called me 'the town sigher.'"

Oliver laughed heartily. "I like that. Very clever. I would have liked to have met your mother."

Claudia exhaled shakily. "She would have liked you. I wish you could have met as well. I wish she were still here."

Oliver pulled her closer. "I know, love."

Claudia reveled in his warm embrace, and they remained silent, content to be together. She wished she could throw aside all her doubts and accept all Oliver offered.

Regarding Danaher," she continued at last. "I know him. The man is intelligent and can tell when people lie to him. So, I gave him the thinnest veneer of truth to ensure my safety and to keep him talking until the police arrived."

"And it was the correct thing to do. You know best how to handle the thug, and I trust you implicitly. As far as dealing with him further, we will cross that bridge when we come to it." Oliver laid hot kisses on her neck, causing her to writhe and moan. "Hell, I wish I had more strength. I want to do more. I want to make you come."

All her thoughts of pushing him away dissipated, at least temporarily. His *words*. Claudia's insides dipped, and she grew wet at her feminine core.

Oliver brushed his hand across her breast, and his fingers caressed her erect nipple. "I want to suck this and make you come apart in my arms. I want—"

Oliver's arm went limp. Then she heard his even breathing.

He's asleep. Unbelievable.

But it's completely understandable, considering the situation and the nature of his injury. All Oliver had to do was touch her and whisper wicked words in her ear, and she was aroused. Trying to keep Oliver at arm's length would be next to impossible.

Why even try?

Because she must guard her battered heart, Oliver endangered her wavering resolve. This was a conundrum that needed further thought. The only way she could do that was to create some distance, at least temporarily.

But it wasn't the main reason.

That protector instinct had kicked in, and putting space between her and Oliver would safeguard him from Danaher. She would do anything, sacrifice anything to keep him safe.

Claudia knew if anything happened to him, she would break apart. Fall into pieces.

But for now, in this moment, she would relish being in his arms.

Claudia knew the truth deep down: she was falling for Oliver Wollstonecraft.

Chapter 23

JEDI DANAHER SAT AND brooded in a small room at the rear of the Black Moon Pub. Since the raid three days ago, he had moved about constantly, hiding in case the police returned to the area and tried to flush him out.

But they hadn't. The coppers hadn't discharged his men as yet, either. Because of that, Jedi did not dare head to the station to talk to his connection within the precinct.

He hated darting about like a rat, keeping to the shadows, but he had no choice until he had a handle on the particulars of the situation.

Cillian burst into the room. "I know who The Sentinel is."

"Well, spit it out!"

"That copper, Detective Sergeant Simpson. The new bloke at the station."

Jedi snorted skeptically. "Give over. Who told you that tale?"

Cillian sat opposite, laying his peaked cap on the table before him. "No one. I figured it out myself. Think about it. That copper just transferred in about the same time that masked nutter started showing up in Notting Dale. This Sentinel beat up Charlie and later rescued some nob walking along the street—right after Simpson's arrival. And get this, he works a lot of night shifts."

Jaysus.

Jedi recalled hearing of the attack on the man in the street. Unfortunately, the assault did not come from any of his men but from vagrants passing through Notting Dale to points unknown. So, there was no way to check up on the incident since it was hearsay instead of tangible information.

Back to his son's declaration. Could it be the copper? What Cillian said made sense. But wait. "I sliced the Sentinel bloke good and proper. And yet, Simpson raids Notting Dale? Why? I saw him marching about, giving orders. He didn't look incapacitated to me." Jedi frowned. "Unless the man giving orders wasn't Simpson at all. We need a good description of him. I will find out as soon as I can speak to my police contact."

Cillian shrugged. "Maybe you didn't slice him as bad as you thought. He's injured enough that he can't leap about buildings but well enough to work as a copper."

Maybe. "So why raid Notting Dale?"

"To rescue Ellingford. That bitch said the coppers would come if we didn't let her go. We had her in that room for hours. When she didn't show up, the coppers swooped in. I will bet you she knows who The Sentinel is."

Jedi rubbed his forehead, his usually agile mind trying to process this information. Some of the puzzle pieces clicked into place. Did Claudia know? Jedi could have sworn she told him the truth about not knowing the vigilante's identity. But she was a clever piece, and no mistake. But if The Sentinel was Simpson, why rescue Claudia and not vice versa? Why would she come back to Notting Dale? Was it to follow some toff as she said?

"Remember, Charlie said he saw a red-haired woman bundled into a police wagon. Who else could it be but this Ellingford?" Cillian absently touched the gauze bandage on the side of his face. "And the night Charlie was attacked? That vigilante was seen running with a woman. What if it was Ellingford with another wig?"

"Still angry Claudia got a slice in?" Jedi cackled. Then he sobered. "When I spoke to Charlie about it earlier, he couldn't say whether the masked eejit was with a woman. But good work, Cillian. I mean it. You've impressed me. Who knows, you may be right. On the other hand, it's a lot of 'ifs.' Here's what we do. Claudia said she worked for an investigative agency. Sniff around. You will find agency ads in the newspapers. See if any redheaded women work for them and report back."

"Fair enough. And what about Simpson?"

"Leave him to me. I'll find out what he looks like and go from there. When the men are released, we will post them at every street, alley, and courtyard." Jedi paused. "Once they are posted, I want every toff who comes into my territory brought to me. There is some connection here, and I aim to find it."

A copper as a vigilante?

It seemed absurd at first blush, but the more Jedi thought about it, the more it made sense. He had heard the oral history of vigilantes, especially in decades past. The vigilante group formed in Whitechapel in '88 during the Jack the Ripper murder spree was one of the more recent ones. It seems strange that one pops up in Notting Dale. Maybe this detective couldn't get his fellow coppers to enter Notting Dale, so he decided to police the area—anonymously.

In days past, Jedi often allowed his emotions to cloud common sense. Not this time. He would gather evidence before acting.

No one threatened him or his domain—police detective or not.

OLIVER TAPPED ON THE connecting door and then entered. Claudia was packing her small case. Miss Callen had brought Claudia a carpetbag with clothing and other essentials yesterday.

Four days had passed since they were rescued from the cache, and although he was walking about, he still wasn't quite fully recovered.

Since the night they cuddled together in his bed, he and Claudia had not much opportunity to talk further.

He leaned against the wall. "I believe it best that you stay."

Claudia turned to face him. "You are far too tempting and too much of a distraction."

That statement gave him a little hope, at least. "I will not keep you here against your will, but what do you suppose Danaher is doing at this moment?"

Claudia returned to her packing. "Checking out various investigative agencies. Looking for me. For he believes I will lead him to The Sentinel."

"You cannot return to Cleveland Street. Not yet, as it is not safe. We need to formulate a plan of attack."

She glanced at him over her shoulder. "Attack?"

"Yes. We cannot hide forever. Danaher should be seen to."

Claudia continued with her packing. "That is the police's job. Not ours."

Oliver strode toward her, gently clasped her arm, and swung her about to face him. "Why are you running from me?"

She gazed up at him. "You know what will happen if I stay. I cannot complicate my life."

Oliver grazed the back of his fingers along her flushed cheek. "There is more to it than that. Something you are not telling me. Do not turn from this—from us." Carefully and slowly, he cupped her cheeks, waiting for her to protest. She didn't.

Oliver nibbled on her lower lip, and she opened in invitation. He took the kiss deeper in increments, tilting his head slightly as his tongue clashed with hers. Briefly, she returned his growing passion until Claudia stepped back, placing a hand against his chest as if to place distance between them.

"We need to stop," she whispered.

"Do we?"

"I agree that I cannot return to Cleveland Street. Olivia invited me to stay with her and Gideon. I think I should. Please understand. What is happening between us? It's too much. Emotional overload. There. I am admitting a weakness."

"Emotions are *not* a weakness," Oliver stated, fighting to keep his disappointment in check.

"You have said that before. Maybe not to you, but to me, it is. We need time and space apart. All right, *I* need it." Claudia exhaled unsteadily. "I know you want more from me, both physically and emotionally. I thought I was incapable of giving any portion of myself to anyone. Part of me wants to throw myself into your arms, but another—is scared witless. There. I admit that, too. I cannot move forward until I understand what is happening inside me."

"I am to have hope, then?" Oliver asked quietly.

"Perhaps." Claudia snapped the case shut. "Please respect my wishes."

Oliver stepped in reverse. "I will respect your wishes. All I ask is that you do not completely dismiss the bond between us. It is more than shared trauma. At least, to me."

Dalton knocked, then entered. "My lord, the Duke of Allenby and the Duke of Chellenham are downstairs. They ask for an audience with both you and Miss Ellingford."

Great timing, Oliver fumed inwardly.

But timing had not been on their side from the beginning. Oliver knew that if Claudia had no interest in him whatsoever, she would have said so—right to his face. The fact she asked for time to think lightened his heart—at least a little bit.

He yanked the ties of his dressing gown tighter across his waist. He wore trousers and a shirt underneath, appropriate enough to greet his friends. "Will you join us? It no doubt concerns the case."

"Yes, but I must leave right after. Olivia is expecting me."

"Of course. I will have my driver take you." He held out his arm to indicate that she go through the door first.

Once out into the hallway, Claudia turned to face him. "Did I sound too cold and dismissive? I do not mean to be. Truly, I don't. Not with you." She gazed up at him. Her eyes had softened. "I am not turning away you, not really. I need a little time."

He took her hand and kissed it. "It is fine, Claudia. I understand. Time you want, time you shall have."

"You were right. That is not the only reason." Claudia took a shuddering breath. "I want—need—to protect you. If anything ever happened to you, if Danaher got to you through me, I-I would die and—"

Oliver pulled her into his arms and kissed her passionately. His heart soared at her heartfelt confession. He tasted every inch of her sweet mouth. Claudia threw her arms around his neck and enthusiastically kissed him in return. This continued for several moments, but they reluctantly broke apart when they heard voices below the stairs. With a smile, Oliver brushed the pad of his thumb across her swollen and well-kissed lips. "You have given me hope."

Claudia took his hand and kissed it before releasing it. Then she slipped her arm through his. "Let us help each other down the stairs."

Despite her protestations, Claudia cared for him—more than she realized. But he would never dismiss her hesitation and fright, for it was real and deeply felt. He respected her too much to make demands. They slowly and carefully made their way to Oliver's study, where the men waited.

"We could have come to you," Christian said as they entered the room.

"We need to be up and moving about," Oliver replied as he gingerly sat on the sofa. Claudia sat next to him but at a slight distance.

"We have some information regarding Shinwell and his father," Damon said as he sat opposite. "The Earl of Darrington's fortunes are not as robust as believed. He did sell the unentailed viscount residence recently, as you suspected. The very one your brother and the others are staying in. The earl worked out a reduced rent for his son."

"As for the earl's past, we discovered Darrington smuggled opium, at least before the law changed in '68. But that money ran out long ago," Christian interjected. "Rumor has it he has his fingers in numerous schemes, including smuggling other goods besides opium."

"But why?" Oliver asked, puzzled. "Since free trade agreements were brought forth in the '40s and beyond, it all but eradicated illegal smuggling."

"Not for some items. Like cheap French wine. That is the main product the earl traffics in," Damon replied. "There are also rumors he deals in stolen goods and is involved with the criminal element. With whom and to what extent, we do not know."

"Why am I not surprised," Oliver scoffed.

"And Shinwell?" Claudia asked.

"Besides the fact he cheats at cards?" Christian replied. "Shinwell is an arrogant, indolent leech, spending his father's money faster than the earl can make it. He also attends orgies. Shinwell attended the late Duke of Chellenham's last sordid function. He's been bragging about it openly."

"Good Christ," Damon shuddered. "Sorry, Miss Ellingford."

"I've heard worse, Your Grace," Claudia replied. "Your reaction is entirely appropriate."

"I have further gossip to share about Shinwell," Christian interjected. "The Countess of Darrington's orphaned niece, Celia Gillingham, came to stay with them some years back. She is the daughter of the late Sir Anthony Gillingham, a baronet. He and his wife were lost at sea when the girl was ten. Anyway, the three-years-older Shinwell wouldn't leave the girl alone. She had to be sent away to school before anything untoward transpired."

"That deviant reprobate," Damon snarled. "Where is the niece now?"

"My mother said Countess Darrington hasn't mentioned her for some time. I can task my mother with finding out if it is important," Christian replied.

"Wait," Claudia interrupted. "In the conversation I overhead at the afternoon tea, the countess said her niece was married and had moved away. Because of that, the countess would probably holiday in Italy come winter."

"Well done. I don't believe we need further information on the niece. Thank you both for the data. I would say this portion of the investigation is ending," Oliver stated. "Rett and I have a plan on what to do next."

Claudia stood. "On that note, I will take my leave. Olivia is expecting me. No need to get up, gentlemen. I will collect my bag and see Dalton about the carriage. Good afternoon."

Oliver watched Claudia depart.

"Oh, you have it bad," Damon tsked after Claudia closed the door. "I am certain I showed that same yearning look on my face after spending time on my case with Althea. As did Christian, if memory serves."

"She is going to Olivia and Gideon's to 'take time to think.' We haven't had a chance to explore the attraction between us, with recovering from our injuries—outside of a few heated kisses."

"And how do you feel?" Christian asked. "Or tell us to shut it if it is none of our business."

"I do not feel whole unless she is in my arms. My heart doesn't beat. And—"

"Tell Claudia, at least do it soon," Damon interrupted. "Althea asked for time, and now we are engaged. Be patient. I have a feeling it will all work out for everyone."

Yes, he could wait. But it was more than beating hearts, yearning, and the like.

Oliver was falling in love. There was no mistake.

Chapter 24

CLAUDIA SETTLED IN at Olivia and Gideon's. She sat with Olivia in the morning room. Olivia explained it was for the lady of the house to correspond and plan her day while basking in the sun's rays. Or so it was said. Olivia clarified this small room only caught the sun toward the end of the afternoon, like now. A tea tray was set before them, and they were left alone.

"I have news," Olivia beamed. "Gideon and I are taking in a little girl from Chellenhome and making her part of our family. Her name is Marie, and she is six years old. Oh, you should see her. Marie is a sweet, kind child. We fell in love with her immediately. We are getting to know her better and giving her time to adjust. She will come here to live with us in January."

Claudia smiled. "Congratulations. That is wonderful."

"And that is not all," Olivia said excitedly. "I am expecting. Can you believe it? I thought I would have difficulties, considering I am well into my thirties. We are over the moon."

"No wonder you have been glowing lately. I am pleased for you both. You—and Gideon—deserve every happiness."

"Did I hear my name mentioned?" Gideon smiled as he strode into the room. "Do not despair. I only popped in to grab a few raspberry tarts. And maybe a raisin biscuit or two." Gideon withdrew a handkerchief from his pocket and deftly gathered baked goods from the 3-tired silver tray.

"I just told Claudia the good news," Olivia said brightly.

"A family. I always desired one," Gideon murmured. "And Claudia, we want you to be part of that family."

She blinked rapidly, looking up at Gideon. "I am an illegitimate stepsister. Sired by a contemptible being we all despise."

"That may be, but to me, you *are* my sister. And we want you to be an aunt to our children. Will you consider it?" Gideon asked, his look expectant.

There is that annoying lump of emotion.

She nodded. "Yes, I will."

"Good. I am glad to hear it. That is a start. Ladies, I will leave you with your tea and varied discussions. See you at dinner."

Gideon swept from the room, closing the door behind him.

"If you had met him a year ago, you wouldn't believe it was the same man. He has opened up in all ways, embracing life and love. So have I. If ever there were two damaged people—but you know of what I speak."

Claudia nodded. "So much has transpired. My emotions are a complete mess. I am so confused. I barely had time to adjust to my new situation when Tensbridge entered my life. I don't know where to begin."

"Why don't we start at the beginning? At our time on the streets? That is the root of your muddled trepidation in allowing yourself to feel anything. I know, believe me. We shall meet here in the afternoon over the next few days, and we will puzzle this out. I promise."

That would mean telling her story again, for the second time in a week. But who would understand how past events can shape one's present life? Olivia would.

With a shaky sigh, Claudia sipped tea and began her narrative. "It all began at Eaton Place, in Belgrave Square..."

THE PAST FEW DAYS AT Olivia and Gideon's home had been a revelation. To witness a loving couple openly express their affection was not something Claudia was used to seeing. The consideration for the other's needs, the teasing and playfulness. The trust.

Hearing of Gideon's and Olivia's pasts put much in perspective. At times, it felt as if only Claudia suffered, but deep down, she knew others had it worse. To find out that, in different ways, Olivia and Gideon had horrible pasts as sinister as—or in some respects—worse than her made her question her lingering fright when dealing with emotions. And within The Rakes stratosphere, Baroness Wenlock suffered trauma from living on the streets. The Duke of Chellenham suffered trauma from an emotionally abusive and neglectful father. But to hear that Winstone physically and mentally abused Gideon as a boy was more than she could bear. Her so-called father deserved to rot in prison.

Being wealthy did not guarantee happiness. Yet, despite Olivia and Gideon's damage, they survived. They thrived. They *loved.*

Why can't she do the same?

Claudia harbored deep feelings for Oliver. She could admit that much. Why risk her life to bring him food while he hid in the cache? He was right. A bond had formed between them beyond their shared hazardous experience. She initiated kissing him more than once, which proved she found him attractive. Oh, why couldn't she move past her paralyzing fright?

Olivia breezed into the library with a basket of flowers. "Good afternoon! I hope I am not disturbing you."

Claudia glanced down at the book in her hands. She had read the same page over and over for an hour. She set it aside. "Not at all."

"Good. Because I ordered a tea tray to be brought up." Olivia placed the basket on the table and arranged the flowers in a crystal vase. "Michaelmas daisies and autumn crocuses. Or so the gardener tells me. When I married Gideon, I knew nothing of flowers or how to craft an arrangement."

"I like the lilac-colored daisies. They are stunning," Claudia stated.

"I do as well. We are having a small dinner party tomorrow night. We would like for you to attend. Eleanora and Christian, Asher and Charity, Gideon's Aunt Mirella, and Gideon's good friend, Brandon Knight, who is in London temporarily on business. Brandon, his wife, Angeline, and his stepson, the young Earl of Oakby, plan to return to England sometime in the next fifteen months. Before you object, I have the perfect gown for you to wear. I wish to give it to you. The coloring never complimented my hair shade. It is gold, with lots of lace and silk."

A dinner party. Hell's bells.

Her first instinct was to say no, stay in her room, read a book, and shut herself off from any social situation. But Claudia was slowly realizing that interacting with people was not something she should or could avoid. Everyone had been so kind and giving, from those at The Velvet Vine to the ladies at the Galway Agency, to Olivia and Gideon and the rest of The Rakes.

But how does she take those baby steps toward Oliver? It was too big of a leap, the emotions much more intense, the risk too great.

Or was it?

Claudia rubbed her forehead to stem the annoying flash of pain behind her left eye.

Olivia sat next to her on the settee. "Oh, my dear. I understand your inward struggle. Our little dinner party is a first step out into the world—a chance to try and place your past behind you enough that the only way is forward. But I do not wish to force you. Just say the word, and I will cross you off the guest list."

Claudia sighed. "It would be easy to stay in my room."

"Very easy. I did it for years, never venturing out much in public. But you couldn't stay hidden away. You had to protect your girls. I admire you so much for doing that. And you cared and protected your dear mother as well. Oh, you have feelings, Claudia. And your instincts are correct. Once you landed at The Velvet Vine, you could have done the same as me—hiding away in your room. But you didn't. You grabbed the opportunity with both hands and accepted the job with the Galways. Good for you."

Claudia nodded as she wiped a wayward tear from her cheek. "And now?"

"You seize even more opportunities. Friendship with me and the ladies within The Rakes and at the Galway Agency. Family, with me and Gideon. But most importantly, love. Or the possibility of it—with Oliver Wollstonecraft. He is a fine, honorable man and devilishly handsome to boot. I do not know all the particulars of how you both came to be injured, and I know you must keep confidence when dealing with an investigative case. But you care for him. You admitted as much yesterday." Olivia took her hand and squeezed it assuredly.

"Perhaps I more than care. I may be falling in—hell's bells, I cannot even say the word. It is so much more than his looks. It is his outward confidence, his desire to help others, how he embraces and acknowledges his emotions and speaks his mind—at least to me. He loves his family and friends. He took in a stray cat, can you imagine? No man should be so perfect."

Olivia laughed, then sobered. "I assure you he is not perfect. No one is. But the fact you see him in this light shows you are definitely falling for him. There is nothing like it," Olivia said dreamily. "To find one's soul mate. To be friends as well as lovers, sharing everything. And it doesn't happen to everyone. There are many lonely people in the world—and alone."

That was true. Everything Olivia said made perfect sense. "Oliver said he sometimes felt lonely, even with his huge family and circle of friends. He said a doctor told him that feeling that way is caused by a fear of intimacy. And tragedy, although I don't believe that aspect relates to him."

Olivia nodded. "Yes, it is true what the doctor said. Even the most confident of people can have doubts and fears. Oliver admitted this to you?"

"We shared quite a lot when we were alone."

"Yes, that is the beginning of building a relationship. Trust and sharing your past."

"It is, and I am so glad I shared it with you as well," Claudia said softly as she squeezed Olivia's hand. "And I will attend your dinner party. Let's try on the dress."

Olivia squealed and jumped to her feet. "I hoped you would agree. I have it laid out on my bed. Come, let's have a look before the tea tray arrives."

As they dashed toward Olivia's room, hand in hand, laughing and talking, a pang of emotion wrapped around Claudia's heart. She had missed this since her mother died, not that they had much to laugh and smile about those last few years. The friendship, the joy of sharing secrets. Actually smiling—and meaning it.

If telling Oliver about her past lifted a weight from her shoulders, then confiding with Olivia removed most of the remaining burden.

Claudia felt lighter. And perhaps, at last, ready to move forward with her life on all fronts.

Chapter 25

OLIVER FELT RESTLESS. The stitches were taken out this morning, and Doctor Drew stated the infection and fever had passed and that his recovery was remarkable. Thank God he was young and fit enough to bounce back from the injury swiftly.

But much had been left unresolved.

What to do about Bryan. What to do about Danaher.

And more importantly—Claudia.

He tapped the wrapped parcel sitting on his desk. He had bought Claudia leather-bound editions of *The Picture of Dorian Gray* and a Sherlock Holmes novel, *The Sign of Four.* Lady Ainsworth mentioned the fictional detective to Claudia. Claudia told him about stopping at Mitchell's place, meeting Lady Ainsworth, and how much she liked her and promised a visit soon.

Claudia lamented about not having any books or time to read. Oliver should send a note, but what should he say? Should he pour his heart out? The message should be short and concise, giving her something to contemplate without encroaching on her time. Perhaps he shouldn't have it delivered, for sending a gift could smack of trying to buy her affection—which is not his intent. Frustrated, he pushed the books away as Rett strode into the room.

"What is wrong, Cousin? Woman troubles?" Rett teased.

Oliver snarled in response. "Yes. And I will not be discussing it. To change the subject. I have an idea."

Rett plopped into the seat before his desk. "What?"

"The two of us? We go into Notting Dale."

Rett's eyes widened. "Has the fever cooked your brain? What if we run into Bryan, or worse, Danaher?"

"I contemplated us stumbling into Notting Dale as drunken swells, but I soon set that aside. Especially after Claudia said that Danaher would question any well-to-do person who crosses into The Piggeries. She mentioned to Danaher that she was following someone for a wealthy client. I do not wish to come face-to-face with Danaher. Not yet. And we could run into Bryan, as you say."

"Very well. But more importantly, *why* do you propose this?"

Oliver sat forward, clasping his hands on the desk. "Why? Bryan is in danger whenever he steps into The Piggeries. Danaher will question him if he hasn't already. The miserable bastard will no doubt compile a list and start methodically checking each name to find Claudia because he believes she will lead him to The Sentinel."

"Then it was wise for her to stay at Watford's," Rett observed.

Perhaps. But it didn't make the ache in his heart hurt any less by her absence. "Sooner or later, Danaher will have to be dealt with."

"And that is for the police. You know this."

"Yes. But Danaher must also pay for his treatment of Claudia—in the past, and most especially in the present."

Rett shook his head. "You are out for revenge. How bloodthirsty of you. I never thought you had such an overt, violent side, but I was mistaken. It is why you became a vigilante, isn't it? Anger at the injustice in the world. Or, more specifically, here in London."

Oliver frowned at Rett's description, for he went out of his way to avoid violence. Or did he? No, not really. He had been involved in plenty of scuffles since donning his vigilante disguise. "You have to admit the city and the world at large would be a better place without Danaher. Come now, I am not suggesting murder. You know me better than that. I want us to go into Notting Dale disguised as working-class blokes to get the lay of the land. You heard Mitchell when he was here yesterday. Danaher's men were released, and Inspector Stanhope told Mitchell to stay out of Notting Dale."

"For the time being. Again, I reiterate. This is a police problem." Rett folded his arms in defiance. "Mitchell said they will be dealing with it—and soon."

"Yes, but when? We cannot wait. I cannot sit here and do nothing when Bryan and Claudia are involved."

TWO HOURS LATER, IN complete disguise, Oliver and Rett made their way toward Notting Dale. They had taken a hansom cab as far as a few streets away and would walk the rest. They had stopped at a pub, ordered cheap gin, then spilled it all over each other. Oliver wore a fake bushy mustache, and Rett wore a long-haired blond wig under his peaked cap. They wore gloves because their smooth hands would be a dead giveaway about not being working-class men out for a lark. Rett carried a giant pickaxe, not only for protection but also as a prop. Oliver had a claw hammer tucked into his coat.

Their fabrication? A fancy town house near the Notting Hill-Notting Dale border was undergoing a renovation to turn it into small flats. Oliver and Rett would pretend to be laborers on their way home, stopping to imbibe along the way. As they came upon the border of the new park area, the cousins halted.

"Look there," Rett whispered. "Men guarding the entryway into The Piggeries. No doubt the ones who were released. There are some even in the next alley over. Do you think they will question everyone who crosses the street?"

"Yes. Claudia said Danaher is thorough. I know we knocked at Bryan's flat, and no one answered, but even if we see them here, Bryan will not recognize us, especially after we rubbed dirt on our faces," Oliver replied *sotto voce*.

"I still say this is madness."

Oliver smiled. "But you are here."

"It appears I have a sense of adventure after all. If allowed in, we go to the pub, order a drink, then circle about and leave, correct?"

"Aye, Tommy boy," Oliver replied, mimicking a working-class accent.

"Not bad, Alfie, old sock," Rett replied in an even better rendition of the accent. "We'd best crack on afore I'm skint like."

"You are really taking to this, aren't you?" Oliver whispered.

Rett chucked as they crossed the street, staggering a bit to give the impression they were half in their cups.

"Hold up, you two blighters," one of the men called out. "What's with the weapon?"

"On our way 'ome from work, over yonder. Laborin' at one o' those toff 'ouses. We be needin' a drink," Oliver said, ending on a hiccup.

"Goin' to the Black Moon for an ale or three," Rett nodded. "Let us through, yeah? What's all the to-do?"

"Never you mind," answered the second man, who looked Oliver and Rett over thoroughly. "Go have your drinks, then leave. No wanderin' around."

Oliver gave a drunken salute. "Aye, Cap'n. We be as quiet as mice."

Rett snickered loudly. Then sobered. He leaned in toward the two men. "Aye, don't want to rile Danaher, yeah? He still be the boss hereabouts?"

Oliver froze. What in hell was Rett doing?

The tall man's eyes narrowed. "Don't be mentioning his name again, you follow me? Or we'll be using that pickaxe to dig your grave."

Rett snorted. "Steady on, mate. No need to go all argy-bargied on us. We're not complete eejits. A few drinks and out. Ta!" Rett grabbed Oliver's arm and pulled him forward as they staggered down the street.

"Look back, are they watching us?" Rett whispered.

Oliver turned and gave a silly wave to the men. "Oh, yes," he replied quietly. "Watching our every move. Continue down this street and take the first right."

Once they rounded the corner, Oliver halted and faced his cousin. "Why mention Danaher?"

"To see their reaction. The fact that they threatened harm shows the situation is dire. Rooting out that bastard will be next to impossible. Again, I say that it's best left to the police. Miss Ellingford has made her official complaint. Now it is up to police to follow through."

Yes, Rett was correct. This place was locked down tight. But he would pass on the information about where the sentries were located to Mitchell.

They continued onward. It wasn't easy to see as the sun had all but set, and hardly any street lamps were lit. They were about to cross the cobblestones to the pub when the door burst open, and Shinwell, Tolwood, Bryan, and one other man stumbled out, loudly laughing and generally acting like complete—what working-class word fit—plonkers? Pillocks? Prats? Cretins? Imbeciles? Morons. That was the word. It fits them to a tee.

They crossed the street, passing a bottle of cheap gin back and forth, walking by Oliver and Rett without giving them a second look. Rett stuck his long pickaxe low to the ground, and Shinwell tripped over it, sprawling to the dirty cobbles.

The other men burst out laughing, and judging by Shinwell's look; he was livid.

"Oh, sorry, me lordship, sir," Oliver said, making a pretense of trying to assist. He purposely stepped on Shinwell's hand, causing the man to yelp in pain. Then Oliver reached for the lapels of Shinwell's expensive wool coat and started to bring him to his feet, dragging him toward a large muddy puddle. Then Oliver released him, and Shinwell tumbled facedown into the putrid water. "Sorry again, me lord. 'ard to see in the bloody dark. Lemme 'elp—"

The men laughed harder. "Be quiet, you cretins!" Shinwell shouted angrily at his companions as he tried to stand. They silenced. Then he looked toward Oliver. "You drunken oaf! Don't touch me again with your greasy hands, or I will have you flayed alive!"

Rett took Oliver's arm and led him away. Shinwell was still yelling as they stepped into the dimly lit pub.

"Well done," Rett said. "Do you think he will come after you?"

Oliver shook his head. "No. He is too drunk and too humiliated. My manhandling of him was not gentlemanly and reeks of school-age shenanigans, but I know this much. The sooner we tear Bryan out of that man's clutches, the better."

And Oliver felt all this would come to a head sooner than anyone believed.

"GENTLEMEN, WE LEAVE you to your brandy and cigars, that is, if any of you even smoke cigars," Olivia smiled.

"Not usually," Gideon replied, giving his wife a wink. "But we might tonight."

Olivia stood, and the men immediately jumped to their feet. It had been a lovely meal of crown roast of pork, baked salmon, and all the accompanying side dishes of whipped potatoes and the like. Claudia especially loved the desert, a trifle with whipped cream, custard, fresh raspberries, and blackberries. She had fretted most of last night about this dinner, but it had gone better than she hoped.

The ladies followed Olivia down the hall to the sitting room, where a tea tray with biscuits and small frosted cakes awaited.

Gideon's Aunt Mirella slipped her arm through Claudia's as they headed toward the settee. "I am so glad you are strengthening family ties with Gideon and Olivia, even though they are not blood ones. We all need people around us who care. And I would very much like for you to think of me as your aunt and call me so."

Gideon's aunt spoke to something Claudia was beginning to realize. Regardless of someone's independence and dogged determination to remain aloof and removed from complicated emotions, 'we all need people around us who care.'

Claudia wanted that, after all.

She had it with her mother and, when she passed, acknowledged she would never experience it again. But she found refuge with her ladies in the East End and now with the Galway Agency ladies, The Rakes, along with Gideon and Olivia, taking her into the protective, trusting circle of love and family.

Claudia patted the older woman's hand. "Of course, Aunt Mirella."

"Well done," Mirella beamed. "Olivia and Gideon will be so pleased. You all deserve happiness."

Yes, blast it; Claudia deserved happiness. And if she could accept it within these groups, there was no reason she couldn't take that final step toward Oliver Wollstonecraft.

A footman entered the room as they were taking their seats. "A parcel has arrived for you, Miss Ellingford. Shall I bring it in?"

"Yes, thank you."

Once seated, Claudia placed her teacup on the table before her. The footman laid the parcel next to it. "It came with a card, miss." The footman bowed slightly and departed.

"Who is it from, Claudia?" Olivia called out.

"I am not sure." She broke the wax seal and flipped open the paper.

MY DEAREST CLAUDIA,

You have destroyed me for any other woman. You have captured my heart and soul and are the very air I breathe. Our bond is profound and fundamental. I want to hold you close and share everything, including laughter and tears. These emotions are overwhelming. Believe me, I know. But if you search your heart, you may discover that you feel the same. I could write pages about how you fill my heart, but I will say three words encapsulating it all.

I love you.

I am in utter misery without you.

With the deepest and most steadfast love,

Oliver

TEARS FILLED HER EYES at the heartfelt words. Claudia reread it, and her heart soared. The joy tearing through her was powerful enough to topple down the last of her reserves.

He loves me.

Setting aside the note, she grabbed the heavy parcel and tore the paper off, tossing it aside. It was two beautiful leather-bound books from two authors she had longed to read, Oscar Wilde and Arthur Conan Doyle. Oliver had remembered her mentioning it. With a gasping sob, Claudia grasped the note and stood suddenly, her heart banging against her ribcage.

I love him.

Claudia had the irresistible urge to tell Oliver that exact thing this very minute. The declaration could not be delayed. Just like his note to her could not wait.

Olivia came to her side. "What is it?"

"I must go to him," she whispered fiercely. "Can you call the carriage for me?"

"To Oliver?"

Claudia held the note to her heart and nodded.

"Then you shall. William!"

The footman entered the room. "Your Grace?"

"Call the carriage to the front entrance for Miss Ellingford, William. At once, if you please."

"Yes, Your Grace."

Olivia clasped Claudia's free hand and squeezed it gently. "Tell him what is in your heart, my dear. Hold nothing back."

Claudia gave Olivia an affectionate kiss on the cheek. She would be forever indebted to Olivia and Gideon for generously opening their home and lives to her, but most of all for sharing their pasts and showing her that regardless of catastrophe and tribulation, a person can open their hearts to love.

Excited and smiling, Claudia dashed into the hall, and William stood with her cloak, ready to lay it across her shoulders. They were off once William assisted her into the carriage and the Hill Street address given to the driver.

Claudia reread the note. Sighing, she tucked it into her cloak pocket as she anxiously watched out the window as the horses' hooves clattered on the cobblestones. What seemed like forever, they arrived in front of the white brick and marble town house. Without waiting for assistance, Claudia tossed her cloak aside, rushed to the door, and banged the brass knocker.

Dalton opened the door. "Miss Ellingford."

"Is his lordship in?" she asked breathlessly.

"Why no, miss. His lordship went for a walk. You are welcome to come in and wait."

Claudia's heart crashed to her toes in disappointment.

Dalton must have seen her distress, for he pointed toward the end of the street. "His lordship often perambulates about Berkley Square, Miss Ellingford. I am certain you will find him there. He's been going for walks there the last few nights since he was well enough to do so."

Claudia stared in the direction Dalton indicated. She could see the square, brightly illuminated by the street lights and the moon above. "Thank you, Dalton. I will find him."

It was a good thing it was mild tonight for late October. Lifting her gold gown, she rushed down the steps and called up to the coachman. "Stay here, Murphy. I won't be a minute."

And with that, she was off down the street as swiftly as her slippered feet could take her. Pins fell out of her hair, causing her upswept style to loosen, but Claudia hardly cared. All that mattered was finding Oliver.

The park was quiet, except for a slight breeze through the remaining large golden leaves of the London plane trees along the perimeter of the main path. Claudia could hear water trickling and discovered a fountain of a nymph holding a vase. Turning about, she spotted a stone gazebo lit from within, no doubt from gas lamps.

A figure emerged from the shadows, heading toward her. It was a man with his coat slung over his shoulder. There was no mistaking those broad shoulders. His head was down, and his dark hair tousled from the breeze. The man was Oliver. Claudia knew in an instant.

"Oliver!" she cried.

His head snapped up, and their gazes met. Dropping his coat, he ran to her, slipping his arm about her shoulder and pulling her close. Their cheeks touched, and they stood together, reveling in the intimacy. Claudia sighed contentedly, resting her arm against his torso. His free hand stroked the bare skin of her arm.

"Claudia, my Claudia," he whispered. "My love."

Claudia knew. Then and there.

She had found her home.

Chapter 26

OLIVER COULDN'T BELIEVE it. Claudia here, in his arms. It was beyond any dreams he had, beyond all expectations. "I know you asked for time. I am sorry I sent the note. It was arrogant of me—"

Claudia turned enough to place two fingertips against his lips, effectively silencing him. "You have destroyed my stubborn wall of resolve. The bricks fell away every time you touched me, kissed me. Oh, hell's bells, when you walk into a room." She stroked his cheek tenderly. "I have had such wicked dreams about you. I cannot wait for night to come to lose myself in those heated fantasies."

Oliver's heart soared at her words, for he did the same every night. "You do want me?"

"Yes, I want you—as the viscount *and* the vigilante. When those yearnings merged, I could not fathom the depths of my overwhelming feelings for you, so I tried to place them behind that barrier." Claudia laid her head against his chest. "But they kept seeping through. I am not afraid anymore. I love you, Oliver. I am so in love with you that I—"

It was all he needed to hear. Oliver kissed her passionately, trailing his hands down her hips until he grasped her rear, bringing her in tight against his arousal.

Claudia moaned softly, writhing in his arms as if desperate to get closer. Breaking the kiss, he took her hand, and Oliver led her off the path behind a large plane tree. With her back against the tree trunk, he kissed her again as his hand tunneled under her gown.

"You are utterly stunning in this dress," he murmured between kisses. "Beautiful no matter what you wear, laborer clothes included."

Claudia laughed softly, then gasped as his fingers stroked her inner thigh.

"Remember what I said? About what I wanted to do?" he asked huskily.

"Oh, yes. Word for word. You said, 'If you only knew how I wanted to vault across my desk, hold you in my arms, and kiss you senseless. Back you up against the wall, trail my hand up under your skirt, finding the wetness therein.'"

"Yes. I want to touch you. Are you wet?" Oliver whispered fiercely.

"I am. Touch me."

Oliver needed no further invitation. His fingers burrowed through the slit in her drawers, and wetness coated his fingers. He moaned at the sensation. It would be tempting to drop to his knees and bury his face there, licking her until she screamed. But it *was* a public park. This is as much as he dared do under the circumstances.

He stroked her folds and, finding that sensitive nub, rubbed it with his thumb as his fingers moved in and out of her. This continued for several moments, and Oliver could feel her peak building. The ecstasy showing on her lovely face urged him onward. Claudia went limp against him, stifling her moans against his shirt sleeve.

"Come for me," he urged, his voice rough with passion. "Come apart in my arms."

It took no time at all. God above, he was close to spilling in his trousers. Claudia's breath came in short gasps until she cried out, covering her mouth with her hand to stem the noise. She shuddered against him, and the tremors sent bolts of desire all through him.

After gaining control of her breathing, Claudia laid her hand against his aching cock. But Oliver heard voices in the distance before they could say or do anything. "Stay here," he whispered. He ran toward the path, gathered up his coat, and returned to her before anyone saw him.

They stood together, holding each other close behind the tree's large trunk, and waited until the voices passed. Oliver stroked her silken hair, laying kisses on her forehead. He could not stop touching and kissing her.

"What about you?" Claudia said as she trailed the tip of her finger along his arousal. Oliver trembled in response.

"Soon. I would like nothing more than for you to bring me to release, but not here." He motioned toward the pathway as more voices could be heard in the distance. "We will have other opportunities. We love each other, and everything is possible." Oliver kissed her again but soon halted as he neared the point of no return. "Did you arrive by Gideon's carriage?" Claudia nodded. "I will escort you to it." He slipped on his coat and buttoned it. It would not be prudent to walk about the city streets with an obvious erection.

"Everything *is* possible, isn't it?" Claudia smiled.

Oliver tenderly stroked her cheek. "We have all the time in the world. I will come by Olivia and Gideon's for breakfast. When do they serve it?"

Claudia took his hand and kissed it. "Half past nine."

He absolutely loved it when she kissed his hand. "We will discuss what to do next about Danaher. That must be resolved before we move forward with our future. Or am I advancing this too swiftly?"

"Not at all. Not in my eyes," Claudia murmured.

Oliver chuckled. "Society will say this all happened far too quickly. That there should be months of courtship before discussing a future together."

"To hell with society and their rules." Claudia threw her arms about his neck and kissed him ardently.

"I so agree," Oliver growled. He clasped her breast, his thumb moving across her erect nipple. He wanted to take her to his bed right this very minute. Have them explore together and make love all night. He was about to suggest that very thing, but those faraway voices drew closer, and common sense again came into focus. Sighing, he took a step back, took her arm, and placed it through his.

Together, they strolled along the moonlit pathway toward Hill Street.

Oliver could not envision a more perfect evening.

JEDI DANAHER SAT BEHIND a table, watching his men drag in two well-dressed nobs. Jedi wore a long cloak with a hood, which he had pulled over his head and hauled low over his eyes to partially obscure his face. His men removed the burlap bags they had over the men's heads.

"Names!" he barked menacingly. The place was shrouded in darkness, so there was no possible way the men could identify their surroundings.

"Viscount Shinwell," the one on the left sniffed arrogantly. "And this is Mr. Bryan Wollstonecraft, son of the Earl of Carstone."

Wollstonecraft kicked Shinwell in the leg; no doubt annoyed the viscount gave away his aristocratic family ties. *Shinwell.* Of course, Darrington's contemptible son. Jedi had done business with Darrington on numerous occasions. Did Shinwell know of his father's criminal enterprises? Probably not.

"They've been at The Black Moon many times and on Bangor Street," Birch said. "And next door."

Buying opium.

"Then you owe me a luxury tax," Jedi growled. He didn't bother using his street accent any longer. What was the point?

"I think not, and you have no right to drag us here like this," Shinwell said, crossing his arms defiantly.

"I have every right. Notting Dale is mine," Jedi replied, then pointed at the viscount. "I know your father very well. We've done many deals together over the years."

"I highly doubt it."

Jedi laughed cynically. "How do you think the earl has financed his life and paid your bills? He's a smuggler and more besides."

The blood drained from Shinwell's face.

Jedi was correct. The pampered bastard had no clue. "You, Viscount. Answer my questions, and I might consider letting you go. Do you know a detective named Simpson?"

"N-no."

Not so arrogant now. "Does Carnstone have any wealth? Is he in the city?"

"Yes, and no, not in London. But his oldest son is Viscount Tensbridge. He lives at 5 Hill Street, Mayfair."

"You miserable bastard," Wollstonecraft hissed through clenched teeth.

Perhaps the viscount brother hired Claudia's agency to follow this wayward whelp. It was plausible and worth a look. "Shinwell, you can go. I will collect the tax from your father. Don't show your face around here again until he settles your account. As for Wollstonecraft—" Jedi paused. "You will stay here as my guest. I will contact your brother about paying your fee. And Shinwell? Don't get it in your empty head to go to Tensbridge about this. Or I will find you and silence you permanently. Go now before I change my mind."

Shinwell scrambled toward the door.

"Troy!" Wollstonecraft called out beseechingly.

Shinwell turned and shrugged. "Sorry. Self-preservation and all that." One of Jedi's men grabbed Shinwell roughly by the arm, pulled the burlap sack over his head, then pushed the viscount out through the creaky door, banging it shut behind him.

"Not much of a friend, is he?" Danaher laughed cruelly.

"No. He is not."

"Put him below," Jedi ordered Birch.

"What? Below?" Wollstonecraft cried.

How ironic Jedi used the same cache The Sentinel hid in, and probably Claudia as well. "It's a bit dark, but there is a pallet and a bucket. Keep quiet, and I might even feed you. Don't try to escape, not that you could. I installed bolts to secure the trapdoor, and my men will be watching."

The panic on Wollstonecraft's face was palatable. Danaher could make it out by the dim light of the candle. He probably didn't like the dark or enclosed places—or both. Who bloody cares?

"Don't put me down there. I have money," Wollstonecraft rasped.

"How much?"

Wollstonecraft dug into his pockets with shaking hands and brought forth a few notes. "Four pounds," he whispered miserably.

Jedi and his men burst out laughing. "Not near enough. But we will take it and buy bread and cheese for you to nibble on. Maybe you can share it with the rats." Jedi hadn't seen any rats below, but he thoroughly enjoyed seeing the blood drain from Wollstonecraft's face at the prospect.

Birch snatched the money from Wollstonecraft and then pushed him toward the large fireplace. In a manner of minutes, Wollstonecraft was secured below.

"What now?" Birch asked.

"Let the toff stew a bit down there. Bring him bread and water at midnight. Then we will send a note along to his viscount brother. If he pays the money, we will let the sniveling bugger go. If The Sentinel *is* involved in this somehow, he will show up, maybe with friends in tow."

"What about the coppers? The viscount could call in the police instead of paying."

"Maybe. But I will put in the note no coppers, or else—" Jedi made a slashing motion across his neck. "That's why you are going to the station to bring Constable Nigel Lindon to me immediately. He works nights and feeds me information."

Birch rushed out the door.

Jedi sat patiently and waited. He cocked his ear toward the trapdoor. There was a noise which sounded like whimpering. A slow, satisfied smile crept across his face.

LINDON STOOD BEFORE him fifteen minutes later. He described Simpson as about six feet, dark blond, blue eyes, early thirties. The description fits the man who gave orders during the raid. Was it Simpson? Some of the puzzle pieces snapped into place; others did not.

"What else can you tell me about him?" Jedi asked.

"I heard he's mates with a bunch of nobs. He's been hanging about at a viscount's place lately."

Jedi's head snapped up. Viscount? It would be too much of a coincidence. In the paper, Jedi read there were over one hundred viscounts currently. What were the odds it would be Tensbridge? Regardless, it was a nugget of information that Jedi tucked away for future use.

"Is Simpson at the station now?"

"Aye, he is. He was just made Detective Sergeant, the miserable bastard. Everything by the book, strict orders and such, and—"

"Enough. Take Birch with you and point him out. Birch, stick to this bloke Simpson like glue. I want to know his comings and goings."

Both men departed, leaving Jedi with his thoughts. He was not wholly convinced Simpson was The Sentinel, but he would pursue this to the end on the outside chance that he is.

No one would interfere with his business.

Copper or not.

Chapter 27

OLIVER ARRIVED FOR breakfast, and to Claudia's amazement, Gideon and Olivia said they would take their meal upstairs, allowing them to be alone. They no sooner departed when Claudia vaulted herself at Oliver, throwing her arms around his neck.

The restraints were off, and all lingering doubts were vanquished. These intense emotions were exhilarating, and Claudia would relish each and every one.

He kissed her passionately, and in return, Claudia cupped his cheeks and rained urgent kisses all over his handsome face.

Oliver laughed and, in placing his arms about her waist, spun her around. Then he plopped onto a chair, bringing Claudia down with him so she straddled his lap, facing him. She continued kissing him. She would never get enough.

"Marry me," Oliver whispered in her ear.

Claudia stopped short and pulled back far enough to stare at him, incredulous at the suggestion yet overcome with complete bliss. "You are serious?"

"Completely. We already agreed we want a future together. Hear me out, for I have a suggestion: a quick, short wedding and a long honeymoon. Perhaps to Spain or my great uncle has a place in Scotland we could stay—or wherever you like. I mention the quick wedding because I want you so much, but I want our first time to be as a married couple. Does that sound strange to you?"

How utterly romantic. "No," Claudia replied softly, her eyes shimmering with unshed tears. "Not strange at all. But married? How do we make it work? I mean, interlocking our lives?"

"All we have to do is observe the examples of marital bliss around us. The Rakes and their partners make it work. So can we. If you wish to stay with The Galway Agency, do so. I would never ask you to be less than yourself. Perhaps I will act as The Sentinel a while longer. We are young and can do whatever we want, including getting married on our terms."

Oliver sounded resolute and confident, and his words made sense to her. As she said last night, everything was possible.

"My family will adore you," Oliver continued. "We can be married once my father and mother arrive, which will be in ten days or less. When we return from the long honeymoon, we can stay in London as long as you like. I have the Tensbridge country house in Kent. We can reside there whenever you wish. These are just some recommendations. I would never dictate our lives. I want a partnership in all things."

It all sounded like a fairy tale, and hell's bells, after everything she has gone through, Claudia deserved happiness with the man she loved. And a partnership? Exactly her thoughts on the matter. "And children?"

"There is no rush. As heir to the earldom, I should try and continue the line at some point and think of the fun we will have to do that very thing." Oliver nuzzled her neck as she giggled.

When in hell had she ever giggled? She was utterly smitten and so in love she could not contain it.

But then, a dark thought entered her mind. "And what about Danaher?"

"Rett and I traveled to The Piggeries," Oliver told her of them dressing up as laborers and their run-in with Shinwell and Danaher's men. "I have been slowly comprehending that Danaher is best left to the police. I admit I had my blood up, ready to exact revenge for holding you captive. I was ready to tear the place apart, but Rett eventually made sense. You also said to leave it for the Met police."

Claudia stroked his cheek. "It is too perilous to deal with him. Danaher is like a trapped rat in a corner. He knows the end is near and will lash out. We should stay out of Notting Dale."

"Then it is all the more imperative we snatch Bryan out of Shinwell's clutches and away from Notting Dale and the danger therein."

Claudia kissed him and stood. "Agreed. I am famished. All this planning for a life together has made me ravenous."

"Only for food?" Oliver teased.

She smiled. "For now. I agree about getting married as soon as your parents arrive. I am eager to meet them and begin our lives together—in all ways."

"I am tempted to sweep the dishes off this table and make love to you right here," he growled seductively.

"But we will wait," Claudia said softly.

Oliver nodded. "Then, we wait."

Claudia clapped her hands together as she strode over to the sideboard. She lifted the covers off the chafing dishes. "We still have much to learn about each other. For example, what breakfast foods do you prefer? Shirred, scrambled, or soft-boiled eggs? Or perhaps hard ones?"

Oliver jumped to his feet, came up behind her, and slipped his arms about her waist, bringing her close. He rolled his hips. "I know of something else that is hard."

Claudia's insides fluttered. Hell's bells, can they even wait until the wedding? Not at this rate. "You are incorrigible. But I love it—and I love you."

Oliver laid kisses along her neck. "I prefer scrambled, served with ham or bacon, preferably both. I don't care for kippers. I am also partial to a mushroom and cheese omelet."

"Good to know. Now, take your seat, and I will serve you. But not all the time, mind."

Oliver laughed and sat at the table. "I would never expect you to. But I will treasure it when you do."

"Pour our tea, love," she called out.

After placing the piled-high plate in front of Oliver, Claudia selected scrambled eggs, sausage, bacon, fresh bread, and marmalade.

After chatting and eating, they were nearly finished the meal when Hobson, the butler, entered the room. "My pardon, my lord, Miss Claudia. There is a Mr. Rett Wollstonecraft to see you. He says it is urgent."

"Show him in, Hobson," Claudia replied.

She exchanged a questioning look with Oliver. This could not be good news. Rett wouldn't disturb them unless something happened—something serious.

Rett strode into the room, holding a note aloft. "It appears we waited too long fetching Bryan from his flat. Danaher has him and is demanding money for his release."

OLIVER TOOK THE NOTE from Rett.

"*Luxury Tax Due: two thousand pounds,*" Oliver read aloud as Rett sat beside him.

FOR THE RELEASE OF Bryan Wollstonecraft, now being held for taxes owed. Viscount Tensbridge, come alone with the money in a leather pouch, a mixture of pounds, guineas, florins, and shillings, and no harm will come to your brother. I will give you two days to gather the tax. Be at the Black Moon pub Thursday night at nine, and the exchange will be done. Call the police in, and I will slit your brother's throat—the King of Notting Dale.

"KING?" CLAUDIA SEETHED. "Oh, that evil man."

"We waited too long," Oliver shook his head. "Damn the man." He hesitated. "Does he know I am The Sentinel?"

"I doubt it. Danaher would have mentioned it in the note," Rett replied. "Or would he?"

"Yes," Claudia replied. "He would have mentioned it. He would have taunted you, luring you into his trap. You see, Danaher has done this before, holding wealthy young men for his own twisted version of compensation. He figures the toffs are using his facilities; they should pay a luxury tax. I am certain he does not know your identity."

Oliver pounded his fist on the table as a wave of rage tore through him. Immediately sensing his distress, Claudia rose from her chair and embraced him. He slipped his arms about her waist, holding her tight. She was his anchor in the storm.

"So I take it things have progressed between you?" Rett asked.

Oliver exhaled, then released Claudia. He took her hand and kissed it. "Claudia has agreed to be my wife and partner. As soon as possible."

"Then, my hearty congratulations. Truly, I am pleased to hear it. But first, Bryan. Correct?" Rett said.

"Yes. What do you propose? Claudia? What say you?" Oliver asked.

Claudia sat next to Oliver, still holding his hand. "It would be best to pay the money and recover your brother. As far as telling the police? That depends. We can take this legal opportunity to be rid of Danaher once and for all. It would involve Mitchell."

Rett shook his head. "Mitchell told us in no uncertain terms he wanted no part of our schemes."

"But this isn't a scheme. It is a criminal act perpetrated by a known villain. Holding someone and soliciting payment is against the law, correct?" Claudia asked.

"It is," Oliver answered. "This may work. Is Danaher holding Shinwell for ransom, I wonder?"

"Before we make any plans, I think we should head to Bryan's flat immediately," Rett suggested. "And see if Shinwell is about."

After a flurry of activity and explaining to Olivia and Gideon where they were going, the three were off in the carriage. They arrived just in time, for Shinwell and a footman were loading his trunk and other cases onto a carriage. The front door hung by one hinge. No doubt when Coldbridge arrived and kicked in the door.

After assisting Claudia from their carriage, they ran toward the harried viscount.

"Where is Bryan?" Oliver shouted.

"How would I know?" Shinwell snapped in reply.

Rett and Oliver each took an arm and dragged Shinwell into the flat, with Claudia close behind. She shut the sitting room door on the footman and turned the key in the lock.

"Danaher has Bryan. I received a note demanding payment for a luxury tax. Tell me all you know about it, and I may just let you live," Oliver seethed.

"I do not know any Danaher, nor do I know what you are talking about."

This interrogation will take far too long.

Claudia strode toward Shinwell as she lifted the hem of her gown to grab her knife from its holder. With a swift motion, she had the blade against the trembling viscount's throat. "Tell us everything."

"Tensbridge, call off your rabid doxy!" Shinwell cried.

Deftly, Claudia nicked his throat, and a trickle of blood stained his cravat.

"You had better tell us what you know and watch your mouth. Another insult toward any of us, and Claudia will slice and dice you for certain," Oliver barked.

"We were nabbed near Bangor Street, sacks placed over our heads. We were taken before some man in a hooded cloak, and he said we owed a tax. He asked me about a copper named Simpson, then said I could leave because he knew my father and would collect from him. He kept Bryan there. I cannot tell you where this shack is because I was escorted out with the sack on my head. The hooded man asked about the earl—your father. I told him about *you*."

Rett snorted. "What a coward you are."

"Now release me. I know nothing more," Shinwell demanded, though his voice shook.

Claudia looked to Oliver, who nodded. She released the viscount. "You should not repeat this conversation, or I will find you. Go home to your criminal father!" Claudia yelled after him.

After fumbling with the key and door, Shinwell ran to the carriage and departed.

"Danaher does not know about you being The Sentinel," Rett offered. "But why ask about Mitchell?"

"That is concerning. We had better find Mitchell this very moment," Oliver said. As Rett exited the room, Oliver gently grabbed Claudia's arm, spun her about, and kissed her soundly. "Have I told you how magnificent you are?"

"May I never tire of hearing it."

As Oliver took her hand, they sprinted toward the waiting carriage. Claudia never felt so alive.

And she was so blasted happy.

Chapter 28

IT WAS TEN MINUTES to nine on Thursday evening, and Rett strolled along Cut-Throat Lane toward The Black Moon pub. Beside him was Claudia, in disguise as a gardener, complete with a bushy beard and appropriate clothing, carrying the satchel with the money.

There had been heated discussion in crafting this rescue plan, and ultimately, they decided that Rett would act as Viscount Tensbridge. During the lively conversation, Mitchell suggested Oliver's residence may be under surveillance since Shinwell gave Danaher the address. Oliver could only hope he was not followed to Watford's two days ago and then followed to Shinwell's. Claudia cleverly wore a long woolen cloak with a fur-trimmed hood so no one could see her face or vibrant red hair.

They finally decided the risk was worth it, and Rett would act as the viscount, with Oliver as The Sentinel, following close behind. As for Claudia, she fervently insisted she be part of the plan. Oliver, initially reluctant only because he wished to keep her safe, agreed, for he knew Claudia could handle herself.

They also discussed using The Rakes but eventually decided against it. Mitchell promised to keep a small contingent of uniformed constables on the outskirts of Notting Dale. He told the men they were conducting a training exercise. Despite Mitchell's initial reluctance to assist in any of Rett's schemes, that all changed when Oliver showed him the ransom note. After all that had occurred, hiding in the cache, the injuries and recovery, to have their confrontation with Danaher come to this—rescuing his brother. Any scenario could play out, but recovering Byran safely was paramount.

Oliver had a revolver tucked in his belt to fire when the police were needed. As Mitchell explained, retrieving Bryan meant keeping to the directions of the exchange as closely as possible. Oliver understood the logic. Storming in with the police and The Rakes would imperil Bryan's life. They could only hope Bryan had the good sense to keep his mouth shut when he saw Rett instead of Oliver.

This strategy had many mechanisms, and anything could go wrong, but swiftness was of the essence. The quicker they put this plan into motion, the more likely they would retrieve Bryan from Danaher's greedy clutches.

It wasn't easy to slink about Notting Dale, for Danaher's men kept a constant vigilance. But as Oliver observed, the criminal's minions had lessened since the raid. The police undoubtedly scared off many, especially after being held in the police station's cells for several days. The one known as Shorty was still there but had not given up much information. Mitchell relayed the dolt probably had no information to pass on, as Danaher did not confide or reveal his thinking to anyone.

Oliver stealthily entered the shack next to the pub. The rear door had a wooden sliding bolt, but the front door's simple latch proved uncomplicated enough to jimmy open. The place was empty. The police raid meant the opium trade had been temporarily shut down. It was a wonder the structure still stood since the wooden walls were rotten, though it leaned against the pub for support.

Oliver cracked open the front door. Rett and Olivia stopped before the pub's front entrance. Two of Danaher's men came forward.

"Himself said to come alone," one of them growled.

"I cannot carry all this money by myself. It is much too heavy for me to handle," Rett sniffed haughtily. His cousin waved a handkerchief around to punctuate his foppish point.

Oliver smiled. Rett was quite good at this.

"My gardener's assistant, Joe. He wouldn't harm a fly," Rett continued. "He also won't say a word."

Oliver watched as one of the men stepped forward to take the valise.

"I must see my brother first. I must have proof of life. And I will speak to the author of the note. I *must* be satisfied." Rett crossed his arms defiantly.

The door opened, and Danaher stepped outside. "I've your brother. Who in bloody hell is this?" Danaher pointed at Claudia.

"Just a gardener's assistant. He carried the money. There is a good deal of shillings and other coins in the case, and far too heavy for me."

"Search them!" Danaher yelled.

Rett stepped in front of Claudia. "I think not. No one will lay a hand on me or the boy." Rett opened his long coat. "I carry no weapon. I would not know how to use one. Neither does he. I must say I am quite insulted."

Danaher hesitated, and Oliver held his breath. "Feck that, search them."

The two men quickly patted Rett down, then turned to Claudia. One of the men's hands slid between Claudia's legs, patted under her arms, and stood aside. "They're clean—and they're male, though I have my doubts about his lordship there."

Danaher and the other man chuckled.

Oliver released the breath he held. The fake phallus passed muster. As far as weapons, Claudia's knife was hidden in her boot. Rett also had one, and a thin sword was cleverly hidden in his walking stick.

"Let's go inside," Danaher ordered.

"I think not. We will do our business in the street," Rett sniffed arrogantly. "And a dirty business it is at that."

"Through those doors, your lordship. Now," Danaher hissed menacingly.

They headed inside the Black Moon, with Danaher's two men following behind. The door slammed shut.

Opening the shack's door wider, Oliver hurriedly glanced up and down the dimly lit street. There was no one else about it. But that didn't mean that Danaher's few remaining men were not nearby. He would have to chance it. Silently, he closed the door and padded toward the pub's front entrance. There was a large window in the front, so he could see in, but all was in darkness. They must be in the room in the back of the pub. Oliver searched his memory. Was there a bell above the door? No, he did not recall one when he was here with Rett. He opened the door and slipped in.

Muffled voices came from the rear. Oliver leaned in and listened.

"Be patient. I have two men bringing the sniveling gobshite here. I kept him in a dark hidey-hole I recently discovered. Ever hear of Sergeant Simpson?" Danaher asked.

Asking about Mitchell again, why? And a dark hole? Dear God, he hadn't kept Bryan in the cache? His younger brother harbored a genuine fear of enclosed places, and he wasn't all that fond of the dark, either.

"Why would I know of a soldier?" Rett replied.

"He's a copper, and maybe more besides. Like a masked bastard who won't keep his nose out of my business," Danaher snapped.

Wait. Danaher thinks Mitchell is The Sentinel?

The front entrance opened, and Oliver could barely dive behind the counter before the men entered. He waited until they passed by before he chanced a glance. Two men held Bryan's arms, and his brother had a burlap sack over his head.

"How do I know that is my brother?" Oliver heard Rett say. "Remove that hood at once!"

While Oliver planned his next move, someone must have entered through the rear door, for he yelled to Danaher, "There are coppers near the park!"

So much for any element of surprise.

Oliver retrieved the Webley revolver from his belt, pointed it to the ceiling, and fired twice, waited a few beats, then fired twice more. Slipping the pistol in his belt, he swiftly kicked the door in and entered the room.

"You!" Danaher hissed through clenched teeth as he tore off his cloak and tossed it aside.

Rett pulled the slim sword from his walking stick, and Claudia reached into her boot to retrieve her knife. They stood back-to-back, ready to take all comers. Oliver grabbed Bryan's arm and pushed him through the door, slamming it shut.

Then, all hell broke loose.

Danaher's four men were on the attack, while Danaher pulled out his revolver. He fired, missing Oliver by mere inches.

It was then Mitchell and seven constables burst through the door. The police officers held their truncheons aloft and quickly subdued the four sycophants. The men were marched from the room.

Danaher looked from Mitchell to Oliver. "This is not possible." He pointed at Mitchell. "*You* are The Sentinel."

"No," Oliver replied. "He is not. He never was. Lay down your weapon and surrender peaceably."

Danaher lowered it partway, but in a rapid movement only Mitchell saw, or so Oliver surmised, Danaher brought it upward and aimed straight at Oliver.

"No!' Mitchell yelled as he knocked Oliver aside. The gun boomed, and Rett and Claudia rushed Danaher, knocking him to his feet as the gun skittered across the floor. The oil lamp also crashed to the ground, and flame licked across the rotting wood floor, engulfing it. The rapidly spreading fire drove Rett and Claudia back. A wall of flame separated them from Danaher, who quickly scrambled to his feet.

Oliver glanced down. Mitchell lay, not moving, blood pouring from his leg. Rage overtook him, and he leaped on the desk. The fire spread to the surrounding walls, and Rett and Claudia took hold of Mitchell's coat and started dragging him from the room.

Danaher crawled along the floor, retrieved his revolver, and fired. Oliver quickly crouched down. The bullet whizzed over his head. Luckily, the smoke filling the room partially obscured Danaher's accuracy. Seething, Oliver looked above him. He located a steel beam attached to the ceiling, undoubtedly used to hang sides of beef and the like. Would it hold his weight? He would soon find out, for he wasn't waiting for Danaher to shoot him. Oliver wished to avoid using his gun, and only as a last resort.

Grabbing the bar, Oliver swung forward with his legs outstretched and kicked Danaher square in the chest, sending the man reeling across the room toward the worst of the fire. The floor gave away with an almighty crash, and Danaher fell through the hole into the cellar below, with the flaming rotten floor boards falling on top of him.

Moments later, there was a bloodcurdling scream—then nothing.

Oliver couldn't get close enough to check if Danaher was dead because the fire intensified. Instead, he grabbed the leather valise filled with money and fled the room just as pillars of flame ignited the ceiling.

Once outside, he found Rett speaking with one of the policemen. Oliver ran up to them and handed Rett the valise. "We will take Sergeant Simpson to a doctor. We have a carriage on the next street."

"Claudia has already gone to fetch it," Rett interjected.

The constable frowned. "I should head to the station and call the ambulance wagon."

"We can get the sergeant to a competent doctor in twice the time. We will send word to Lancaster Station as soon as he is treated. You might want to call in the fire brigade instead."

The constable nodded, touched his forelock, then raced toward the police station.

"Where is Bryan?" Oliver asked as it was hard to see from the billowing smoke and the dark sky.

"There," Rett pointed.

Bryan lay on the ground, the sack still on his head.

Looking around and finding no one, Oliver removed his hat, scarf, and mask and handed it to Rett. He crouched down by his brother. "Bryan. You are safe. Come, stand up." Oliver tore the sack off his head, then took his brother's arm and assisted him in standing.

Bryan's eyes squinted as if trying to focus. "Oliver?" he rasped hoarsely. Then Bryan threw his arms around Oliver's neck and began to cry softly.

Seeing his brother broken like this tore Oliver's heart in two. "It is all right, Bryan. We have you. All is well."

A loud crash caught their attention. The Black Moon Pub's roof caved in from the fire, and billows of black smoke climbed higher in the night sky. The shack next door, where Oliver had hidden, was also aflame.

"Here's the carriage!" Rett yelled. "We have to get off the street right away."

"Here, help Bryan."

Rett took Bryan's arm just as Claudia jumped down from the carriage. She had removed the beard and wig. She called to Kennedy, the driver, to assist Rett in loading the unconscious Mitchell into the conveyance.

Claudia ran straight to Oliver's arms, hugging him tight. "I was scared to death," she whispered. "If I had lost you. Oh, Oliver, never scare me like that again."

"My love." He kissed her, took her hand, and ran for the carriage. This was enough adventure for one night.

For a lifetime.

Chapter 29

WITH MITCHELL TUCKED away at Damon's residence and Doctor Drew Hornsby called in to attend to him, Claudia and Oliver returned to the viscount house with Bryan. Drew Hornsby would call in on Byran and give an update on Mitchell as soon as possible.

Mitchell had told him recently that when detectives were allowed to carry a firearm after the murder of two policemen in '84, very few took the option, Mitchell included. Oliver wondered if he now wished he had?

Meanwhile, his brother was upstairs, hopefully sleeping. Bryan waved away any food, but he did sip brandy before heading upstairs. Oliver had never seen him so subdued. He also did not want to speak about his ordeal. Rett stayed with Mitchell and would report his condition to the inspector while discovering any updates on the Danaher situation.

A plate of uneaten sandwiches sat on the table between him and Claudia as they remained deep in thought.

"I think a long honeymoon is just what we need," Claudia murmured. "I will gladly lounge about on a beach in Spain. And as soon as possible."

"In San Sabastian, I have read the water is turquoise, and the sand is the most beautiful golden shade. We can rent a villa there, right on the beach, and make love to the sounds of the crashing waves with the moon reflecting on the water."

Claudia jumped and vaulted herself at Oliver, straddling his lap and facing him. "Oh, I am so tempted to ravish you here and now. It must be the excitement of our adventure. My heart is pounding like a battle drum."

Oliver cupped her face and stared into her lovely eyes. "Only because of the adventure?"

Claudia wriggled her hips until she firmly placed her feminine core against his aching, erect shaft. "No. Not only." Claudia started rocking back and forth, rubbing his cock for all its worth. Even through the layers of leather and wool, he felt her heat.

Why not indulge in a little simulated sex?

"Ride me," Oliver demanded.

HELL'S BELLS.

Rett and Doctor Hornsby could return at any time, but the prospect of someone walking in on them merely heightened Claudia's desire. Rubbing against Oliver's stiff shaft excited her beyond compare, and she lost herself in the stunning sensation. She moaned, keeping as quiet as possible. But it was near impossible, for the feelings tearing through her made her giddy with joy. What will making love be like? With the man she loves? Claudia couldn't wait.

"Yes," Oliver growled. "Right there. Faster."

Faster it is.

Claudia could feel the peak building, like climbing a mountain. Then it slammed her hard. She cried out, smothering her release against his leather coat, quaking from the sheer bliss of it.

Oliver thrust his hips faster until he groaned, burying his face in her neck. Their breathing was erratic as they reached their peaks. Their bodies shuddered as one. They held each other close until, at last, they calmed.

"My," Claudia whispered. "That was rather intense."

The door burst open, and they started.

"My pardon, I should have knocked first," Rett said, laughter in his voice. "I can come back later."

Grasping Oliver's shoulders, Claudia reluctantly stood. Then, she quickly took a seat next to Oliver at the table.

"Great timing, Cousin," Oliver admonished as he pulled his chair closer to the table. "What news?"

He sat across from them with a smile still plastered on his face. "I would guess you two will be married as soon as possible, am I correct?"

"I have said yes to Oliver's proposal. And it will be as soon as his parents arrive," Claudia replied.

"Then my heartiest congratulations, and welcome to the family, Claudia."

"Thank you." Impulsively, Claudia jumped from her chair, ran to Rett, and kissed him on the cheek before returning to her seat. "I am looking forward to meeting everyone. I love Oliver to distraction. I know we will be happy."

Rett glanced between them. "Yes, I can see that. You both look completely blissful."

Claudia exchanged a knowing look with Oliver.

"The news?" Oliver said, not taking his eyes off Claudia.

"Oh, right you are. Mitchell has been stabilized, but Drew worries infection will set in. The bullet damaged some tendons, which may mean a longer recovery. He also lost a lot of blood, but it did not nick a major artery. Drew will know more tomorrow."

"Oh, poor Mitchell. He jumped in front of Oliver. He is a hero in my eyes, as are you both. Running into danger to save Bryan," Claudia stated.

"And you, Claudia," Rett replied. "You did not hesitate to volunteer. Anyway, Drew will be here shortly to look in on Bryan.

I went to the police station, and they informed me a body was discovered in the pub's basement, burnt beyond all recognition. There is no way to tell if it was Danaher. They are assuming it is him and closing the book on the case."

"I do not see how he could have escaped that," Oliver mused. "The building and the fire fell on top of him. Did the fire spread?"

Rett shook his head. "Not far. The shack next door is gone, and another condemned building on the other side of it sustained damage. But the fire brigade got the fire under control quickly. This will be the death knell for Notting Dale."

"Perhaps sooner than the city committee planned. Did the police inspect the basement area?" Oliver asked.

Rett cocked an eyebrow. "I don't believe so. They took out the corpse and departed. Why?"

"I do not know. A nagging feeling Danaher somehow escaped his fate? It is not possible. Danaher's men?"

"Scattered. What the police have planned next for the area? They did not share the information with me. I spoke to Inspector Stanhope, Mitchell's boss. He was not best pleased by the whole affair. As long as Mitchell sticks to his story of holding a training exercise nearby and acting once the gunshots rang out, he should escape unscathed. Well, except for his injury."

Oliver clutched Claudia's hand. "We will go see Mitchell as soon as we can, and I will put in a good word with the inspector. I imagine a viscount and heir to an earl has some sway."

"All of a sudden, I am exhausted. It is nearly midnight. I should head to Olivia's and Gideon's," Claudia yawned. Fatigue covered her like a rogue wave. All she wanted was sleep.

Oliver kissed her hand. "Come, I will escort you there."

After saying her goodnights to Rett, they were off in the carriage. Claudia curled up in Oliver's arms, sighing contentedly.

"I would like to pick you up at nine sharp tomorrow morning if you are available," Oliver said softly.

"Hmm. Is it a surprise?"

"Yes, of a sort."

Oliver kissed her tenderly when the carriage stopped before the Watford residence. "Dream of me tonight, for I will be dreaming of you."

"Oh, yes."

Oliver assisted her out of the carriage and walked her to the door. Then he kissed her hand. "Sweet dreams."

"Sweet but heated," she whispered.

Oliver laughed and blew her a kiss as he headed toward the carriage.

Never had Claudia been so happy.

AS PROMISED, OLIVER arrived at nine sharp. Sitting close to Oliver, his arm about her, Claudia stared out the window as the carriage turned onto Harrow Road.

"Can you not tell me the surprise?"

"This isn't it, but I asked Rett to locate the washerwoman while I recovered. It took some doing, but he found her. She was alone with her three children, with no money or food. Her husband, Charlie, one of Danaher's minions, after being released from the police cells, left for points unknown."

"Oh, no. That poor woman," Claudia murmured.

"I agree. We had Mrs. Nettles and her children moved out of Notting Dale. She has a sister in the East End, so Rett saw that she was settled near her family with some money and a decent job while she recovered from her broken arm."

"I am so pleased. As I said, you and your cousin are heroes."

Oliver kissed the top of her head. "Here we are."

"A cemetery?" she questioned.

"Yes, Kensal Green Cemetery. Also, while recovering, I contacted Edwina Callen and hired her to complete a task for me: to locate where your mother is buried."

"You did?"

"I gave the directions to Kennedy. He is driving us there now."

"But why here? I thought this burial ground was for people with money?" Her point was proven as they drove by marble mausoleums and massive Gothic monuments.

"This place is seventy-six acres, and there are many sections, like one for children and one for those who cannot afford an expensive funeral and burial."

"In other words, a section for the poor."

"Yes. That is where your mother is buried."

The carriage came to a stop before a large parcel of land. There were a few scattered wooden crosses, but for the most part, there was not a tombstone to be seen. Oliver assisted her from the carriage.

"In some of these plots, there is room for up to six coffins. It is how they bury the indigent," Oliver said softly.

Claudia slipped her arm through Oliver's as he led her over to the right side of the grounds. Tears burned hot in her eyes, and a lump formed in her throat. Since her mother died, she did not have the luxury to mourn her properly, for surviving took over every instinct.

"How startling to find, "Oliver continued, "that your mother is alone in this plot." He stopped before a section by a pathway. "Here, on the border of the path. I contacted the cemetery and paid to have no one else put in with her. We can order a tombstone right away. Or, if you wish, we can move her to another cemetery section."

The tears that threatened now spilled down her cheeks. "Oh, Mama," she whispered miserably. "I am sorry I left you. Forgive me."

Oliver pulled her close. "Under the circumstances, she understood there was no other option. It is why your mother told you to leave. My dearest Claudia."

She cried softly against his wool coat. Then, she sighed, grabbed a handkerchief from her reticle, and dabbed at her eyes.

"The cemetery said they have a lovely plot surrounded by rosebushes and a flowering shrub. We can have your mother moved there. Would you like to see it?"

Claudia sniffled, then nodded.

"I have tasked Rett to handle this for us while we are on our honeymoon. He will be with your mother all the way. She will be placed in a proper coffin and interred at the new plot with a tombstone."

"Nothing too elaborate," Claudia whispered. "Mama wouldn't like that."

"I made an appointment with someone in the office. We can see them now, have them show us the plot, and you can pick out a stone. Just in case you wished to move your dear mother."

Claudia gazed up at Oliver. "I do. Have I told you how much I love you?"

"Tell me again," he whispered, tenderly stroking her tear-stained cheeks.

"I love you so much. Thank you for this."

"Claudia, I would do anything for you. Anything. You are my life. My heart. My very soul."

IT WAS NOON WHEN OLIVER returned home after dropping Claudia at Watford's. She would be visiting with them until their marriage. Before he took her home, they dropped in to see the Galway sisters and told them the news of their upcoming nuptials.

They heartily wished them well and informed Claudia she had a position in the agency when she returned and could decide how many hours to work.

He handed his coat and hat to Dalton. "Has my brother arisen from his room?"

"No, my lord. We sent up a breakfast tray, but it remained untouched."

"Fix one for luncheon, for me as well. I will ring you when it can be brought up."

"Yes, my lord."

Oliver took the stairs two at a time. He turned the handle and entered. The room was encased in darkness. Oliver immediately strode over to the draperies and pulled them open, allowing sunshine to pour into the room.

Bryan groaned as he sat upright, his eyes blinking rapidly, adjusting to the light. Oliver took the damask dressing gown from the foot of the bed and tossed it to his brother. "Put it on. We have to talk."

Bryan turned slightly to slip it on. There were bruises down his left side.

"Wait." Oliver strode over, then leaned in to inspect it. "Danaher?"

"I am surprised Hornsby didn't tell you after he examined me last night. One of Danaher's men when he brought me water and bread. He kicked me twice, calling me a sniveling toff with no guts or gumption.' He's not wrong."

"No, he isn't." Oliver dragged over a chair and sat on it. "Is that all they did?"

"I wasn't violated, if that is what you mean," Bryan replied bluntly. Then he exhaled a shuddering breath. "They put me in a dark hole," he whispered miserably.

"I am sorry. I know you don't like it."

"Like it? I nearly went mad. I was barely in there twenty-four hours, but it felt like twenty-four days. Thank you for coming for me. Did you pay him?"

"No. There was a fight; the oil lamp was knocked to the floor, and the rotten wood ignited. The burning building fell on him. A corpse was found. The police believe it is Danaher, though no identification can be feasibly done as you can imagine."

"It is all a blur. Rett was there?"

"Yes, and Claudia, my fiancée. You have missed quite a lot while you wallowed in dissipation, but we can place all that in the past. Mother, Father, Grandmother and the rest of the family need never know what depths you sunk to or about being held for ransom. I will keep your secret on one condition."

"What?"

"That you become a functioning member of this family. Tomorrow, I want you to seek out these solicitor offices," Oliver took a folded piece of paper from his coat. "Pick one for your apprenticeship. Then, you will serve in the free law clinics for six months as you work toward your Postgraduate Certificate in Laws. No more immersing yourself in vice, alone or those with a deviant bent. No opium or heavy drinking. Understood?"

"Do I have a choice?"

Oliver crossed his arms. "No. Your selfishness ends here."

"I have acted as an egocentric, entitled bastard. I am sorry. May I never see Shinwell again. He gave me up and left me there. Told Danaher where to find you. I will do as you say."

"Yes, you will. Unless you want to be sent to the Hertfordshire Sanitorium." Oliver's look softened. "You are my brother, and I love you. If anything was ever to happen to you—" Oliver cleared his throat and passed Bryan the list. "Do this because you want to do it. Not because I am forcing you."

"I want to do this."

"Good. And I wish you to stay with Rett while I am away. You can look after Caramel, my cat."

"Cat?"

"As I said, you've missed quite a bit. I received a telegram from Father. He and Mother will be here in seven days. Let me ring for luncheon, and we can discuss how you can assist me in planning this small but whirlwind wedding."

Bryan nodded. "Yes. I can eat now."

Oliver stood and strode to the bellpull.

"And Oliver?" Bryan said. "I love you, too. Thank you."

AND SEVEN DAYS LATER...

AFTER DISCOVERING A civil wedding ceremony had stricter rules concerning wait times for obtaining a license than most churches, Claudia and Oliver opted for a special license within the Church of England. By the time his parents arrived, all the rapid preparation had occurred.

It was a small gathering that bright autumn morning with Oliver's parents, his cousins Rett and Ronan, and his brother Bryan. On Claudia's side, Olivia and Gideon, Aunt Mirella, and Edwina Callen attended. Gideon had walked her down the aisle. They had hoped Mitchell would recover enough to attend, but he developed an infection which prolonged his recovery. They did stop by and see him briefly yesterday, and he wished them well. Claudia and Oliver vowed to stay in touch while they were away on their honeymoon trip. Otherwise, they decided to keep the ceremony small and intimate, and their friends within The Rakes and the Galway Agency said they understood and wished them well.

Claudia could not believe it as she stood staring into Oliver's lovely green-gray eyes. The love that radiated from them caused her heart to soar. It felt as if she were in a fairy tale. The vicar's words faded into the background. All she could see and feel was Oliver, so handsome in his black dress suit with a boutonniere of lavender Michaelmas daisies, which matched her bouquet.

As for her dress, her wedding attire consisted of the gold gown she had worn the night she found Oliver in Berkley Square and declared her love. Olivia had a shimmering gold veil made for her in record time. Never has she felt so beautiful.

At last, the vicar came to the "I do" portion and the exchange of rings. When that concluded, he said, "Although it is not part of the Church of England ceremony, Claudia and Oliver asked that it be added. Oliver? You may kiss your bride and seal your commitment to each other."

Reverently and gently, he cupped her cheeks, mouthed, 'I love you,' then gave her a sweet, tender kiss that melted her heart. Everyone in attendance applauded.

They were married.

A few tears escaped the corner of Claudia's eyes, but then, Olivia told her it was good luck for the bride to cry at her wedding.

After hearty congratulations, they were off to the Carnstone town house, where a wedding breakfast awaited. The plan was to head to Oliver's residence for the wedding night before catching a train and then a ship to the port of Cadiz in Spain. All during the breakfast, Claudia's insides were in knots.

Oliver laid his hand on top of hers. "Are you all right, love?"

"Yes." Claudia leaned in and whispered, "Let us depart. Now. I need you most desperately."

That was all Oliver needed to hear, for he stood immediately.

AFTER WELL WISHES AND warm embraces, Claudia and Oliver were off to Hill Street.

When they arrived, Oliver halted at the door. "Shall I carry you over the threshold as they did in medieval times to ward off evil spirits?" he smiled. "Or as some do now, to show I will protect you, come what may?"

Claudia laughed. "How about we go through the door together? It is wide enough. We will start our life as partners—on equal footing. We will protect each other."

"And love?"

"Most definitely love," Claudia replied softly. "Until death do us part."

Oliver hooked his arm. "Then, let us go forth, my lady."

Claudia slipped her arm through his. "My lord."

They walked through the door together, then burst out laughing. Then Oliver looped his arm about her waist and spun her around. When they stopped, they found Dalton standing nearby.

"Dalton! We are not to be disturbed for anything unless the house is on fire until seven o'clock in the morning," Oliver cried happily.

"Yes, my lord, my lady. The trunks are packed and ready for your departure."

Oliver took Claudia's hand, ran for the stairs, and ascended. Once inside the bedroom and the door secured, they wasted no time divesting each other of their clothes and tumbling onto the bed. Their hands were everywhere, exploring and caressing while they kissed. Oliver clasped her breast, his mouth closing over the erect nipple. Claudia moaned as she grabbed fistfuls of his hair.

Oliver couldn't wait. He must be inside her. Reluctantly, Oliver broke the kiss. "I have sheaths," he murmured silkily.

Claudia nuzzled his neck. "Good. But for our first joining, let us go without. We can use them the rest of the day and night."

Oliver chuckled. "Day and night, eh? I am all for that. But, are you sure?"

"I doubt I will become pregnant. I know my cycles. I am fine."

"Always straight to the point, I adore you. We will be learning as we go, my love."

Claudia rolled over so that she lay flat on the bed. "Then let us begin."

Oliver positioned himself between her thighs as his fingers trailed toward her feminine core. *Oh, so wet.* He found that sensitive nub and rubbed it until Claudia writhed with pleasure. Taking his time, Oliver entered her slowly, allowing her to adjust. He also paused to savor the feeling of her tight, wet heat. Her inner muscles clutched him, causing him to moan loudly at the devastating sensation. He slipped in deeper.

"Oh, hell's bells."

"Have I hurt you?"

"Not at all. A little pinch. But right now? You being inside me feels wonder—oh!"

Oliver moved in and out, leisurely strokes that built to a rising crescendo as their moans and heavy breathing filled the room. He couldn't stop kissing and touching her. Claudia wrapped her legs around him, her nails scoring his back. Faster, he moved, hoping his deep thrusts were stimulating her enough. "Come for me, love," he urged.

Claudia cried out, shuddering in his arms. A mere few seconds later, he joined her. It was the most intense and earth-shattering moment of his life.

Lying in each other's arms, they cuddled until their breathing slowed. "And to think, Oliver whispered huskily. "This will only get better."

"I don't see how, but I cannot wait for us to explore. Our adventure is just beginning." Claudia nuzzled his neck. "I love you so much."

"And I love you with every beat of my heart."

Oliver kissed her deeply, becoming aroused once again.

Adventure? Theirs started before tonight. From almost the moment they met.

And Oliver could not wait to see what further escapades awaited them.

****Scroll ahead to read a sneak peek at book one of a new series, a spin-off from The Rakes of St. Regent's Park. The Detective and the Baroness (The Duke's Bastards #1) is Coming soon from Dragonblade Publishing. It concerns Mitchell Simpson and Baroness Addington, who both appeared in this story!****

Epilogue

SUMMER 1908
  Tensbridge House, Kent

"OLIVER! ARE THE TRUNKS in the carriage?" Claudia called out.

They were already late, for they had to catch a train to Bamford Park in Essex for the yearly retreat of friends and family at the Duke and Duchess of Allenby's country home.

Eleanora Galway and Christian Bamford held this get-together every summer. It was quite the crowd, and Claudia looked forward to it, not only for the relaxing holiday but seeing everyone and catching up, for they all led busy lives.

"They are, love!" Oliver called back.

Coming down the stairs were the twins, Aidan and Aileen, both six years of age.

"Be careful, you two!" Claudia called as they ran outside to join their father. Claudia stood by the window and pulled aside the draperies to watch. Oliver hugged his children tight, then assisted them into the carriage. Her heart swelled at the sight of him. She loved Oliver more than ever, if that were possible.

As she had predicted, their life together was certainly an adventure and had its share of tragedy, as most people experience.

Claudia knew more than most that life was not a fairy tale. After three years of working at The Galway Agency and Oliver acting as The Sentinel sporadically, Claudia decided to try for a child. Unfortunately, the baby boy was stillborn. It had smashed both their hearts to pieces, but together—and with the help of family and friends—they managed to put those shards back in place, and a year later, they tried once again. Claudia became pregnant, and their joy knew no bounds when they discovered she would have twins.

Aidan, the heir, named after Oliver's beloved grandfather, and Aileen, named for her darling mother, happily took up all of Claudia and Oliver's time, and they retired from their detective and vigilante doings and focused their energy on their children, and charitable endeavors within their group of friends and family.

Oliver bounded into the room. The breeze had tousled his hair. The sight of him still took her breath away. He was still handsome and very fit. "Ready to depart, love?"

"I am."

Oliver brought her into his embrace. "I thought we might nip away for a short trip, just the two of us, toward the end of the Bamford Park holiday. I already broached the subject with Christian, who said the children could stay with them. He has the extra nanny for the summer."

"That would be wonderful."

"Not as long as our honeymoon, but just as welcome."

They were gone for nearly six months for their honeymoon, and after Spain, they traveled to other locales, finishing off with Scotland in the spring. The trip was much needed after all they had experienced, but that precious time alone made them all the closer—and more in love.

"Scotland?" Claudia asked hopefully.

"You read my mind."

Oliver bracketed his hands on either side of her face and gazed lovingly into her eyes. Then he kissed her, long and deep, causing her insides to flutter.

Slowly, he ended it by kissing the tip of her nose. "Shall we join the children?"

"And continue the adventure?"

Oliver laughed as he took her hand. "The journey continues. Let's barrel ahead."

And they did, for many years to come.

Author's Note #2

Like Claudia Ellingford in my story, many women joined or created private investigative agencies. Lady detectives were also famous in fiction books during the Victorian era, starting in the 1860s.

Oliver's cat, Caramel, is based on my cat, one we recently adopted from a shelter. To see pictures of my sweet Caramel, check out my Instagram. She has been my constant companion while writing this book.

I researched Notting Dale thoroughly, pouring over Victorian-era maps. Between 1878 and 1899, 45,334 men, women, and children were evicted from the area due to clearances. The city ejected the pig farmers in 1878. I also researched all the facts mentioned in this story concerning the history of Notting Dale. Notting Dale did become an area containing a mixture of public and private housing. It was the site of the tragic Grenfell Tower fire of June 17, 2017, where 72 people died.

Although I mention many streets in London, the addresses are fictitious.

Bayer claims that in the 1890s, the German chemist Felix Hoffmann discovered acetylsalicylic acid, or ASA. Bayer began to distribute it in powder form in 1899. They sold it under the name 'aspirin.' I set the date back a few months to fit my autumn 1898 timeline. There are disputes to this Bayer narrative, as many scientists throughout the 1800s had a hand in making this discovery. The product was sold in pill form starting in 1903.

Berkley Square did not have a gazebo, then or now, but I just had to include it when I received my lovely cover.

Characters from my other historical romances appearing or mentioned in this story:

Aidan Wollstonecraft. Check out his story in *Love with a Notorious Rake* (The Men of Wollstonecraft Hall #3)

Garrett Wollstonecraft. Check out his story in *Scandal with a Sinful Scot* (The Men of Wollstonecraft Hall #2)

Riordan Wollstonecraft. Check out his story in *Marriage with a Proper Stranger* (The Men of Wollstonecraft Hall #1)

Drew Hornsby. Appears in *The Vicar with the Frozen Heart* (The Hornsby Brothers #2)

Tremain Hornsby. Check out his story in *The Vicar with the Frozen Heart* (The Hornsby Brothers #2)

Damon and Althea's story: *The not so Perfect Duke* (The Men of St. Regent's Park #5)

Gideon and Olivia's story: *The Duke of Pain* (The Men of St. Regent's Park #4)

Christian and Eleanora's story: *Protecting the Duke* (The Men of St. Regent's Park #1)

Brandon and Angeline's story: *Knight of Christmas* (The Men of St. Regent's Park #3)

Asher and Chastity's story: *The Baron and the Mistress* (The Men of St. Regent's Park #2)

Author Biography

A multi-published author from the East Coast of Canada, Karyn Gerrard loves to write sensual historical and contemporary romances. Tortured heroes are an absolute must.

Karyn's been happily married for a long time to her own hero. His encouragement and loving support keep her moving forward.

To learn more about Karyn and her books and places to follow her for book news, visit www.karyngerrard.com[1]

Also, visit her on Facebook, Twitter-X, Instagram, and Threads.

"Looking for a swoon-worthy read? You can't go wrong with the lovely and emotional romances from Karyn Gerrard." ~**Vanessa Kelly, USA Today Bestselling author**

"Karyn Gerrard writes very enjoyable, richly textured historical romances." ~**Kate Pearce, New York Times and USA Today Bestselling author**

---

1.   http://www.karyngerrard.com/

More Books by Karyn Gerrard

~H istorical~
    The Spinster and Mr. Glover (Book #1 Blind Cupid Series)

The Governess and the Beast (Book #2 Blind Cupid Series)

The Copper and the Madam (Book #3 Blind Cupid Series)

Protecting the Duke (The Rakes of St. Regent's Park #1)

The Baron and the Mistress (The Rakes of St. Regent's Park #2)

Knight of Christmas (The Rakes of St. Regent's Park #3)

Duke of Pain (The Rakes of St. Regent's Park #4)

Bold Seduction (of Professor Hornsby) (Book #1 Hornsby Brothers Series)

The Vicar's Frozen Heart (Book #2 Hornsby Brothers Series)

Marquess of Secrets (Book #3 Hornsby Brothers Series)

Beloved Monster (Book #1 The Ravenswood Chronicles)

Beloved Beast (Book #2 The Ravenswood Chronicles)

Marriage with a Proper Stranger (Book #1 Men of Wollstonecraft Hall Series)

Scandal with a Sinful Scot (Book #2 Men of Wollstonecraft Hall Series)

Love with a Notorious Rake (Book #3 Men of Wollstonecraft Hall Series)

The Not So Perfect Duke (The Rakes of St. Regent's Park #5)

The Viscount of Shadows (The Rakes of St. Regent's Park #6)

COMING SOON! The Detective and the Baroness (The Duke's Bastards #1)

~Contemporary~

My Highlander Cover Model (Heroes of Time Travel Anthology Series #1)

Timeless Heart (Heroes of Time Travel Anthology Series #2)

My Wicked Soul (It's Never Too Late for Love Anthology Series #1)

That Christmas Feeling (It's Never Too Late for Love Anthology Series #2)

He's the Wicked Bad (Wicked Men of Rockland City #1)

His Wicked Celtic Kiss (Wicked Men of Rockland City #2)

His Wicked Cold Heart (Wicked Men of Rockland City #3) is coming soon!

Sneak Peek of The Detective and The Baroness (The Duke's Bastards #1)

Coming soon!

Prologue

EARLY NOVEMBER 1898
London, England

"DETECTIVE SIMPSON!"

Mitchell groaned and strained to open his eyes, but it proved impossible. He heard a woman's voice and one somewhat familiar. His bewildered brain tried to place it. There was a familiarity, to be sure, and the sound of the breathy voice sent frissons of pleasure through his aching body.

"Sergeant, please wake up!" The woman gripped his arm and gave it a shake.

The haze started to clear. What had happened? The villain, Jedidah Danaher, had shot him, leaving him to bleed out in a condemned building. He recalled that much; after that, he could only extract brief snippets, and Mitchell couldn't tell what was true and what was not.

Someone transported him to his half-brother's house, where they called in a doctor. But Mitchell remembered her voice through his numerous fever dreams while slipping in and out of consciousness. He recollected her soothing touch. The lady had laid a cool cloth on his forehead when hot and covered him with blankets when Mitchell felt cold. She told him that all would be well, that he would recover.

Not that he genuinely believed it.

"Mitchell!"

The sound of his name brought him the rest of the way of the mist. He groaned and placed his blurry gaze on the sound of the frantic voice.

When his vision cleared, and he saw who had awakened him, a powerful yearning tore through him. Baroness Corrine Addington. The Honorable Corrine Edgeworth, daughter of Viscount Rothley. The recently married baroness, bride to Travis Addington, the new baron. Travis Addington was a distant cousin to the recently passed old baron, Gilbert Addington.

He was sick and injured, yet his mind still could pluck out relevant facts stockpiled in his organized detective brain. It boded well for his recovery. Why was Lady Corrine here? Right. In a previous life, she had been a nurse. Yes, he had asked about her.

"We have not been properly or officially introduced. I was at the Galway's residence when you came looking for Viscount Tensbridge and Miss Ellingford. There was no time for conversation, only a passing acknowledgment. We saw each other again when I assisted in nursing Miss Ellingford's injuries."

Mitchell remembered it all. He recalled locking gazes with her and how a potent blast of awareness and arousal had gripped him tight—just like now.

"I was at the Galways again," she continued in her husky tone. "When the Duke of Chellenham came to tell Althea Galway your injuries resulted from a police raid. I offered my services again."

"How long have you been here?" Mitchell croaked.

"Since your friends brought you here five days ago."

Five days? "What about the baron, your husband?"

"What about him?"

"Isn't he wondering where you are?"

The baroness shrugged. "I highly doubt it. We are separated, at least temporarily."

Already? Weren't they married only a few months ago? Why did the prospect of her estrangement from her husband fill him with hope? It was inappropriate, especially since Mitchell had met the baroness only recently—and briefly, not so formally.

"I must tell the others you are awake."

"Others?" he rasped.

"Your family and friends. They are all here at the moment. I will fetch them."

Family? He had no family.

Mitchell groaned. Damon, his recently revealed half-brother, was the new Duke of Chellenham. Why was he brought to Damon's residence instead of a hospital to recover? What did it matter?

Discovering you are the bastard son of a duke was just one of the shocking twists and turns Mitchell's life had taken lately. Before he could reply, the baroness departed, leaving an enticing odor of vanilla and roses in her wake.

Damon stepped into the room, closing the door behind him. Unfortunately, the utterly alluring baroness did not come with him. And damn it, he never thanked her for her care.

"I am relieved," Damon exhaled. "It was touch and go there for a few days. You may stay here as long as it takes to recover," Damon added. "Olivia will be by later this afternoon."

Their half-sister. He had more family than he thought.

"Thank you," Mitchell replied quietly. "The baroness, why is she here?"

"Lady Corrine was with the Galway sisters when word of your adventure reached them. She volunteered once again to assist us."

Why was the baroness meeting with the ladies who ran The Galway Investigative Agency? And multiple times? The questions he longed to ask were piling up. Although, how tempting it would be to have Damon call her back into the room. "Where am I, Clarendon Place or the Duke's house at Queen Anne's Gate?"

"Clarendon Place. The duke's residence is in the last weeks of its renovation. The children wish to see you, but I said you were still too ill for company. And by looking at you, that seems to be the case." Damon smiled. "No offense."

Children?

His assorted much younger half-brothers and half-sister. Mitchell had only met them a few weeks ago. Yes, he had more family than he knew what to do with. All of them, he, Damon, and Olivia included, were the progeny of the detestable Edward Cranston, the late Duke of Chellenham. But Mitchell couldn't deal with the confused emotions tearing through him on all fronts.

"Thank you. I cannot see the children in this condition. Not for a while." His mind was still in a fog. "Is everyone well? Tensbridge and the rest? Is Danaher dead?" Mitchell could hardly keep all that had transpired straight in his head as the events occurred swiftly.

"A body was discovered in the burned building. The police allege the corpse to be the villain Danaher but state that, scientifically speaking, it will be difficult to know for sure. Everyone is well. And as far as seeing the children, I surmised you would not be up to having rambunctious tots running about your room. I will explain it to them. By the by, your supervisor, Inspector Stanhope, came to see you, but you were not up to visitors. He wanted an update on your medical condition."

Mitchell's blood chilled. "Why?"

"Doctor Drew Hornsby will relay that to you." Damon strode toward the door, opened it, and waved in the young doctor. Once Hornsby entered the room, Damon left them alone.

A sickening feeling settled in Mitchell's guts. The news wasn't good, and Stanhope would take immediate steps to replace him if he weren't up to co-running the F Division Lancaster Station near the Notting Dale district.

Mitchell tried to move his injured leg but couldn't. Panic tore through him, and he elevated his head and looked down the length of the bed.

Oh, thank Christ.

He still had his leg.

Doctor Hornsby stood by his bed. "Awake at last, Sergeant Simpson. How gratifying. I will be blunt: we almost had to take the leg. Sepsis started to settle in the wound, but I used carbolic acid on the bandages, and luckily, the danger has passed."

Sepsis? Isn't that derived from the Greek word *sepo*, which translates to 'I rot.' His late adoptive parents ensured he obtained a good education, which came in handy more than once. Mitchell flared his nostrils. Thankfully, there was no putrid smell. "And what is my diagnosis?"

The young doctor pulled the chair closer to the bed and sat upon it. "It will be several months before you can return to duty, Sergeant. I am sorry."

The crushing disappointment moving through him was potent, indeed. "If at all?"

"I believe with a sufficient recovery period and rehabilitation exercises, you will regain full use of your leg, at least enough to return to work. Your inspector said he will come by tomorrow to discuss your sick leave."

Mitchell groaned. Medical leave for the Metropolitan Police was barely sufficient for basic survival. How in hell will he live? His savings were for his retirement rather than for everyday living.

"You will have to use a cane in the interim. And there may be sporadic pain," the doctor continued. "But with focus and determination, you shall recover. I place my reputation on it."

"In other words, don't wallow in self-pity and get on with it," Mitchell growled, allowing himself a moment of temper for his unfortunate fate.

Hornsby pushed his spectacles further up his nose. "Yes. That is the gist of it. I believe your brother will offer that you stay with him as you recover."

Oh, no.

They hardly knew each other, and besides, Damon was to be married next month to Althea Galway, and they were taking in those younger siblings. The duke didn't need a grumpy older half-brother lurching about the residence like a restless beast.

"I can make my own arrangements. And Chellenham is my half-brother."

"The duke guessed you would say exactly that. I have another proposition. You can stay with me. That way, I can assist you in your recovery. I live in a large flat not far from here, a lucky side benefit from being the adopted son of a viscount and nephew to a duke."

Mitchell blinked several times, shocked at the suggestion. "Why would you make such an offer to a perfect stranger?"

"Well, it turns out we are not exactly strangers—in the biological sense."

Mitchell stared at the doctor in disbelief.

No. Not another one.

Damon's father, the old duke, was a miserable, egotistical excuse for a man with a deep conviction in eugenics. Edward Cranston believed he possessed a superior bloodline and ensured he spread that lineage as far and wide as possible. There were dozens upon dozens of his progeny out in the world. It was a long, complicated tale, not one Mitchell wanted to discuss. He would leave that conversation for another day. But observing Hornsby, he could see it: those sky-blue eyes, the light-colored hair, and the tall frame. Almost all had the same physical attributes, himself included.

"How and when did you find out?" Mitchell whispered.

"Only recently. My mother passed when I was nine, and Viscount Hawkestone adopted me shortly thereafter. On her deathbed, she told my adopted father, then a vicar, who my birth father was and made him swear never to tell it. When Edward Cranston died a few months ago, my father decided to inform me of the truth. You see, my mother and I lived under a fake name. She was hiding me from Cranston. A long, sordid story for another time."

Mitchell could not be more shocked if Hornsby had smacked him with a pine board across the head. "Have you told Damon?"

"Yesterday. Chellenham promptly invited me into his club. And more generously, into his life and family."

That sounded like Damon. The club in question was The Rakes of St. Regent's Park. "Me as well. I am thinking about joining the club."

"Perhaps we can join—but later. Let's form one of our own. I appreciate the duke's offer concerning The Rakes and their charity work, but I would like us to focus on another purpose besides that." Hornsby reached into his coat pocket and pulled out a piece of paper. "This is the list Damon's mother gave him that started him on his journey of discovery. It is the names of the illegitimate children that the duchess knew of. I say we find these people."

The list Mitchell's name was on. He had no idea what to say.

"I am overwhelming you. I do apologize," Hornsby said softly. "I am still trying to digest the news myself. I did not expect this turn of events. I cannot explain why I feel compelled to seek out these people. It is not for family's sake, as I have a wonderful family with the Hornsbys as you did with the Simpsons. Damon told me of the particulars."

"We were fortunate to be taken in by good people," Mitchell murmured.

"Yes. But how many on this list were not? I say we band together and form a support group. Do good works from within for those who need it."

The idea began to germinate. Mitchell liked Damon more with each passing day, but joining his half-brother's exclusive club with those aristocratic and wealthy members did not appeal, even though they were honorable men. At least, not at this time. "Let me see the list."

Hornsby handed him the paper. Eight names. Six males and two females. "Damon told you of Olivia Durham here on the list? She is married to the Duke of Watford, a friend of Damon's, and a member of The Rakes."

"Yes. Chellenham also mentioned that August Donaldson, a footman at the country estate, came to him recently to ask for money. Donaldson claimed to be heading to North America to start a new life, but Damon doesn't know if he left the country."

"There is a ledger full of names beyond this list."

Hornsby nodded. "The duke told me about that and the foundling home."

Yes, the foundling home—yet another discussion to add to the growing agenda. Mitchell returned his attention to the paper. The next name on the list after he and Olivia? Liam Hallahan, pub owner.

This idea would be like ripping off a bandage and exposing a better left-alone wound. But this quest would give Mitchell some purpose while he recovered. He was a detective, after all. He could do some private investigative work by opening a temporary agency.

"You need to think about it, I understand," Hornsby said solemnly. "Take all the time you need."

Mitchell didn't need time. Be damned if he would lie about bemoaning his fate. Doing good works was why he considered joining Damon's group, but Hornsby's proposal intrigued him more. Why not offer assistance to those who share an unfortunate bloodline? What better way to expunge Edward Cranston's loathsome legacy than banning together and rising above it?

"I say we forge ahead," Mitchell declared firmly. "And I have just the name for our group. The Duke's Bastards."